Plantation Christmas

Weddings

—Four-in-One-Collection—

Plantation Christmas
Weddings

SYLVIA BARNES

LORRAINE BEATTY

CYNTHIA LEAVELLE

VIRGINIA VAUGHAN

BARBOUR
PUBLISHING

Christmas at Dunleith

Sylvia Barnes

Dedication

To my Lord and Savior, Jesus Christ; to my husband and family; to the Bards of Faith; and to the loving members of Pelahatchie Baptist Church, who have supported and encouraged me. And thanks to Rebecca Germany, my editor, for giving me a chance.

Chapter 1

Thanksgiving Week 2010

Marilyn McLemore looked at the car rental attendant with disdain. Her flight from Denver to Baton Rouge had already put her in a foul mood. Stormy weather, quick seventy-five-foot drops, and now they were telling her the vehicle would not be available for two hours. She strummed her fingers on the counter.

"What do you expect me to do?" She saw the attendant look down at her hand and immediately pulled it from the counter.

"This is the Monday before Thanksgiving, ma'am. It's a busy time. You'll just have to wait." Her speech indicated impatience.

"Really? Where?"

"There is a coffee shop right down there."

Marilyn followed the direction of her finger. "Fine." She turned back and studied the attendant, her lawyer face on. She glanced at her name tag while positioning herself closer to the counter, her hands folded on top. "If I may be blunt,

Rosie, it occurs to me that you could show a bit more concern when customers have to wait. I mean your company actually advertises someone will pick up the customer. How long would that take?" She shook her head. "But, hey, what do I know?" It wasn't the girl's fault. "I'm sorry, bad day."

"It's okay. You're right. I've been fussed at all day. I let it get to me."

"I understand." Marilyn stared at her before offering a slow smile. "Truce?"

"Yes, ma'am. Check back in an hour. I'll try to get you a car."

"Thanks, Rosie. Coffee sounds good, anyway." She touched the young lady's hand in an effort to fortify her apology. "Want me to bring you a cup when I return?"

"That's sweet. But no, thank you. I'm good."

Marilyn turned her carry-on around and pulled it toward the designated shop. She ordered black coffee and looked around for a seat. Her order came quickly, and she hurried to a vacant table in the corner, positioned her bag by the table, and removed the top off the cup when she sat. Taking a deep breath, she relaxed and took a sip of the steaming brew. The aroma made her smile. Besides bacon, it had to be the best smell in the world. Well, maybe along with Perry Ellis Original. She smelled her wrist to validate her point.

Now, in a better mood, Marilyn could think about the upcoming wedding. She looked at her watch and realized it would be after dark when she arrived in Natchez. She let her thoughts wander. Her daughter, Constance, married to a Mississippi farmer. Justin was a good-looking guy with impeccable manners. But she had pictured Constance marrying an attorney, or at least a white-collar suit. She essentially wanted her daughter to be happy. Maybe she was being judgmental in her connotation of Southern men, in particular, cattlemen. She wished Dan were still alive to witness his princess's passage to another culture. But then, he would have been blatantly opposed. She could only hope Constance was secure in her choice. At least they were getting married at Dunleith Plantation. Marilyn had searched online and found pictures of past weddings, which had given her some encouragement. A Christmas Eve wedding in the hot South. Marilyn suspected this trip, on the pretense of finalizing plans, was primarily for her and Justin's widowed dad to become acquainted before the wedding. She sipped the strong, now tepid, liquid and pondered the following days. *A cowhand. Huh.*

⬥

Beau Burnham hugged his son and future daughter-in-law in the lobby of the Main House before finding his way to the Dairy Barn where he was staying. At dinner the kids had explained it had been used years before as a real dairy, but that it was built like a small castle. He chuckled. If it still smelled like cows, he would feel right at home.

After driving his truck to the separate structure, Beau got out and looked at the miniature chateau. Charming. He removed his bag from the backseat of his king-cab Ram and stalked to the building, shaking his head. "Lord, just get me through." Beau thought of his deceased wife and knew he would not have to do this if she were still alive. Or maybe he would. Dark memories invaded his head as he unlocked the barn and walked into the warmth of his temporary home.

A lamp was on. The living area looked comfortable. Beau glanced around to the kitchen and headed for the bedroom, where he threw his bag on the floor, opened it to retrieve his pajamas, and dressed in the bathroom. He was tired and went straight to bed, much earlier than his normal bedtime.

❧

Marilyn used the map she had printed to wind her way to the Dairy Barn. Seeing another vehicle, she pulled up beside it and removed her bags, pulling the large one with one hand, her carry-on with the other, and her purse tucked under her arm. The turbulent weather had been followed by a chilly wind, which kept blowing her hair across her eyes. She puffed her breath upward so she could see. She tried to open the front door. Locked. Choosing between bothering someone at the Main House and knocking on the door, she rapped gently. No answer. Using her knuckles, she knocked. Silence. Focusing on the difficulties of her day, she gritted her teeth and banged with her fists. The door slowly opened. A broad chest blocked her vision.

She looked up. Way up. "I'm sorry, the door was locked. And you are?" Marilyn could barely see a face but was surprised to see a man. Sharing the cottage with her?

"Well now, little lady, who are you?"

Marilyn gasped. "I'm a guest."

"Is that so? So am I."

"That's nice. It's getting cold out here. Could I please come in?" She was tired and didn't want a struggle.

"Sure. Need some help?"

Marilyn hesitated. Being an attorney, she had learned long ago to not cut off her nose to spite her face. "Yes, thank you. I'm Marilyn McLemore."

He grinned. "Well, I'll be a jack rabbit. I'm Beau Burnham."

Marilyn drew back. The image she had drawn in her mind suddenly came to life. Oh goodness. She forced a smile. "Nice to meet you, Beau. Could we please go in now?" She shivered, more to prove to him the chilly temperature rather than be redundant.

"Oh sure, ma'am. Here, let me get the big one."

Marilyn picked up the carry-on and followed him in. "This is nice. I think I'm upstairs."

"You bet you are. Unless, of course, you want to change rooms. I went to bed already, but hey, some messed-up covers wouldn't hurt."

"Uh, gee, that's nice of you. But no thanks." Just as she thought. Redneck.

Beau led her upstairs and asked which room was hers. She pointed to one, and he tried to open the door. Locked. "Well, I guess you need to go to the office and get a key. Did you check in?"

"This late? Someone's at the office now?"

"Yep. It's right down the drive. I'll walk with you."

She assented, and they walked to the office together. After checking in and returning to the Dairy Barn, they walked back upstairs and Beau opened the door for her and set her bags in.

"Is this satisfactory?"

Marilyn looked around. Light blue walls, soft green accessories, and a lamp barely glowing created a relaxing atmosphere. She wanted to crash into the folds of the thick comforter and never come out. "It's wonderful." She looked over at him. "Well, I guess I'll see you tomorrow. Planning meeting at ten?"

"That's what they say." He hesitated and looked around the room again before staring at her a few seconds. "Well, good night."

"Good night." When he closed the door, she sat on the bed and thought what a long few days this would be. A Mississippi farmer. How much worse could it get?

⤳⤳

Marilyn slept later than usual. She reached for her cell phone on the nightstand. Six o'clock. Knowing she would not be able to go back to sleep, she showered and dressed for the day, lazily pulling her light brown hair up in a semi-ponytail. She looked down at her soft silk slacks and picked fuzz from the taupe-colored material. The mirror reflected her colorful Izmir jacket, the gold threads of the tapestry accentuating the gold flecks in her brown eyes and the subtle highlights in her hair. She smiled as she lifted her shoulders for a final look. Okay, let the day begin. She lightly sprayed perfume on her neck and left for the kitchen. Coffee would definitely get her going.

Trying to be quiet so she wouldn't awake "Bubba Beau," she started brewing the coffee. She giggled at the name, which had come to mind as she inhaled the smell of the tantalizing liquid. Not one she could speak aloud for sure. She was still laughing when the door to the first-floor bedroom opened and he appeared.

Beau walked to her side. "Glad to see you chipper this morning, Marilyn. Mmm, coffee smells good. I'll have a cup as soon as it's ready."

Marilyn felt her smile fade. She glanced down at his T-shirt. She must have missed seeing the print the night before. "Cows Rule?" She glanced back at Beau.

He was smiling. Broadly. "Sure do, little lady. Pads my pockets for sure."

If he kept calling her that all week, she'd have to take medication. "Well, that's good to know. It's a bit of information I wasn't privy to." This sounded maybe a little too sarcastic, even to her.

He must have missed it, because he never responded. Instead, he said, "I'll go dress. You look mighty fine. Holler at me when the coffee's done. We'll stop off and have breakfast at the restaurant before the meeting."

Marilyn gave him what Constance always called her *look*. "Sure thing, Beau. Be mighty glad to." Maybe that sounded like his kind of talk. She surely wanted to fit in. Oh yeah.

❧

Beau and Marilyn walked across to Dunleith's Castle Restaurant for breakfast. Beau remained quiet as he watched Marilyn appraise the plantation, her lips turning up at the corners as she approached the restaurant.

He spoke softly. "Nice, huh?"

"Absolutely."

"Lawyers' kind of words?"

He saw sparks form in her eyes as she turned toward him. The sun reflected on their amber flecks and the golden highlights in her hair. She was a fine-looking little lady. He'd give her that.

She retaliated, "What kind of question is that?"

"I mean most women would have said, 'Yes, it is,' or some sort of soft, tender statement about the beauty of the place. 'Absolutely' seems so hard and final. Like you want to end the conversation right there."

Those beautiful, full lips hinted a smile. "Yes, I see. You're used to Southern women who flutter and chatter with emotion."

"Wrong. I'm used to strong Christian women who are gentle and kind. Who speak softly from the heart." His thoughts drifted for a moment to his deceased wife. All Southern women were not like that, but he would not go there with her.

"Of course. I'm sorry. Sometimes I come across very differently from what I actually feel. Trained attorney and all." A sudden sadness crossed her face. "Again, forgive me."

"No problem." They lingered in front of the restaurant. "Another mini-castle. Amazing, huh?" He was giving her another chance.

Her laugh sounded with relief. "Oh yes, it is. I read it was once the carriage house."

"There you go. The little woman has done her homework." He rested his hand on her back. "Ladies first."

When they were seated, Beau watched Marilyn review the menu before glancing at it himself. "I see what I want."

She looked at him over the menu and raised her eyebrows in question.

"The usual Southern fare. Eggs, grits, biscuits and gravy, sausage and bacon."

"Grits, huh?"

"Yep. Never tried them?"

"No. Should I?"

"Please. You should always try local dishes."

"Good point."

The waiter came and took their order. When Marilyn ordered grits, toast, and coffee, Beau interrupted. He told the waiter, "Bring her some eggs and bacon. She has a long day in front of her."

When they were alone, she spoke. "I'm not used to someone making my decisions."

"Yeah, it shows. But you do have a long day. It's no telling how long we'll be in the planning meeting. We'll probably have a late lunch."

"I don't eat lunch."

"Yeah, that shows, too."

"Are all Southern men so rude?"

"I don't call it rude. I call it taking care of my friends."

"So, I'm your friend now?"

He could tell she was trying to conceal a smile. "No. You're family now."

Her smile faded as her face slightly crumpled. He thought she might cry. But she composed herself as the waiter brought the food, poured the coffee, and asked if he could be of further assistance before leaving them alone with the mixed aromas wafting up toward them.

Beau reached across the table and took Marilyn's hand, a look of surprise telling him she had no idea why. "I always say a blessing before my meals. I hope you don't mind."

"No. Fine."

Eyes closed, he prayed, "Dear Lord, thank You for the joining of two families. For the wonderful institution of marriage. I ask You to be with Justin and Constance as they seek a future filled with love, children, and all the blessings You have in store for them. Guide them in all their decisions, Lord. May it all be to Your glory. Thank You for Marilyn and for this food we are about to eat. Bless it to the nourishment of our bodies. Amen."

He looked up to see Marilyn wipe a tear from the corner of her eye.

Chapter 2

Beau had wanted to walk around Dunleith before the meeting. Marilyn begged off, needing to return to the Dairy Barn to make some calls. The first thing, though, was more coffee. Her fingers touched the pot. Lukewarm. She poured it into a mug, which she stuck into the microwave, remembering a Bible verse she had learned long ago. From Revelation, she thought. God said to be either hot or cold but not lukewarm, as He would spew you out of His mouth. Well, she guessed she was good to go on that one, because she was neither hot nor lukewarm. She had been icy cold. Church had been out of the picture since her daughter was a little girl. She knew Constance had started back when she was in college, and she was proud of her.

She took the coffee to her room, wondering why she was all of a sudden thinking like this. She reflected on Beau's prayer. How surprised she was to hear the soft, sweet words spoken by the large cowhand. Though a handsome one. Then she thought about that. His large blue eyes and sandy hair.

His muscles. Okay, enough. Get to the phone calls. She grabbed her cell and called the office, looking at the time and realizing she only had about thirty minutes.

As usual, her messages were from clients who needed her right away. Well, sorry, they would have to wait until after the meeting. She hurried to the bathroom, repositioned her ponytail, put on fresh lipstick, and left for the meeting, grabbing her briefcase from her car on the way. For once Marilyn took the time to breathe in the fresh, cool air and admire the fall foliage still clinging to the trees as she walked to the Main House. The plantation social coordinator had asked them to meet her there instead of at the office on the grounds behind the mansion.

Constance, Justin, and Beau were waiting outside for her. She hugged her daughter and future son-in-law. She nodded at Beau.

"Well, where did you guys eat breakfast?" Beau's loud words occupied the outdoor space.

Constance rolled her eyes. "McDonald's."

Beau and Marilyn looked at each other, the word "Why?" forming at the same time.

"It was where Justin wanted to eat. And until we tie the knot, I'll let him have his way."

Justin responded, "Sure, baby girl. Wait and see who rules the roost in our family." But he ruffled her hair and smiled.

Beau hooted with laughter.

Marilyn smiled but thought to herself, *"Baby girl," "little lady." Where do they get names like these for women?* She shook her head. "Well, should we go in?"

They entered, walking around a ladder on which someone was balancing on the top, hanging evergreen garland around the door. Isabella, the coordinator, was waiting with Constance's wedding planner, Wreath Anderson, in the hall. They shook hands with each of them and led them to the front parlor, which led into another, similar room, both lavishly furnished with fine antiques and windows draped with fine silk. Ladies after her own heart, Wreath and Isabella got right down to business. Marilyn appreciated this and told them so as she opened her briefcase and retrieved a pad and pencil.

The first order of business was, of course, the wedding itself, and Marilyn addressed Isabella. "I reviewed the wedding package online. I have a copy with me." She pulled it from her case and handed it to Isabella. "Is the information on this sheet still correct?"

Isabella looked over the contents. "Yes. How many guests will you have?"

Marilyn looked at Constance. "Didn't we conclude about fifty?"

"Yes ma'am. Justin's relatives, a few of my friends in Denver, and our friends here. Oh, and a few college friends from out of state. What about you, Mama? Anyone from your office or maybe your friend Lily?"

"No." Marilyn looked back at Isabella. "Fifty, give or take a few."

"Good. We can accommodate that many in the Main House. Usually the guests stand around the wedding party. We can place a few chairs for those who need to sit. You see, the hall can handle any overflow. That's why I wanted us to meet here, so you would have a good idea of what it will be like. Of course, on a warm December day, we can set up chairs on the front lawn, and the wedding party would stand on the porch and the stairs. That can be determined closer to the day."

Wreath spoke before Marilyn could reply. "What about attendants? Same as when we spoke?"

Constance responded, "I'll only have a maid of honor—Bethany, my best friend. Justin's dad will be the best man. Do we need ushers?"

"No." Wreath thumped her pen on her paper. "Everyone can find their own place in this small ceremony. Unless you would like to have them?"

"No, not really." Constance looked at her mom for confirmation.

Marilyn nodded in agreement. She had been observing Wreath, thinking how attractive she was. Constance had told her she had been abandoned at the altar on her wedding day. She couldn't understand why someone would leave this gorgeous young lady. "What about decorations? What do we need to do?"

Isabella regained control. "That's the good thing about a Christmas wedding. I'm sure Wreath talked to your daughter about this. Our facilities are beautifully decorated, as you can see by the progress already made. The Main House will have trees, poinsettias, all mantels decorated. Nothing lacking there. The windows and porch outside will be laden with wreaths and garlands. You can provide your bouquets, of course. You may want something of your own taste on the main table in the reception area. Otherwise, your guests will be charmed by the decor of the house itself, especially when it's fully decorated for Christmas."

"It is beautiful." Marilyn was warming to Isabella. "What about the reception? Will we use the Castle Restaurant?"

"Since you're letting Dunleith cater and I've had the opportunity to see you again and ensure our plans are in place, I'll go." Wreath stood. The reflection of the light played on her dark hair. "That is, if you don't mind. I have a lunch appointment."

Constance stood and hugged her wedding planner. "Thank you for all your help. We'll stay in touch."

"Isabella has a list of the photographers and florists we discussed. She'll give it to you. When you decide who to use, let me know, and I'll coordinate with them."

"Thanks, Wreath. Have a good lunch."

Constance sat back down. "Sorry. Back to using the Castle Restaurant?"

Isabella's expression begged forgiveness. "No, I'm sorry. We only use it for eighty or more guests. We can offer a buffet in the Main House."

Constance nodded her okay. "I was thinking finger foods."

Isabella stood and handed out menus. "You can select what you would like to serve."

Beau, who had dozed and had to be nudged, looked over the menu with his son. "I don't see chicken wings."

"Done—we'll add that." Isabella smiled at Beau.

"Let's not add chicken wings to such an upscale menu." Marilyn glanced at Beau.

"Where I come from, chicken wings are upscale." Beau

drummed the table with his fingers.

Isabella diplomatically replied, "There isn't a problem, really. Many people select wings."

Marilyn looked at Beau and suddenly discarded any pleasant thoughts she had earlier.

"Fine. If I may suggest the duck eggrolls with crawfish gumbo sauce?"

"Sure, Mom, sounds good." Constance's voice sounded like she was trying to keep peace.

Beau put his finger up in the air. "I like the sound of these fried green tomatoes with that stuff on top."

Isabella looked at the menu. "Yes, with the jumbo crabmeat."

"Well, it would suit me fine if we could leave it off and just fry 'em."

Marilyn's briefcase fell to the floor when she stood. She addressed her daughter after picking it up. "Constance, if you don't mind, I'll let you and Justin make these decisions. I have a number of client calls to make. Just don't forget to ask about a local photographer and florist." She kissed her daughter's cheek after seeing the surprise on her face. "I'll check with you later." She turned to Isabella. "Thank you. I'll be in touch. You've been very helpful." Marilyn could feel the heat rush from her neck to her face.

As she walked out the door, she heard Beau ask, "Did I say something wrong?"

To herself, Marilyn muttered, "Everything."

⤜∾⤛

Marilyn made her calls. One woman insisted she return to Denver right away. After all, she said, she was paying an enormous sum of money. Marilyn dispassionately tried to console her client. She was then accused of disparaging the client's predicament. Marilyn assured her when she returned to Denver, she'd be the first on her schedule. Finally, the woman's temper was abated and Marilyn hung up with a sigh. She fell back on her bed and thought about her own predicament. She had to think of a way to keep from being so irritated by Beau. For Constance's sake. She rolled over, retrieved her phone, and called Constance, assuming by now the meeting would be over.

When her call was answered, Marilyn asked if she was happy with the arrangements. Satisfied her daughter was okay with everything, she took a deep breath.

"Constance, I wonder if there would be any way you could check and see if there are accommodations available in the Main House."

"For who?"

"Whom. For me, sweetheart. I just don't think it is appropriate for me to stay in the Dairy Barn with a. . .gentleman." She had to force that word out.

"But, Mom, I wanted you guys to get to know each other. And it is part of the inn."

"Well, I think we have. Now I'd like to stay at the Main House."

Constance's voice sounded weak when she answered her request. "Okay, Mom, I'll see. I'll call you right back."

Marilyn started gathering her toiletries together to pack when the phone rang.

"Mom? No, there are no rooms."

"Well, there is an extra one here."

"But none here." Agitation reflected in her speech.

"Well, dear, would you like to change rooms with me?"

"Good grief, Mother. It can't be so bad. What's the problem? I don't want to be that far away from Justin."

Marilyn considered this. "You're right. I shouldn't have asked you. I'll be fine. What are your plans for the rest of the day?"

"Justin and I are going to go talk to a few people Isabella recommended for flowers and pictures." Constance paused. "Do you and Beau want to come?"

"Oh no, darling. Go ahead. Listen, it seems to me we've about accomplished everything we needed to. That is, if you succeed this afternoon. I have a client screaming for help and wonder if you think I could leave a little earlier than planned."

"What is wrong with you? Justin and I have made arrangements for all of us to do some things together. One is a surprise. Can't you stay at least a couple more days?"

Marilyn felt ashamed. This was one of the most important times in Constance's life, and here she was minimizing it so she could get away from Beau. "Yes, sweetie. I want to share some time with all of you. I just didn't know. Forgive me?"

"Yes, ma'am. I love you, Mom."

"Me, too, dear. Talk to you later."

Marilyn fell back on the bed again. She didn't want to get up anytime soon.

After the planning meeting, Beau drove his truck to the nearest convenience store for a newspaper and a large Coke.

He thought about the women in his life—Beau chuckled—or the lack of them. Women seemed to automatically like him. He'd been told he was charming, larger than life, even good-looking. Some of that was overstated. Probably. He'd been on quite a few dates after Mary Ann died. A prominent rancher, he had the opportunity to meet a lot of folks, had a lot of friends. Someone was always trying to fix him up, trying to saddle him with a friend, a sister, or a cousin. Even once to an ex-wife. He didn't always take the bait. Especially with that one. Beau smiled. But the relationships never lasted. He never got serious, and sometimes the women became disinterested. He never gave it a lot of thought because he really didn't want to settle down with another woman. Mary Ann may have died, but she broke his heart while doing it. That was a hard thing to get over. Only the Lord could have seen him through.

He went in the store and bought the paper, a big Coke, a bag of Doritos, and a can of boiled peanuts. He didn't know what Marilyn was doing, but he knew it wasn't lunch. So he'd just go back to his room and chow down. Maybe she'd like some herself. He wondered as he drove back what had gotten under her skin. It couldn't have been his request for chicken wings. She'd be on a high horse if that was the case. Which he'd decided if she was, she could just take her better-than-you-are ways back to Denver. Somehow, he knew he irritated her, and he would have to fix it. For Justin's sake.

❧

Marilyn heard the front door open and got off the bed to lock her door. She intended to stay in her room all afternoon. She was sure she would have to face Beau for dinner. It would be rude not to. She wondered if Constance had plans for all of them tonight. She had not said exactly which evening. Her thoughts were interrupted by a knock. She moaned as she got up to answer the door.

So much for solitude.

"Hi, girl. Look what I've got." The door had not opened all the way when Beau held a bag of chips through the crack.

"Hey, Beau. Uh-hmm. Looks like you're snacking for lunch."

"Yeah. Got some boiled peanuts, too. And a big Coke. Want to come to the living room and watch television? I'll share."

"No, I don't think so. I was resting. Had a number of calls to return, and I'm a little tired." She saw his hurt expression, and it actually made her feel bad. Sort of. Probably because she felt a little guilty for leaving the meeting so abruptly.

"Not even just a swallow of Coke? I can pour some in a glass over ice."

She had to do it. For Constance. And maybe a little to make up to Beau for being rude.

"Well, something cold would be great."

"Come on out here, girl. I'll be fixing it for you."

"Fixing it? Is it broken?" She just couldn't help herself. She knew what he meant, but *fixing it*?

"You're cute. No, it's not broken. It means I'm making it for you. Ya'll don't say that in Denver?"

"Not really. I'll be just a second."

Marilyn shut the door while she smoothed her clothes

and her hair. She applied a little lipstick and left to spend some time with "Bubba Beau." She needed to make sure she didn't say that aloud. Anyway, there were probably a lot of nice guys named Bubba.

She walked downstairs and found Beau sitting on the couch. She skirted around the coffee table to sit in the chair beside it. Before she could settle in, he was holding the Dorito bag in front of her.

"Have some. Your Coke's on the table."

To please him she took a chip. "Thanks, Beau. I am a little hungry."

"Ought to be. You hardly touched your eggs this morning. Only half your toast. Not to mention the grits. You must not have liked them."

He was scrutinizing her breakfast? "I don't usually eat a big breakfast. Maybe half of a whole-wheat bagel. Sometimes a granola bar on the way to work."

"And you don't do lunch. No wonder you're so skinny."

"I'm not skinny."

He looked her over. "Well, not everywhere."

She chose not to open that door. Instead, she thanked him for the Coke.

"So," he asked, "where are we going for dinner?"

"I'm happy with the Castle Restaurant." It would be quicker. "So, you don't think the kids have plans for us tonight?"

"Oh no, tomorrow night. I'm sure we'll eat there before we leave, but tonight I'd like to do something different. I've heard about Biscuits & Blues downtown. How would you like a good ole shrimp po'boy?"

She would just go along. For a couple of days, she could get through almost anything. "Sounds good. How far is it from here?"

"Just a way down the road. I think we should take my truck."

"Your truck? That's okay. We'll go in my car."

"Don't think so. We'll go in the truck."

"Whatever." She hoped it didn't smell like cow manure. "I think I'll go rest awhile. What time do you want to leave?"

"Let's leave about six. We can walk around downtown, too. Take your coat. We've had a little front come through. And, hon, wear some jeans."

"I didn't bring jeans. Let me handle what I'm going to wear. Hon."

"Sure, babe, sorry. Just wanted you to be comfortable. I thought a woman from Colorado would at least have jeans and gypsy boots."

"I live in the city and practice law." She got up and started walking toward the stairs. "Thanks for the Coke."

"Yeah, no problem."

Chapter 3

Marilyn curled her hair and wore it down. For warmth, she told herself. She washed her face and applied fresh makeup. Just to feel better. She dressed in winter-white wool pants and a red sweater. It was not cold here in November as in Denver, but chilly enough tonight. She grabbed her brown leather jacket and went downstairs to meet Beau. He was waiting at the front door.

"Looking good, kid."

She smiled. "Sounds kind of like a Bogart movie. Thanks."

He nodded and placed his hand on her back as they walked to the truck. He opened her door and helped her into the cab. When he shut the door, she sniffed, mildly disappointed she smelled only a vague, mannish fragrance, which didn't substantiate her preconceived notions. Always an attorney.

They were quiet as he maneuvered the large truck through town. He found a parking place a couple of blocks from the restaurant, and they walked slowly, taking in the crisp air and the historical downtown area.

Beau grabbed her attention by pointing to something down the street. "Look, the town has already hung Christmas decorations on the poles. I bet they turn them on Friday. Celebrations are big the day after Thanksgiving."

Marilyn sighed. "Probably so. I've been seeing Christmas displays in stores for a month. I do wish we wouldn't commercialize it so."

"I know." Beau had slowed the pace, and he stopped and looked at her. They had reached the restaurant, but he didn't seem in a hurry to go in. "I wish you could have Christmas with us. At my mom's. It would take you back in time."

"Sounds nice. Uh, shouldn't we go in?"

He placed his hand on her back again as he led her past the crowd waiting outside. His touch was beginning to feel welcome. . . . Scary.

She was surprised they didn't have to wait for a table. But when the hostess addressed Beau as Mr. Burnham, she realized he had made reservations. How clever. She watched him talking to the pretty blond. He looked dapper in his jeans, white shirt, and brown corduroy jacket. It seems the blond thought so, too. She leaned toward him, laughing at his remarks, her eyes sparkling, her red mouth smiling preposterously. He followed her to the table, Marilyn tagging along behind. She actually felt a bit miffed.

An older woman, thankfully without blond hair, handed them menus. As she studied hers, Beau took it from her.

"We are going to have the shrimp po'boy. I bet you don't

get fresh seafood in Denver. Not like this anyway."

"I told you I'm not used to someone making my decisions for me."

"Seems to me like you would enjoy it for a change."

Marilyn contemplated that for a second. She formed a small smile. "Maybe you're right. I give."

He placed their order and looked seriously at her. "May I ask you a personal question?"

"Maybe. Depends."

"This morning at breakfast, you looked sad when I said I consider you family." He paused before adding, "Why?"

Marilyn, caught off guard, hesitated, thinking about her reply. She decided to be honest. "I have no one besides Constance. My husband had a large family, but since his death, they seem to have disappeared. I have no brothers, no sisters, no aunts, uncles." She choked on the next words. "My parents had me after being married twelve years, and they are deceased now. It touched me. It was a thoughtful thing to say."

"I meant it. Really. You have us now. We're all here for anything you ever need, Marilyn." He patted her hand. "I couldn't help but hearing you say in the meeting you have no friends coming to the wedding. Why not?"

She was somewhat riled by this question. "Must have been before you fell asleep." She still couldn't help herself but softened as she continued. "I don't actually have many friends. There's Lily." She held up one finger. "I guess you could add Courtney and Hazel in my office." Two more fingers rose. "Maybe Elizabeth. Or again, maybe not." Her three fingers folded back into her hand as she made a fist. "I'm so busy. Really. I don't have time to. . ." She stopped and looked at Beau.

"Again, Marilyn. You have friends now. Family if that suits you."

She shook and bowed her head so he wouldn't see the tears gathered in her eyes. She didn't look at him as she spoke. "Thank you." Her words seemed insufficient. She realized she had concentrated on her work and pushed private matters aside. Beau bringing it to the forefront hurt.

The embarrassing moment was erased when the waitress brought their order. Marilyn didn't have to lift her head, because when the lady left, Beau began to pray. What did she feel about this man? One minute he was a crude cowhand, the next, a prince on a white horse.

After the blessing, Marilyn blurted out, "That's another thing."

"What's another thing?"

"We quit going to church after my husband died. Constance doesn't have a spiritual background."

Beau was quick to appease her. "She has it now. She made a confession of faith. Our pastor baptized her a few weeks ago." He paused, as if gauging her reaction. "She wanted to call you. She wanted you there, but she knew you were too busy and you were coming this week."

"Oh, I see. I mean I'm glad. I'm sorry I missed it." She felt her eyes fill. "I made one, too. Long years ago. I'm afraid I haven't been a good Christian."

"Hey, it happens. But God is merciful and loves us

unconditionally. You can repent and begin anew. That part of your life will be wiped from the slate. He is a forgiving God."

She smiled and wiped a tear with her napkin. "Yes, He is. Thank you."

"You're welcome. How's your sandwich?"

"The best seafood of my life."

"Knew it."

⊷∾⊶

After leaving the restaurant, Beau, without mentioning it to Marilyn, drove a few blocks to the river.

He saw her looking out the window and knew the question was coming.

"Where are you going?"

"I thought you might like to get a good look at the river." He pulled beside the street's curb and parked.

She continued looking. "The Mississippi surely is wide. Look, Beau, a riverboat."

"I don't want to spoil any surprises, but I'd bet that's what the kids have in mind for tomorrow night."

"You think so? How wonderful." She turned from the window and looked at him, her eyes sparkling. Not quite the tough bird she pretended to be.

"If it's what they do, don't say I mentioned it."

"Oh, I wouldn't. But it would be lovely."

"Care to brave the cold? We can sit in the gazebo a few minutes.

"Sure."

He opened the door and helped her with her coat. Taking her hand, he guided her to a bench facing the river. Lights reflected on the water like stars on a clear night. She shivered, and he wanted to warm her by moving closer, but that would be a mistake. "You're freezing. We'll only stay a minute."

"It's okay." She looked across the river. "No wonder it's called the 'mighty Mississippi.' "

"Yeah. I've seen it from almost every port. It never fails to amaze me." He looked at her. She seemed different tonight. "Marilyn, what happened to your husband?"

"Brain tumor. He was only thirty-three." She continued to stare at the river.

Beau was sorry he asked. Sadness had replaced the gleam in her expression as she turned to face him. "What about your wife?"

"Car wreck." He felt his jaw tighten, and anger overcame him as it did every time he remembered it.

"What's wrong? Are you mad at me for asking?"

"No. But it's a subject I can't discuss. I try not to even think about it."

She hesitated before replying. "You must have loved her so much."

He slapped his hand on the seat of the bench. "Yeah, unfortunately I did." He stood and turned toward her. "Ready to go?"

"Of course. Beau, I'm sorry I asked." She stammered through an apology. "It's just you. . .so I thought. . .I'm sorry."

"You're right. I did bring it up. Forget it. Come on, let's get back."

He didn't say anything on the way back to Dunleith. He hated that she regretted bringing up his past, thinking she was introducing fresh sorrow to his heart. She would be surprised to know sorrow was the least of his emotions.

~~~~~

Marilyn's cell phone rang. She gave Beau an apologetic look when he glanced her way.

"Hello."

"Mom, where are you?"

"On the way back to Dunleith. Beau and I had dinner."

"I need to talk to you. Can we have breakfast in the morning at the Castle Restaurant?"

"Is anything wrong?"

"No, I just want to run some things by you about the wedding."

"Sure, honey. What time?"

"Eight?"

"I'll be there."

"Thanks, Mom. See you tomorrow."

Marilyn hit the END button and slipped her phone back in her purse as Beau drove up to the Dairy Barn. She unhooked her seat belt and looked at him when he stopped.

He turned toward her. "Problem?"

"No, wedding matters." She took a small breath. "Beau, I enjoyed this evening, and I'm so sorry if I intruded by asking too many questions. I guess I'm an attorney 24-7."

He shook his head. "No, you didn't. I was at fault for asking the first question. Look, Marilyn. Both of us have had a past, maybe good sometimes, maybe bad at times. I really want us to be a family. I love Constance like my own daughter, Heather. I can't wait for you to meet her and my mom. Let's look forward and not relive the past." His look was serious. Steady. "Does that suit you?"

"Yes. Of course, and thanks for this evening."

Beau clipped her chin with the crook of his finger. "You bet, little lady. I had a great time."

What was it about this man? She couldn't figure it out. She waited for him to open her door as she had learned he was prone to do. They walked to the front door, his hand again on her back. She thought she could feel the warmth even through her jacket. Heat rose up her neck, and her face felt warm. She hoped it wasn't red when she faced him inside, glad only the lamp was burning. She patted his arm and turned toward the stairs. "Thanks again. I'll see you in the morning."

Beau grabbed her sleeve and turned her around. "That's it? Wouldn't you like to watch some television, have some coffee?"

She looked toward the TV, as if seeing it would help her with an excuse. "Sounds nice, but I really need to get up early."

"Yeah, breakfast and all. Sure, babe. I'll just see you in the morning. If you make coffee, knock on my door and wake me up when it's ready."

"Sure. Babe." She turned toward the stairs. This time she hurried. Redneck Bubba was back.

⁂

Marilyn waited ten minutes in front of the restaurant before Constance appeared. She couldn't help chuckling when she thought of how she dressed and left without making coffee. She assumed Beau was still asleep. Wake him up when the coffee was ready. *Not in my lifetime.* She resumed her straight face when she saw Constance coming.

"Hi, Mom. Sorry I'm late."

"Déjà vu. Heard that before." Marilyn couldn't help but smile. She missed her daughter, the good times and trials, too. She didn't look much different. Her strawberry-blond hair, inherited from her father, swinging in a ponytail. Her fresh-faced smile. Her glass always half full. She would be a joy to anyone.

Constance hugged her mother. "Let's eat. I'm starved."

"Nothing new there, either." Marilyn received a punch in the arm.

Once seated and order placed, Marilyn asked, "Everything go okay yesterday? Flowers and pictures taken care of?"

"Yes, but I didn't order anything but a vase of fresh flowers for the large table at the reception. Oh, and some white roses to mix in with their garlands."

"Fine. So what do you want to discuss?"

"Mom, you can't even fathom what it's like to be a woman in this state. I guess it would be true in all Southern states." Constance leaned back against her chair and sighed.

"What's this about? Are you having second thoughts?"

"I don't think so. It's just so different from the way we lived. I mean you can't take a crash course in how to become a Southern belle. I think it's something taught at birth and descends from generation to generation."

"What is? What are you talking about, Constance?"

She shook her head. "You have no idea. Did you know making chicken salad is a must? You have to make it to fit in.

You have never made chicken salad. How would I know how?"

"Dear, you are not making any sense. Why do you have to make chicken salad to be a—what did you call it—Southern belle? And why do you have to be one anyway?"

"I told you. You have no idea. Justin's grandmother has this circle of friends. Their daughters have circles of friends. They have church functions all the time. When they do lunch, most of the time they have chicken salad and fruit. If I have anyone over, I can only cook spaghetti. Or pizza."

Marilyn reached across the table and patted her daughter's hand. "You're getting nervous, honey. Everything seems bigger than it is. Chicken salad is not hard, and I have made it before. It's made like tuna salad. We've eaten many tuna sandwiches."

"No, it's not that simple. It has lots of stuff in it. They even put nuts in it. And grapes. And did you know there are only about twelve patterns of acceptable silver? And most of these ladies change their china patterns every season? And Justin's grandmother says you never serve potato salad on fine china. I will never fit in." Constance's ponytail swung back and forth as she shook her head again. "And listen to this. If something falls below the esteemed Southern belle's idea of how something should look or be, they say, 'How tacky.' "

Marilyn laughed. So much for the half-full glass. "I think you are taking these things too seriously. I have never heard such things."

"Precisely, Mom. And neither had I. I'm learning more every day. They make *chicken and dressing* instead of stuffing. And with cornmeal. I'm going to have to visit Paula Deen to learn how to cook like they do."

"Sweetheart, you'll learn. I'm sure Justin's grandmother will teach you. According to Beau, she's a sweet lady."

"She is. They have a large family. I'm not used to that. It's overwhelming. I'm glad we are going to be here for Thanksgiving. This restaurant is preparing a true Southern meal. You'll see what I'm talking about."

"Don't fret. You have premarital jitters. You'll ease into it all. I promise."

"Maybe you're right." Constance's uncommon demeanor tugged at Marilyn's heart.

"I am. Wait and see."

Their breakfast arrived, and Constance reached for her mother's hand when the waiter left. "Justin has taught me we need to always say a blessing. Do you mind?"

"No, dear, of course not. Beau says one, too." Marilyn felt ashamed she had never thanked God in front of her child before. That she had to learn this from others. She bent her head as she listened to her daughter's beautiful words.

"Dear Lord. How can I say thanks for all You have done for me? My wonderful mother, the father I knew for such a short time. The blessings You bestow. And Justin. Forgive me my frivolous concerns, Lord, for I am so very rich. Thank You for this food, and may it nourish us for Your service. Amen."

Marilyn squeezed her daughter's hand when she finished. "I'm so proud of you. Beau told me about your decision to trust Christ. It's the best thing any of us can do in our life. I'm sorry I wasn't there."

"Thank you, Mom. I knew you were busy, but I should

have called you." She sipped her coffee. "Oh, and there's one more thing. I didn't think to ask about a wedding cake for the reception." She laughed. "We were more concerned about the wings."

"Oh dear. We will try and meet with her after breakfast. If they can't do it, I'm sure they will recommend a bakery." Marilyn looked down at her plate. She had splurged and ordered pancakes. Beau would be so proud.

They ate in silence a few minutes. Marilyn used this opportunity to ask the question that had been on her mind since the night before. "Constance, do you know what happened to Justin's mother?"

"She got killed in a car wreck."

"Yes, I know. But is there anything else? Beau seemed to get angry when he told me about it last night."

"No. I can't imagine what else it could be. Justin has only told me how she was killed. I think he was once bitter, but Beau leaned on the Lord during that time. Still does. He occasionally sings a song in church. In his testimony, he proclaims he has been a Christian since he was nine years old. But it was the accident that enlightened him as to what it really means."

Marilyn choked on a bite of pancake. She quickly took a sip of coffee and sputtered out, "Beau sings? What is the song?"

"One made popular by Charles Johnson. 'I Can't Even Walk without You Holding My Hand.' Mother, when Mr. Burnham sings that song, there's not a dry eye in the church."

"Amazing. Okay." Marilyn sat back and took a deep

breath. "Really amazing. Please don't mention I asked. I don't mean to be nosy. It was just odd, is all."

"I won't mention it. Boy, aren't these pancakes good?"

Marilyn nodded. Oh, the minds of the young. From someone's death to pancakes in the time it takes to snap a finger.

Chapter 4

After listening to Constance talk to her wedding planner for ten minutes, Marilyn finished her third coffee refill and deliberately set the cup on the saucer. The noisy clink brought Constance's gaze toward her. Marilyn signaled with her hand to wrap it up. Her daughter smiled and told Wreath she'd call later.

"What?" Constance lifted her eyebrows as she looked at her mother.

"I think you gathered your information in the first two minutes. We need to select a cake?"

"Mom, I think you should leave your alter personality in the office. No wonder you don't have many friends."

"That hurt."

Constance relented. "I know. I'm so sorry. But, really, you need to relax and discover a life outside of the courtroom. But, yes, we need to go into town. I know exactly what I want."

Marilyn was digesting and trying to process what Constance had told her. She knew she was too uptight. After observing Beau and Constance as they displayed their faith, maybe she needed to rediscover hers. She would have to dig deep. She lifted the ticket from the table and responded. "Okay, baby, I'll do better. I'm charging this to my room." She signed the ticket and stood.

Constance sighed. "I need to let Justin know I'll be gone awhile. We could shop for your dress for the wedding, too." She glanced at her mom's clothing. "For sure, I'd like to be in on that."

Marilyn leaned toward her. "You're hurting me again."

⟡

Marilyn turned on Natchez's Main Street. "Oh my. Look, they're putting up a giant Christmas tree. Right in the middle of the street!"

"They have it blocked, Mom. You'll have to turn at the next intersection."

"Where is the bakery, Constance?" Her voice was firm, suspecting. As usual.

"Actually, it's on John R. Junkin. But I thought we'd see a dress shop downtown."

"Let's order the cake first. I can get a dress in Denver."

"Well, according to the map, we can turn right here and hit Franklin, turn right on Homochitto and get on John R Junkin."

"So we're going in circles?"

"Sorta."

Marilyn continued to follow Constance's directions. She was actually not disturbed by this. At least she wouldn't be exposed to Beau for a while. "What's the name of the bakery?"

"Edna's."

"Isn't that it?" She pointed to the sign.

"Yes, pull in."

Marilyn was ahead of her. She had already slowed down and turned on her signal. She stopped in front of the bakery. "Are they open?" It appeared to be dark inside.

"Yes. Let's go.

They were seated at a table with a photograph book of various wedding cakes. Constance exclaimed, "This is it." They were only on page 2.

"Are you sure?" Marilyn was looking at three double layers positioned by the stand at different angles. It was beautiful, with ivory icing and elegant white roses floating across the layers in clusters of four.

"Mom, it's perfect. I want to check and see if they can add a red ribbon with icing, though. My dress, which you haven't seen, by the way, is ivory with delicate white roses trimming the bodice and a white train. I know it sounds strange, but it is so pretty."

"Okay, how many does this serve?" She stretched across the table to read the text beside the photo. "I can't see what it says."

"Up to sixty. Just right."

"Okay, let's order it."

After providing the baker with dates and times and determining the cost, they left with Constance at the wheel. Marilyn thought for Dunleith. But Constance turned west and soon crossed the bridge across the Mississippi River. Marilyn turned and looked at her daughter. "What now?"

"You'll see." Constance pulled an online map from her purse

and began turning soon after reaching Vidalia. Eventually they arrived at a dress shop called Billie's.

"You're determined to help me find a dress. I doubt very much I'll find something here."

"We can look."

Ten minutes later, Constance found Marilyn looking through a rack of long dresses.

"No, ma'am. Try this."

Marilyn looked at the classic dress. Short, black. Peplum lace, cap sleeves. Not what she would select for a wedding, but chic, ultra feminine, and stunning. "You're sure?"

"Try it on."

"Okay." Marilyn asked the salesclerk to direct her to the fitting room. She laid her clothes gently over the door, slipped on the dress, and turned toward the floor-length mirror. Her lips opened with a soft, "Wow." Constance picked a winner. The dress stopped about two inches above her kneecap, the lace of the bodice flaring out about three inches below the waist, making the waistline look slimmer. She didn't want to look better than the bride, but. . .

When she redressed and came back out, Constance was holding a pair of satin heels with peep toes and crystals adorning the tops in one hand. In the other were a crystal stretch bracelet and crystal-accented chandelier earrings. Marilyn shook her head. "You've been busy."

She smiled at her mother. "I wanted to see the dress on you."

"You can. At the wedding."

"You liked it!"

"You, my dear, have excellent taste. Now, what's all this?"

"They will go beautifully with the dress. What do you think?"

"I think I'm set if the shoes fit. Thank you. Now if I can get all this in my suitcase."

"When is your flight?"

"Tomorrow. Three thirty."

"No, that won't do. Tomorrow's Thanksgiving, and we have reservations for a typical Southern meal at the Castle Restaurant. I had all our rooms reserved until Saturday. I want us to enjoy the lighting of the Christmas tree and the street decorations Friday night."

"Oh, Constance. I really have so much to do at work. I'm getting calls from unhappy clients."

"Mom, this is important to me. You will only be here a couple of days for the wedding. Please, let's enjoy this time together. It will be so busy then."

Marilyn saw the intensity in Constance's face. The pleading look she remembered when her daughter was growing up. She gave in to it then, and she couldn't help but give in now. "Of course. I want this time to be memorable for you. For all of us. The grumbling clients will have to get over it. I'll call and see if I can change my flight to Saturday."

Constance hugged her mom, dropping earrings on the floor as she wrapped her arms tightly around her. "Thanks, Mom." She released her and stepped back. "I love you so much."

Marilyn felt her eyes fill. "Oh, sweetheart, I love you, too." Why had she been so work oriented that she had forgotten what was really important? She had already learned much from this trip. Obviously God was working on her. Well, He surely needed to.

Constance drove Marilyn to the Dairy Barn. "Justin and I have plans for you guys tonight. We will pick you up here at five. Wear something comfortable but nice.

"I've had more advice on what to wear in two days than all my life."

"Sorry. You just seem to have so many professional clothes. We relax more down here. Jeans, tennis shoes or flip-flops. You look so uncomfortable all the time."

"I have professional clothing because that's what I need in my world. And pajamas."

"That needs to change." Constance leaned over and kissed Marilyn's cheek. "Don't be hurt. I just want you to be happy."

"I am happy."

"No, I don't think so. But we'll work on it."

Marilyn glared at her daughter. "You do that. I'll see you at five." She forced a smile as she got out of the car.

"Don't forget to change your flight."

Marilyn nodded without turning around. She didn't know if she was hurt or angry.

❧

The door opened as Marilyn reached for the doorknob.

"Hi, kid. Wondered if ya'll would ever get back. Have a good day?" Beau searched Marilyn's face to detect her mood. She looked tired and not happy at all. "Didn't have a good time? You look angry."

Marilyn sat on the couch and hugged her purse to her

chest. "Do you analyze everything? My breakfast, my clothes, now my mood?"

"It's not hard, hon. You're like an open book. Thought lawyers had to keep their emotions intact. I'd love to watch the expressions on your face in the courtroom."

"Good thing you'll never have the opportunity."

He laughed. "You never know." He sat down by her. Put his arm on the back of the couch behind her. "Since we're family now, I just might come visit." He lowered his arm to cross her shoulders. He felt her cringe. He hugged her.

She lifted her arm and removed his. "So proud you care, Beau, but I'd sooner be left alone."

"Seems to me that is your problem already."

She turned to face him. "What do you mean?"

"It doesn't take a rocket scientist to see you're lonely, Marilyn. You close yourself off. Why?"

She looked down a minute. Two. Three.

Beau waited.

"I'm not really sure." She looked at him again. "Ever since Dan died, I have had the responsibility for everything. I have known no one cares one way or another what happens to me. Constance was a child, so she needed my attention. At work my boss gives me accolades if I win cases and bring in large settlements. Then he walks off and thinks nothing of me as a person. I have feelings, but no one with whom to share them." She reached over and patted his hand. "Thanks, Beau, for treating me like family. I'm sorry I seem so high maintenance, but truth is, I'm really not. Just not used to anyone in my life but my daughter. No one to care what I eat or if I had a good day. I guess I don't know how to accept someone might be concerned and be gracious to them for it."

"First of all, if you'd rekindle your relationship with the Lord, you'd see how much He loves you. He cares about everything you do. Beau stroked her hair. It was soft. He was gentle. She didn't push his hand away. "Marilyn, you need a little coddling. And some fun. Let's try to have a good time tonight with the kids. They are so excited about doing this for us."

She smiled. "You're right, Beau. Let's do enjoy ourselves. They deserve it. I guess we do, too. And may I ask you a question?"

"Sure."

"What is coddling?"

Beau's laughter rose from his gut. "You don't know what coddling means?"

Marilyn wasn't smiling. "You think I would have asked if I did?"

"Well, it's cooking below the boiling point, for one. For two, it's like pampering."

"So which do you think I need?"

Laughing, he caught her chin, brought her face closer, and kissed her forehead. "Sweetheart, I think you may need a little of both." He examined her pretty mouth, watched her lips part, and gently touched them with his. Soft and sweet. He pulled away before he became captivated and lost his senses, surprised she had not broken the embrace first. He sat back, waiting for her response.

"Now, was that cooking below the boiling point or

pampering? I mean it was coddling, right?" Her smile eased his mind.

"See, you're being human already."

"Oh, so I wasn't even human?"

"Hmm, almost. You only needed a few lessons. More breakfast, either lunch or snacks, and one of the best kisses you've ever had."

"Arrogant, aren't you?"

"Goes with being an important cattleman. We think we are all man."

"I see. Well, the kiss was nice, but I'll hold my conclusion on the all-man thing until all evidence is in."

"Spoken like a lawyer."

"I prefer attorney." She got up and walked toward the stairs.

"Yes, ma'am. Attorney it is. See you down here about five. That's when the kids are picking us up." He watched her climb the steps. His statement dangled in the air. He felt his lips with his fingers. They were still tingling.

Marilyn steadied herself as she walked up the stairs. She didn't want Beau to see how he had affected her. After closing the door to her room, she headed for the bathroom. Staring at herself in the mirror, she noticed light blotches of pink dotting her face while her cheeks shone like a setting sun. Her fingers touched her lips as she tried to extinguish the simmering that lingered, wondering if it was only her imagination. Then she breathed air in and out, washed her face with cold water, and pushed the feeling aside. Like when the witness on the stand had been dismissed, and Marilyn could head back to her seat, another one down.

To truly cleanse her mind, Marilyn emptied her briefcase and began making notes on a current case that she would face when she returned home. The alarm sounded at four, reminding her she needed to shower and change for the evening. A funny feeling hit her stomach. Like the witness was called back to the stand. She would be bolder.

After her shower, she walked to the closet. What would she wear? She had not packed changes for day and evening. Nice but casual, Constance had said. Huh. She searched and found the black pants she had intended to wear on the plane home. She pulled a pajama top out. Could it serve as something to wear out? Why not? No one seemed to like the alternative. Marilyn slipped the black and gray T-shirt over her head and stretched it to cover the top of her slacks. She pulled the long sleeves down so the cuffs would cover her wrists and walked to the bathroom mirror to examine the look. Not bad. She twisted her hair into a side ponytail before applying makeup. One step back, a sigh of approval, and she grabbed her jacket and joined the party waiting for her downstairs.

"Mom!" Constance's expression showed her approval. "You look great. And young."

Justin agreed, and Beau said nothing. He just looked at her, his face void of expression.

"Thanks, honey. You ready?"

"Yes, ma'am."

Marilyn followed Constance out, Beau and Justin following behind.

After settling in the backseat and buckling her belt, Marilyn glanced over at Beau. He was staring ahead, no expression on his face. She wondered if he was bipolar. He probably thought she was. Finally, she whispered, "Aren't we supposed to have fun?"

He turned his head and faced her, his expression stoic for a few seconds. Then he smiled. She got the impression it was feigned. "I got a call about an hour ago. Two of my cows have been found dead. If more die, it would be really bad news. I don't have a clue what it could be."

"I'm sorry, Beau. When will you know?"

"I have my men out looking. They'll call. Meanwhile, the vet is on his way to check the dead ones. You know, I know them all." He shook his head. "Hey, it's all a part of it. I'll enjoy myself, I promise." He winked at her. And then the smile faded.

Marilyn gave what he said some thought. In her mind, she always placed people in groups. Professionals like herself, who entered tall buildings through glass and chrome doors and dressed in suits, one category. Funny, she placed doctors, dentists, and medical workers in a separate group. Then there were people like Beau. She pictured them in overalls, driving tractors, feeding cows, growing crops, sitting in small-town beer joints, and spitting tobacco. And, of course, the blue-collar workers, standing on an assembly line, their work tedious, metal lunch box, and a thermos keeping the coffee warm.

Maybe she was wrong. When did she begin to think like that? Her childhood had been simple. Her father owned his own hardware store in small-town USA. But she had gone to law school and met Dan. Refined. Handsome. Son of distinguished mother-and-father attorneys. She got caught up in their lifestyle. Yes, they went to church, but now she wondered why. Was it from the heart or pretentious? Networking? Socializing? Marilyn loved Dan deeply and until now never considered he had faults or was wrong or wasn't all he seemed. It hurt. But now she was beginning to see things in another light. In his own world, Beau was obviously a professional, too. And he seemed to care, not only about the profit, but about the animals he tended. She searched her soul. Did she really care about her clients? The answer caused her pain, as well.

The car pulled to a stop. Marilyn looked out but couldn't tell where they were. Justin and Beau got out and walked around to open the ladies' doors. Beau and Marilyn followed Justin and Constance down the street. They stopped in front of the Eola Hotel. Marilyn wondered why. But she followed the children in. Marilyn stopped and stared at her surroundings, momentarily forgetting her depressing thoughts.

"Oh my. This is beautiful." She looked around the lobby at the lovely antiques, the oil paintings, fountains, green marble columns, and then upward to the chandeliers and finally the painted ceiling. Cherubs graced the ceiling, floating amid flowers and ribbons. Real cedar and pine boughs laden with berries and ornaments wound their way up columns. A Christmas tree stood tall, displaying colorful balls and tinsel. The decorations reminded Marilyn that Thanksgiving was the next day and Christmas and Constance's wedding were around the corner. "How old is this hotel?"

Justin opened a brochure. "Opened in 1927. Named after the developer's daughter. Seven stories with balconies that overlook the river." He looked up at Marilyn. "We can tour the courtyard and dining areas."

Just like a man—not big on descriptions; just get to the bottom line. But Marilyn smiled at Justin and thanked him.

They walked through the palm-filled New Orleans–style courtyard and paused to study the fire-and-water fountain. They continued through the dining areas, through arched doorways, and around stately columns—throughout an exuberant interior.

When they returned to the street, Marilyn thanked the kids for the tour, only to see a horse-drawn carriage appear when Justin whistled the driver over. He paid and bowed with an offered hand to his companions to climb aboard.

"This is a real treat, son." Beau actually looked happy in spite of his problems.

"Oh, this is not the finale, Dad."

Marilyn remembered what Beau had said about their surprise. She hoped she could show her excitement so they wouldn't know it was suspected.

The driver urged the horse on and took them through town. Main Street was still blocked as the decorating continued on the huge tree. But the driver skirted close to it before turning so they could see the work in progress.

Beau had not seen it and leaned forward to shout to the driver and anyone else within earshot, "That's one big tree, man."

People on the sidewalk turned and stared. Marilyn cringed and settled back further in her seat. The ride, though, was amazing. They rode by antebellum homes flanked by large white columns and resting under moss-laden trees. She shivered from the cold and slipped on her jacket before folding her arms over her body to hold in the heat.

Justin held the back of the seat, stood, and whispered something to the driver, and soon they were back at the Eola. They thanked the driver while Beau took out a large bill and handed him a gratuity.

Marilyn assumed Justin had included that in his fare, but the "all-man" couldn't help himself. She guessed it went with the territory.

Assembled back in the car, Justin drove to a parking area near the river. When they stopped, he turned to the back. "Surprise, guys. We are going on a Natchez Dinner Jazz Cruise."

Even better. Marilyn was delighted. "Wonderful. Absolutely fantastic."

"There's the lawyer word again." But Beau seemed excited, too.

On deck, they stood along the railing to enjoy the view, waiting for the buffet to be served when they embarked.

Marilyn patted Justin's shoulder. "This has been the best evening I can remember in a long time. Thank you and Constance for planning this for us."

Beau agreed, and then said to Marilyn, "Even better than earlier today?"

"Whoa." Justin stood straighter. "What does that mean?"

Marilyn felt her face grow warm. She retorted, "Nothing. Your dad's being funny. So, is everything in order for the big day? Constance picked out my dress today."

Justin rescued her. "Bet you'll look like a million bucks."

Marilyn laughed. "Not sure about that, but I love the dress."

A shrill noise squealed through the air. The captain introduced himself and told them the riverboat was leaving the bank. The passengers found a spot to watch the paddle in action. Muddy water swirled around the wheel as they pulled toward the middle of the Mississippi River. A few minutes later, the captain announced dinner. While they were eating and the jazz band played "Ain't Misbehaving," Beau knocked over a glass of tea onto Marilyn's lap.

Beau watched Marilyn run up the stairs when they arrived back at the Dairy Barn. They had both thanked the kids for a wonderful evening, but Beau knew it ended when he knocked over his drink. How clumsy could he get? She was wet from the waist down and freezing. He had taken his jacket off and covered her lap. She was brave, finishing her meal, listening to the band, and applauding and laughing appropriately, but he knew she was miserable.

Beau called his ranch manager and inquired about his dead cows. He was told they found one more, but all the rest seemed fine. So far. He and the vet had loaded one on Beau's trailer and taken her to the office. They wouldn't know until the next day. Beau thanked him, changed his clothes, and got in bed.

He couldn't sleep. He wondered which cows died. He ran over the possibilities for their death. His thoughts were intermittently interrupted by thoughts of Marilyn. He knew she wore a facade. He knew she had it within her to be warm. And loving. He had seen it. And what about her faith? She said she had, in the past, gone to church. She indicated she had accepted Jesus as her Savior. Did she push that faith so deep after her husband died that it only surfaced at times? He knew about that. Death would have been hard enough, but the other? Only God could have picked him up. But it took him a while to let Him. And now? Beau couldn't even walk without Him holding his hand. His wife's death had given him a double grief. Sadly the grief of her death had been overshadowed by the horror of the circumstances involved. He still harbored anger, hadn't yielded it completely to the Lord.

Chapter 5

Bright light filtered through the window. Marilyn rolled over to face the door. But sleep wouldn't return. She stretched, pulling her toes along the tightness of the sheet. A faint but familiar scent wafted its way across the room. She sat up and sniffed. Coffee. Throwing the covers off, she headed for the bathroom. She donned her robe and left for the kitchen, running her fingers through her hair as she walked down the stairs.

Beau stood by the pot with two cups in his hands, one reaching toward her. "Coffee?"

"Do you expect exoneration?"

"Yes."

Marilyn laughed. "Well, sir, you have it. Coffee is my weakness."

"I knew that."

Sipping the steaming beverage, Marilyn studied Beau. His sandy hair was in disarray. His blue eyes seemed to search hers. He was a handsome man. A big guy but not overweight.

Just tall and muscular. She could tell by his arms and the flatness of his stomach beneath the funny words, "Cows Rule." She assumed he had not brought a change of pajamas. She set her coffee down. Before it spilled from shaking hands. What was wrong with her? She had not been this affected by a man since Dan.

Beau's amusement reflected in his speech. "You okay?"

"Yes. What time is it?"

"Nine. You slept later than usual."

Now he knows my sleeping habits. "Guess so. What time are we meeting the kids at the restaurant for lunch?"

"Noon. Want some nabs with your coffee to tide you over?"

"Nabs? Are those peanut butter crackers?" She had heard the term but couldn't help teasing him.

"Yeah. They're in my suitcase. I'll get us a pack."

Watching him leave, she observed his muscular back, closing her eyes before her curiosity led her further. "Get a grip." She spoke softly to herself.

The package was already open when he returned. He allowed her to take the first two.

By the time she consumed them, he had finished the other four.

"Sorry. I have some more if you want."

"No. I'm saving my appetite for the meal you all have told me about."

"Great. Do you want to dress and walk around before we eat?"

"No, I have some paperwork to do. But thanks for the

coffee. I'll meet you down here at ten till." Marilyn patted his arm and left the kitchen. An arm she could easily lean on. She ran up the stairs and locked the door to the room. Paperwork could wait. She fell across the bed and envisioned Beau holding her. In those hard, strong arms.

∽

Justin had reserved a table at the Castle Restaurant. The Thanksgiving feast on a buffet table was sending enticing aromas across the room. Beau handed Marilyn a small menu announcing the choices for lunch. He looked over her shoulder as she read them aloud. "Herb and citrus-glazed turkey, Southern corn bread dressing, cranberry clementine relish, bacon-wrapped green beans." She stopped reading until she came across the desserts. "Umm, savory bread pudding with apples."

Beau added, "Southern pecan pie. And pear-walnut Huguenot torte? Not sure what that's about."

Marilyn glanced over at the buffet. "I don't know, but I'm ready to try it."

Beau stood. "Okay, let's have a blessing before we serve ourselves." He turned to a party of eight adjacent to them, noticing they hadn't yet served themselves. "Want to join us in a Thanksgiving prayer?"

One of the men frowned at him. "Are you kidding us, sir?"

Beau was surprised by the answer. "Why, no. I just thought as long as we were saying our blessing, I could say one for all of us."

"You assume a lot. If you don't mind, we'll tend to our own business." The man rose and encouraged his party to follow him to the buffet.

Beau stayed silent. He felt foolish. He had only been trying to be friendly. He looked around the table and saw mixed emotions. Justin and Constance seemed to feel sorry for him. Marilyn looked embarrassed. "I'm sorry. I didn't mean to offend anyone."

Justin nodded in sympathy. "It's okay, Dad. Say our blessing."

Beau sat before praying. He couldn't say it. "Justin, would you say the blessing?"

"Sure, Dad." Justin bowed his head. "Dear Lord, I have so many things to be thankful for today. The first is Your love and saving grace. I thank You for Constance and for my family. Thank You for Your provisions, for this food we are about to eat. Bless it so it will sustain us for Your service. Amen."

Beau reached over and patted his hand. "Thanks, son. Let's eat."

They served themselves and sat back down. Beau glanced at Marilyn's plate. "You should have gotten more dressing. You hardly have a spoonful."

"Beau, I know you love to be 'in charge.'" She glanced at the table next to them. "But if you don't mind, I would like to make my own decisions about what I eat. Just a suggestion."

Beau knew she was embarrassed, but she even seemed angry. "Sorry, hon. I was just trying to be helpful."

She didn't respond.

Justin and Constance tried to bring cheerfulness back to the table. They talked about the good food, the wedding, and Christmas. But Beau and Marilyn remained silent.

At the end of the meal, Beau was pleased to hear Marilyn finally speak.

"I have to say, this was a terrific meal. The dressing was better than I expected. Constance, you'll have to get me a recipe from Justin's grandmother."

Beau said, his voice soft, "I'm really glad you liked it. And I'm truly sorry I ruined our first Thanksgiving meal together."

Marilyn stood, and while hugging Justin and Constance, replied, "It's okay. Maybe you learned something."

Beau watched her walk out of the restaurant, and then he turned back to the kids. "Again, I'm sorry."

❧

Everything inside Marilyn congealed. The shock of Beau imposing on the people seated next to them had momentarily paralyzed her. Oddly, this morning she had forgotten how boorish he could be. So much for the strong arms to lean on. She hurried back to the Dairy Barn, wishing she had not promised her daughter she would stay until Saturday. She didn't feel like going to the lighting of the Christmas tree. Denver seemed so far away right now. But her mind took her there. Her heart was safe there.

Once in her room, she locked the door. In an attempt to buffer her thoughts, she turned on the television. A Paula Deen rerun on making dressing. She turned to the news. Depressing. She found a movie. Cary Grant wooing Deborah Kerr. She turned it off and stared out the window. Colorful leaves fluttered across the lawn. The limbs would soon be bare. Much like her soul.

Paperwork still waiting, she sat on the bed and opened the

nightstand drawer. The book stared back at her. Holy Bible. She lifted it and began to flip through the pages, hoping God would help her find just the right passage. One to soothe her. She stopped in John and looked at the page. Her eyes fell to verse 27 of the 14th chapter. "Peace I leave with you, My peace I give to you; not as the world gives do I give to you. Let not your heart be troubled, neither let it be afraid."

Marilyn let the Bible rest on her lap and glanced out the window. Shame flowed through her. She had put her only hope, her first love, on the back burner. The Lord was surely the source of peace. Of joy and happiness. She didn't need Beau or anyone else. She bowed her head and prayed for forgiveness. And then she eased the rest of her body on the bed and slept.

⟨∽⟩

After lunch Beau didn't bother Marilyn. He went shopping with Constance and Justin. They browsed the few open antique shops for accessories for their new home—a house eighty years old and only five miles down the road from Beau, but the most beautiful place in the world to the kids. They wanted to furnish it in keeping with its era. Beau smiled as they bantered with each other over items they wanted. He slipped behind their backs and purchased a few things they had reluctantly returned to the shelves. When they questioned what was in his bags, he responded, "I can shop for my house, too."

It was dark when they returned to Dunleith. Beau, noticing her car hadn't been moved all day, was anxious to check on Marilyn. Once inside the Dairy Barn, he eased up the stairs to find her door closed. He knocked softly, but no one answered. Knowing he shouldn't, he turned the knob. Locked. Disturbed, he went back downstairs, ate a pack of nabs, and dressed for bed. He stretched across the bed and wondered what tomorrow would bring. He had dated a few women since his wife's death, but he had not felt the sensations plaguing him now. And why? Marilyn wasn't exactly a bundle of womanly tenderness. Not exactly who he had expected to care for, or even like very much. But he did. Guilty on both counts.

&

The knock on the door had awakened Marilyn. She also heard the knob turn. Wow. How brazen was this man? Despite the slight growls in her stomach, she would not leave her room. Instead, she delved into her briefcase and worked until midnight, finally giving in to sleep when her eyes started feeling heavy.

Marilyn woke up and jumped from her bed to check the time on her phone. Six o'clock. She showered, washed her hair, and dressed for the day. Warm air had blown in from the Gulf, so she dressed in a pair of khakis and a pin tuck, buttercream blouse over a vicuña-brown tank. After applying a light coat of makeup, she fashioned her hair in a short braid that fell just past her collar. Then she grabbed her purse and set out for the day.

Her feet fell light on the steps as she tried to keep Beau from hearing her. Once in the car and on her way—to where she didn't know—she called Constance.

"Sweetheart, what is the plan for this evening? I know

you wanted me to stay for the Christmas lights, but do you have an agenda?"

"Mom, are you in your room?"

"No. I'm driving."

"Where are you going?"

"I'm not sure. I just want to know when to return."

"What's wrong? Are you mad at Mr. Burnham?"

Marilyn hesitated as she thought about the question. "Not really. I just need some time to myself."

Constance's voice drew out—"Okaay. Well, I guess we'll walk around downtown and grab a bite to eat while we wait for the lighting of the tree. Do you have anywhere you want to eat?"

"No. But I'm sure Beau does. Ask him."

"You *are* mad at him."

"No, Constance, I'm not. I just need some space."

"Okay, but be nice. Remember, this is mine and Justin's special time. Don't mess it up. Please."

Marilyn cringed as she was reminded of this. "I know, baby. I promise I won't. Just tell me what time you think we'll leave."

"I guess about five thirty. I think they light the Christmas tree at seven. That will give us time to find somewhere to eat. I hear Main Street will be crowded. They block it off for this."

"Okay. I'll be ready. Have a good day, honey."

"You, too, Mom. Just don't get lost."

"I won't."

As Marilyn hung up, she spotted a McDonald's. She pulled in, anxious for a sausage biscuit and a good cup of coffee. Since she missed dinner the night before, she was starving.

As she ate, she observed the older couple sitting next to her. She picked up her tray and turned to them.

"I'm sorry to bother you, but I was wondering if you could tell me somewhere near Natchez I could visit today."

The gray-haired woman smiled, crinkles framing her light blue eyes. "Where are you from, dear?"

"Denver. I'm here to help my daughter plan a wedding at Dunleith."

"Such a lovely place." She looked at her husband. "Fred and I have spent a weekend there. Even though we live in Natchez." She patted his knee before looking back at Marilyn.

"You need to drive down Highway 61 to St. Francisville. The town has beautiful homes and neat shops. I think you would enjoy it."

Marilyn rested her hand on the lady's shoulder. "Thank you so much. I'll do just that."

She pulled her keys from her purse and walked out, looking forward to her adventure.

⌘

Beau had no idea where Marilyn was. But he waited for her all day to return. He started getting dressed for the evening at four, and before he could pull his turtleneck over his head, he heard her come in. He couldn't see to walk to the door—his head stuck as he tried to get his arms in the sleeves—but he tried and stumbled over the nightstand, hitting his knee on its corner.

"Ow!"

By the time he stuck his head through the tight neck of the shirt, he heard her last two steps on the stairs before she opened and shut her door. He would have to wait until she was ready to go. He finished dressing and looked in the mirror. Stonewashed jeans, white cotton-knit turtleneck, and his brown corduroy blazer. He combed his sandy blond hair, which badly needed to be trimmed, and applied Old Spice. Justin had tried to get him to upgrade his fragrance, but he had always worn his favorite cologne and he always would.

Satisfied with his appearance, which he knew concerned him only because of Marilyn, he went into the living room and turned on the television. And waited. For an hour.

He watched her walk down the steps. She looked young like her daughter. She was beautiful. As she took the last step, she looked at him and smiled. Was it forced? He returned it as he stood.

"Are the kids picking us up?" She stood by the chair.

He looked at his watch. "Yes, any minute now. Have a seat."

"No, if it's time, I'll stand."

"Okay. How was your day?" He somehow knew not to ask where she had been.

"Good. I enjoyed it." No comment as to her whereabouts.

"I'm glad." Strained. Kids, hurry up.

Beau stood at the sound of the horn. "Well, they're here." *Thank goodness.* "After you, Marilyn." He held out his arm toward the door.

They climbed into the backseat, Beau allowing Marilyn to fend for herself. What else should he do, the way she was acting?

Justin turned toward his father. "Okay, where to?"

"I think we should park on the street by the river, if possible. Then we can walk wherever we want."

The streets were congested with traffic because so many people were going to the tree lighting. But Justin maneuvered the car patiently and pulled into a tight spot on South Broadway by the river. They got out and started walking toward downtown. Only one street over, Beau hollered.

"Whoa. Look at that."

They all looked toward where his finger pointed.

"Fat Mama's Tamales. Let's do it."

Constance looked at her mother. "Mom?"

"Whatever."

Beau turned toward them. "Okay, I just thought it would be fun. And who doesn't like hot tamales?"

Marilyn seemed to relent. "Of course. It sounds great." She even offered a pleasing smile.

"Good, then. Let's go." Beau seemed eager to get to the restaurant, which didn't look crowded at the moment.

Beau ordered a dozen tamales for the table, but each decided on a different entrée. Constance ordered a taco salad, Justin, two gringo pies, Marilyn, Natchez nachos, and Beau, well, more tamales.

Watching Marilyn eat her nachos was a treat for Beau. "You hungry, girl?"

Marilyn stopped eating and glared at Beau. Beau saw Constance elbow her mother, who suddenly smiled. Again, forced. "Yes, matter of fact, I am. No lunch."

He wanted so badly to inquire where she'd been, but

refrained. "Well, go to it, then. Glad to see you enjoy your food." He was beginning to wonder if he felt anything for her or not. Obviously, she didn't care much for him. That thought brought a little hurt to his heart. Guess his emotions were doing a two-step. Didn't matter. She would be leaving the next morning. He would be glad to get back to his cows. Which were happy just to graze. No worries. Then his thoughts turned to the ones that died. He still didn't have an answer.

Beau paid the bill and plopped a large tip on the table. He glanced at Marilyn, who was watching him with no small amount of disdain. *What?*

Justin and Constance thanked him for the wonderful meal, after which Marilyn expressed her sentiments. At least she enjoyed it.

They left and walked north toward Main Street where the lighting event was to take place. Once there, they assembled as close to the Christmas tree as the crowd allowed.

Beau looked at his watch. Five more minutes. They remained quiet, waiting for the big moment.

Christmas carols floated down the street as cool air from the northwest blew the warm air back toward the Gulf. And suddenly the colorful lights exploded on the huge tree. A chorus of "aahs" commemorated the spirit of Christmas as "Joy to the World" brought to light the true meaning of the celebration. The crowd sang along. And Marilyn put her hand over her heart. As if to commend that act, all the lights decorating the streets came on. The Christmas season had begun. And soon a marriage.

Chapter 6

Marilyn's alarm sounded at five. Because of her earlier flight change, she had a layover in Dallas. She had told everyone good-bye after the lighting of the tree downtown and the return to Dunleith. After dressing, she closed and snapped her suitcase and eased down the stairs so she wouldn't awaken Beau. The scent of fresh coffee rose up the stairs to greet her. Maybe the coffee was worth another good-bye.

"Good morning, Marilyn. Thought you might like some coffee on your ride to Baton Rouge."

"Cows Rule" caught her eye as she stepped off the stairs and reached for the cup. She wanted to remind him that a washer and dryer were available but decided she should just take the coffee and go. "Thank you, Beau. It will make my trip much nicer."

"Look, kid, I'm sorry if I have irritated you or embarrassed you in any way. I guess I'm not used to big-city girls."

"No, you're good. I just have a lot of work back at the office and so much on my mind. You know, with this wedding and all." She braved a look into those blue eyes. Then she swam out of that ocean as quickly as possible. "Well, if you can carry my bag to the car, I'll take this delicious cup of coffee and get on my way."

"Sure, hon."

She watched his muscled arm pick up the suitcase. Not even a pause. He took his left hand and pushed a sandy blond lock out of his eyes before opening the door and leading the way. She actually heard her intake of breath.

When she and her luggage were tucked away safely, she started the engine, smiled out the window, and drove off. She caught his salute in the rearview mirror. Was that sarcasm?

Thirty minutes past Natchez, her cell phone rang. By the time she fished it out of her purse, it quit. Constance. She pressed the callback button and heard her daughter's first words this morning.

"Mom, did you tell Beau good-bye?"

"Yes, dear. He fixed me coffee."

"He is sweet. I don't know why you had to be so rude to him. I honestly feel he's a very attractive man."

"Yes, he is."

"But?"

"Constance, don't take this the wrong way. I don't feel Justin's like his dad. Not really."

"What does that mean? Like what?"

"Well, I guess I have always had preconceived notions about Southern men. Especially farmers. Don't get me wrong. He's a super guy, but I'm used to a little more class."

"Like in the men you work with?"

"Yes."

"The men who wouldn't bother coming to your daughter's wedding or being your friend outside of the office?"

Marilyn slowed the car. Stunned. "I don't suppose I expect them to do that."

"Mother, may I share something I recently read about rednecks? And I assume it's what you think Beau is. Who happen to only fit in that group because of people like you, by the way."

"Constance, I—"

"Let me finish. I grew up in Denver. But I guess because I'm young, I had no preconceived notions like you. But redneck jokes have been around for years. I read an e-mail the other day. It said we need to take a look at the core beliefs of a culture that values home, family, country, and God. If I had to face terrorists who threaten my life, I'd choose these so-called rednecks to back me up. They are never offended by the phrase 'one nation under God.' You've never seen them protest the Ten Commandments being posted in public places. They are true and loving and care about individuals—like you, Mom—who are lonely and don't have a very large network of people who care. All I'm saying is judging Beau by such a demeaning standard is wrong. He would give anyone the shirt off his back. What about those men at your work? Would they do the same? Don't answer. Just think about it. And when we meet the week of Christmas, maybe you'll be willing to give Beau a break. Oh, and please be nice to his whole family. They are farmers who work hard. They love me, and I surely love them. And one last thought, Mom. Beau and his family do have class. Lots of it. They don't prejudge people. They value everyone. And the ladies can set a table even you haven't seen the likes of. They use china and silver and absolutely beautiful arrangements. They know which fork to use for each course. Actually, they are more refined than any of your associates. Don't you remember our chicken salad conversation?"

"Oh, honey, I'm so sorry. You are right, of course." Marilyn took a deep breath. "Please pray for me, Constance. My own daughter has pointed out my shortcomings. I'm like a Pharisee. I promise I'll be a different person." She wondered if Constance could hear the break in her speech as she felt the break in her heart. She wiped tears off her cheeks. "I do love you. So very much."

"It's okay, Mom. I guess even old people still learn, huh?"

Marilyn laughed. "And the old people would be whom?"

"Who." Constance laughed. "I better go. Have a safe trip, and I'll talk to you later today."

"You stay safe. And tell Justin and Beau I'll see them soon. Let me know when they find out what happened to the cows."

"That sentence seems so strange coming from you. But it sounds good. Love you."

"I love you, too, Constance. I'm really glad you're happy."

"Oh, Mom, before you hang up, I found out something."

"What?"

"I asked Justin about his mom. He told me his grandmother let it slip one day she got killed in a wreck while leaving with another man. They had suitcases in the car. He overheard her talking to her friend."

"Oh dear. No wonder he seemed angry. I'm so sorry."

"So, you'll be nice to him?"

"I will. I am so sorry." Marilyn knew she could never mention to Beau what she'd learned. He was too proud. But she could be nicer. She hurt for him.

❧

Beau drove straight to the vet's office before going home. He pulled up to an old white house his friend had bought and restored. Over 100 acres of woods and pasture surrounded the building. Dr. Rhodes had plenty of fenced area to accommodate sick horses, cows, and an occasional goat.

Barking dogs greeted him when he opened the front door.

"Hey, Michelle. Doc in?"

"Sure, Mr. Burnham. Go on back."

Beau stepped over a calico cat, which showed no interest in him. Had that experience already this week. He grunted and wound his way through the doors to the back, where he found the doctor.

His friend Kevin looked up. Then shook his head.

"So, what's going on with my cows?"

"Just got the report. Blackleg."

"You're joking."

"No, wish I were."

"So, my soil is contaminated?"

Kevin scratched his head. "I think maybe just a patch somewhere, or more of them would be dead by now. What say we go on over to your place and look around. I need to vaccinate as many as we can get ahold of. We can take some random soil samples to send the lab."

"Sounds like a plan. The sooner the better."

"Beau, you go on ahead while I gather up what I need. I'll meet you at your house."

"Good. Just come on in. I'm going to take my luggage upstairs and check the house. I've been gone almost a week."

"Sure thing. See you in a little bit."

Beau left with a sick feeling in his stomach. Driving home, he contemplated what this could mean. He hoped Kevin was right about it being just a patch of soil these particular cows had grazed. He felt if they could get them all vaccinated and they hadn't yet been exposed, it could work out all right. Ironically, his first inclination was to go home and try to contact Marilyn. Like she'd care.

❦

The moon cast enough light for the taller structures in her neighborhood to loom like ominous gray forms in a horror film. Marilyn felt loneliness engulf her. She pulled onto the driveway of the garden home she had purchased when Constance left for college. She sat in the car and stared at her house through her tears. She didn't even know her neighbors.

Oh God. How did I become this person? She blew her nose and closed her eyes. *I need You so much. I always have. Did I somehow blame You for our loss? Give me something, please. Something to make me feel whole and happy again. Hold me, Lord.* Marilyn pictured herself in Jesus' arms. He wrapped His loving arms around her, soothed her hair, and promised everything would be okay. These were her thoughts, but maybe, just maybe, He gave them to her for comfort. She wiped her last tears and smiled. Her heart felt light. She could change.

Marilyn opened the front door before retrieving her purse and bags. She pulled out the shopping bag holding her dress and smiled. She thought of Beau. How she hoped she had not ruined their friendship. The realization of how tender and caring a man he was almost brought her to tears again. How ignominious she had been. Mean. Despicable. Beau, who wanted only to invite her to be a part of his family. Beau, who loved everyone. Who even cared for his cows. And the tears started again.

After setting her bags down by the front door, Marilyn called Constance to say she was home. She dialed the number, walked into the kitchen, and put on a kettle of hot water for tea.

When Constance answered, Marilyn's first response was to inquire of Beau's cows.

"Oh, Mom. They had blackleg. That comes from contamination in the ground. They checked the pastures until it got dark and will finish tomorrow, but it's not good. They're hoping it is in a small area and the other cows somehow avoided eating there."

"Oh, I'm so sorry. Will you tell him I asked and I wish him the best of luck?"

"Are you sick?"

"No, why?"

"This doesn't sound like you. I thought you didn't care for Beau."

"I haven't cared for a lot of things. Coming home to a lonely house made me see that. Constance, I really want to change, and I realize God is my answer."

"Mother. How wonderful. I'll be praying even harder for you."

"You've already been praying?"

"Yes, ma'am."

"Seems He's answering your prayers, sweetheart."

"I love you, Mom."

"I love you, too. I'll see you in a few weeks."

"Yes. I can't wait. I wish for you the happiness I feel when I'm with Justin."

"Thank you. Maybe one day."

She took her tea to the living room and sipped it. She would unpack later. She smiled at the thought of returning to Dunleith. To family. To a special friend.

❧

Beau walked through the chilled house to the kitchen, poured cold coffee into a cup, and microwaved it. He had been out all day fixing fence and feeding cows. The results of the samples had come back negative, meaning there'd been a small patch of contamination. He hoped, since the weather was getting colder and almost all the grass had died, he could keep them fed and happy through the winter. If they could get some snow or ice, it would probably kill whatever was in the ground. The *ding* brought his attention back to the coffee. He carried it with him to his den and set it on the fireplace mantel while he built a fire.

Fire blazing, Beau turned on a floor lamp and pulled the wingback recliner closer to the hearth to enjoy his coffee before the blazing flames. He studied the flames changing colors, reflecting on, not for the first time, the trip to Natchez.

He tried to recall all the things he had done that seemed to irritate Marilyn. He wanted to avoid them on his return trip next week. This was to be his son's special day. He wanted everything to be perfect for him and Constance. After that, well, the ball would be in her court. If she wanted to be part of this family, she could. If not, then so be it.

He looked around the old house. It had never seemed so lonely.

He moved his Bass Pro catalog over on the hearth and picked up his Bible. He always kept it there when he wasn't at church. He read it every night before going up to bed. He was studying Kings, but tonight he flipped through, trying to find a verse to give him comfort. He was even at a loss at what to pray.

He ran his finger across random verses until he stopped in chapter 8 of Romans. He read verses 26 and 27. "The Spirit also helps in our weaknesses. For we do not know what we should pray for as we ought, but the Spirit Himself makes intercession for us with groanings which cannot be uttered. Now He who searches the hearts knows what the mind of the Spirit is, because He makes intercession for the saints according to the will of God." Beau bowed his head and prayed what was in his heart, knowing his Lord already understood. He stood before the warmth of the fire, the loneliness fading, his heart full, his hopes sealed by the One who directed his path.

Chapter 7

Marilyn arrived at Dunleith the afternoon of December 23. She briefly paused to look at the mansion, its banisters draped with fresh greenery, the front door adorned by a huge wreath tied with red ribbon. She drove slowly and parked outside the office, which was close to the Dairy Barn. She glanced that way and saw Beau's truck. Of course a big wreath was secured to the back. She'd bet there was one on the front grill, too. She didn't know if she would be glad if her room was in the Dairy Barn or not. But when the woman at the desk affirmed she would be staying there again, she stifled a smile. She was determined to be different. She thanked the woman, took the key, and hurried to move her car closer to the Barn. She had little time to dress and get ready for a short rehearsal and dinner.

The wreath swung out as she opened the front door, and she had to move her head back to keep from getting hit. She was disappointed to see the door to the living area closed. Only the stairs were visible, so she trudged up, pulling her suitcase behind her. She unlocked her room and at least felt at home in the familiar surroundings. She sat on the edge of the bed and started thinking about the wedding. She panicked. She didn't know who was marrying them. Was it someone locally? Living so far from here, she didn't feel involved like she needed to be. She dug in her purse for her cell phone and dialed Constance.

"Mom, are you here?"

"Yes, just arrived. Constance, who is marrying you?"

"Are you nuts? Justin."

Marilyn chuckled. "No, I mean who is officiating?"

"Oh. Pastor Guy. From Beau and Justin's church. He was nice enough to bring his family during this busy time. I think they're staying through Christmas."

"Good. It has occurred to me there is a lot I don't know."

"Don't worry, Mama. I have everything under control. I should be the apprehensive one."

"I know, dear. I'm sorry. What time do I need to be at the Main House for the rehearsal?

"A little before six. It won't take long. With only one attendant and Beau as best man, there won't be much to do. Then we all have reservations at the Castle Restaurant."

The mention of that name brought back memories to Marilyn. Not all good. But then she remembered how kind Beau was to her by inviting her into his family. Not all bad.

"Sounds nice, baby. See you there."

Marilyn unpacked her clothes and hung them in the closet. She laid out the black silk pants and jacket she would be wearing this evening, shaking her head already. She looked back in the bag and found her red lace-trimmed tank and her red-and-white crinkle cotton voile scarf. Yes. Then she took a long, hot shower before dressing. She wanted to look her best. She smiled at the tingle in her stomach.

⌇

Beau had heard Marilyn arrive, but he was about to dress, and he didn't want to do anything that would cause problems before the rehearsal. He would meet her there. But he felt anxious. Like he was going on a first date. Or the last time he would see her. He glanced upward, as if he were reminding God it was all in His hands. But Beau would do his part.

He walked the brick path to the Main House where his pastor and several more had gathered. Pastor Guy reached out and shook Beau's hand while patting him on the back with the other. Beau wanted to hug him.

"This is a beautiful setting, Beau." Pastor Guy had wanted to marry them at the church. Constance had informed him God would be present wherever they married, after which he smiled and relented that it was true.

The men turned to see who was approaching. Beau stepped forward and took the girl's hands in his.

"Bethany, thank you for supporting us. I know you should be home with family at Christmas." Beau glanced at the young man beside her. "Hi, I'm Beau Burnham, Justin's dad."

Bethany made the introductions. "Mr. Burnham, this is Chase. I hope it was okay for him to come."

"Of course." He looked at Chase and patted his back. "We're glad to have you, son."

They all turned to see a beautiful woman open the back

entrance to the hall. Beau squinted to see if he recognized her. She was all smiles, and it took a minute for him to realize it was Marilyn. He stiffened, waiting for her response to him. But he smiled and held out his hand, which she graciously took and kissed his cheek. The eighth wonder of the world. He had to suppress looking her up and down.

"Marilyn."

"Beau. How good to see you."

They stared at each other before remembering people were standing around awaiting introductions. Beau took the honor.

Bethany hugged Marilyn. "You look wonderful, Mrs. McLemore."

"You, too. I haven't seen you since you and Constance left for college and your parents moved from Denver."

"They couldn't let me get too far away, and Dad was able to transfer."

"Yes, I wish I had done the same."

❧

The rest of the party arrived, and rehearsal began. When Marilyn stepped into the two open rooms where the wedding would take place, she let out a breath. "Oh my, it looks beautiful." Fresh greenery covered the mantels, a mixture of pine and cedar. The white roses Constance ordered had not yet been delivered, but large, glittering, white Christmas balls peeped from the stems among candles glowing through pristine glass. The lights in the chandeliers cast a warm glow over the floral carpet and antique furnishings.

A gentleman appeared and took his seat at the grand

piano situated in the corner of the room. The ceremony would take place in the middle of the two rooms to allow enough standing room for the guests.

Wreath Anderson called for silence and began directing the players into place as the rehearsal began. Marilyn, softening, but still in attorney mode, timed the event. Eighteen minutes. Perfect. Now they could eat. Her growling stomach reminded her she had not eaten anything but a bagel before her flight. She stood back and allowed the wedding party to lead her out the back entrance and down the walkway to the Castle Restaurant.

Marilyn watched Beau walk with Constance's friend, Bethany, and her friend, Chase. He looked resplendent under the soft lights in the courtyard. She was not even repelled that he wore jeans with his white shirt and tie. A good-looking man. She assumed, like her, he was in his middle forties. Very well preserved.

The rehearsal party was smaller now, just Beau, Justin, Constance, Bethany, Chase, the pastor and his wife and son, and herself. Beau's mother and daughter would not be down for the rehearsal. Mrs. Burnham was busy cooking for Christmas Day.

The Castle Restaurant was almost empty. Marilyn spotted a party of four at one table and a party of six at another. A long table in the middle had been elaborately set for them. Marilyn was disappointed when Beau and the kids were led to one end, the pastor's family in the middle, and she, Bethany, and Chase at the other end. She watched Beau and the children through the flickering light of the candles as they laughed and talked quietly. When did Beau start speaking so softly?

The waiter handed out menus and took their drink orders. He advised them hot apple cider and appetizers were provided for them downstairs while they waited for their entrees.

After ordering, the party went downstairs. Since it was a pub, Marilyn and Beau had not visited this area. But it was so beautiful. A small room with a large fire crackling behind two wingback chairs, a table laden with grilled marinated oysters, lump crab cakes, and a cheese tray. A small wooden keg produced fragrant apple cider. Marilyn fixed a small plate and stood in front of the roaring fire. Beau behaved like a perfect gentleman, but he had few words for her. When the waiter announced the entrees were ready, they went back upstairs to dinner. Marilyn glanced at Beau talking to the others, but he did not make any eye contact with her. She tried, for Constance and Justin's sake, to contribute to the conversation, forcing laughter when appropriate. Why had it come to this? Why was he acting this way? Why did she care? Fighting nausea, she forced herself through the meal.

When everyone was through eating, they continued to chat. Marilyn stood and walked to the other side of the table to hug and thank Constance and Justin for the fine meal, offering the excuse of being tired after a long flight. She addressed the others and said she looked forward to seeing them the next day. Beau only smiled and nodded. Conflicting thoughts swirled through her head on the walk to her room. Where was the Beau she remembered? Realization hit her in the gut. She wanted him. So wanted him.

Beau didn't know if he'd behaved like Marilyn would have wanted or not. He'd tried to be reserved so he wouldn't get on her nerves like he did before. But she didn't seem very happy. Maybe he was too cool. Maybe it didn't matter. She'd be gone after the wedding. He doubted he'd see her again unless she visited Constance. But he figured they'd go to Denver since she was such a busy lawyer. Justin's hand on his arm broke his thoughts.

Beau paid the waiter for the meal and thanked him for their hospitality. The pastor shook Beau's hand, offering his gratitude before leaving with his wife. Constance and Justin planned to take Bethany and Chase on a short tour of Natchez and the river. So Beau walked over to the Dairy Barn, and hearing no sounds, closed his door and relaxed on the bed while he pondered how he felt about Marilyn. Tomorrow was the big day. Wedding at four. Reception following. Then the next morning an early drive back to Carroll County for Christmas at Mother's. He supposed there wouldn't be enough time for any connection with Marilyn. But that was in God's hands. Beau had no answers, not being sure how he felt.

Chapter 8

The guests began arriving at three. They milled around, looking at the beautiful rooms and walking out on the grounds until almost time for the wedding. Marilyn counted thirty-five. Beau arrived about the time Wreath called the party to the front porch to wait for the arrival of the groom and bride-to-be. It was very cool outside, but not so bad that five or ten minutes would hurt anyone. Marilyn held the hankie Constance had placed on her bed the night before. The engraved gold lettering said, *Mom, to dry your happy tears on my wedding day, as you have always dried mine. I love you, Constance.* Tears filled her eyes now.

She heard the sound of horses before she could see anything. A white carriage, driven by four white horses, rounded the brick drive and stopped in front of the guests assembled on the curved steps. Justin, princelike in his white tux with a red rose boutonniere, jumped from the carriage step to the ground then turned to help his bride. Constance, carrying a bouquet of red roses, looked radiant in her straight white-satin gown, its bodice covered by lace and white roses. The crowd separated and allowed them entrance. They walked to the middle of the drawing rooms and were joined by the bridal party. Bethany, the bridesmaid, looked lovely in a red strapless gown, carrying a bouquet of white roses. Beau, the best man, debonair in a black tux with a white boutonniere, took Marilyn's breath away. With the backdrop of the greenery on the mantel, the lit candles, white ornaments, and the white roses Constance had chosen, it looked like a Christmas fairytale.

Marilyn looked at Beau more often than she did the kids. Occasionally, she caught his eye. What did she see? Her sentiment should be with her daughter and not the father of the groom. She wondered if those around her could hear her heart beating. How could she have been so arrogant, so stupid? She wiped a tear as Constance and Justin said their vows. Her daughter looked lovely, and Marilyn was so proud of her commitment to God and her affection for these people in small-town Mississippi. How wrong she had been to judge them. She looked back at Beau. He was watching her. She attempted a smile. He gave her one in return. Her hand flew to her chest and covered her heart before she could stop it. He winked. She turned back just in time to see the groom kiss the bride. She felt the heat moving up her neck, she so wanted to be kissed like that. She returned her focus to Constance, her wise and precious daughter. How sorry she was for doubting her choice. And for the way she had felt about Beau.

❧

Beau considered Marilyn's reaction to him. Maybe she was different, or at least wanted to be. He took Bethany's arm and followed the bride and groom out of the room. The reception was set up in the two rooms across the hall, the food in one, the wedding cake and punch in the other. The pastor announced for all to enjoy the reception and held his hand out to show the way.

The pianist played soft music for those who wanted to dance. Beau looked forward to dancing with Constance in the absence of her father. The guests flowed easily around the tables, the wedding cakes served after pictures were taken of the bride and groom feeding each other. And guests walked to the doors of the drawing rooms to watch Beau gracefully glide his new daughter-in-law across the floor before passing her on to Justin.

Beau followed Marilyn to the buffet table. He drew up beside her. She smiled, picked up a crispy chicken wing, and mischievously ate it in front of him. He raised his eyebrows in question. She smiled playfully. He took a napkin and wiped the sauce from her face.

"Would you honor me with a dance?"

"Why, I'd be glad to. Just let me eat one more of these delicious wings. I'm really hungry."

"You've changed."

"So have you."

"Kind of like meeting in the middle?"

"Suppose so."

He tipped her chin up and dabbed it with a napkin. "Let's dance before the pianist goes home." He took her plate and handed it to a waiter.

Beau led her to the drawing room. He took her hand and

looked her over. "The dress becomes you. You look lovely."

"As do you."

He pulled her toward him. After a few steps, he pulled her closer. "I missed you, Marilyn."

"I missed you, too."

He smelled the sweetness of her hair before briefly tasting the sweetness of her lips. Just a light kiss. "Would you consider taking a few extra days and driving to Carroll County in the morning? I can promise you the best corn bread dressing this side of the Mississippi River."

"I didn't bring any jeans."

"And why is it a problem?"

"If I'm going to a farm, don't I need some?"

"We'll find you a pair."

"That settles it, then. But I haven't met your mother yet."

"She's here. Heather, too. So, no problem."

"Then I'd love to go to Carroll County."

Beau lifted her up and swung her around, shouting with joy. He saw Marilyn look around to see if they had caused a scene. Constance and Justin laughed, and all at once, the whole wedding party burst out in applause.

On that note, Beau took the opportunity to let her slide to the floor and kissed her again, embracing her, so this time she would know he meant it. And if she was embarrassed, she could get over it.

But she wasn't. She looked happy. He looked up again and said a silent prayer. Just before she pulled him back to her for another kiss. When she stepped back, she said, "I love you, Beau Burnham, redneck or not."

"And I love you, Marilyn McLemore, arrogant attorney or not." He drew her back into his arms and tasted again the full, pretty lips that had tantalized him since the day he first saw her.

Christmas at Longwood

Cynthia Leavelle

Dedication

To my beloved husband, Tommy.
You are my hero.

Chapter 1

*Mary pulled the trigger as the bandits
drew even with Jim's horse.
One fell off his saddle, giving Jim the time
he needed to take out Big Al.
She grasped the reins, trying to curb the runaway horses'
headlong drive for the bluff.
Could she stop them in time?*

The ringing cell phone penetrated Meredith's consciousness and stopped her typing. It took a few seconds for her agent's voice to register. "What's that, Linda? I'm sorry, my mind was somewhere else."

"I said *Prairie Firebrand*'s a bestseller." Linda had her attention now.

"Really? How did that happen?"

"Silly, you sold a lot of books. And *Wagon Trails* sales have picked up again since your new book came out. It may hit bestseller range soon."

"Oh wow." Dazed, she stared out the window at the brick wall across the alley, trying to understand what this meant for her.

"I've been getting calls from the editors. They want to sign another contract as soon as you have a proposal."

Meredith's mind churned. "I haven't really thought of a new line."

"What are you working on now?"

"*Kansas Railroad Bride*. I'm almost finished with the first draft."

"Work that up and send it on. I've been thinking. Southern antebellum's hot right now. Why don't you do something from your hometown?"

"Natchez?" Meredith could hear the squeak in her voice.

"Sure."

"I don't know, Linda. Let me think about it."

"Don't take too long. You need to get stuff out there. You're doing great. Keep it up."

"Thanks. I'll be in touch." She pushed the red button and stared at the phone—bestseller status, at last. She wanted to call someone to help her celebrate but couldn't think of anyone. Standing up, she stretched her stiff muscles and looked around.

The tiny apartment she'd taken when she decided to live on her writing looked awful. Dishes waited in the sink, and dust bunnies floated under her coffee table. What time was it? Eight? Five hours straight without a break. No wonder her neck ached.

She moved to the sink, started the hot water, and added

detergent. Mother always said that cleaning up helped her think. Dear Mother and Daddy. She would never stop being their daughter, no matter how long they'd been gone. If she hadn't moved away from Natchez, she could have spent more time with them. "But I had to go somewhere else. I couldn't stay in Natchez." Realizing that she had stopped thinking and started praying, she went on. "God, You know my situation. What am I afraid of?"

The thought that came to her then must have come from God, because she never would have come up with it herself. "Go back to Natchez? Why?"

Deep in her heart, the answer resonated. She'd never find what she wanted until she made peace with her past.

The uneasy feeling she got when God wanted her to do something she didn't want to do plagued her as she went downstairs to her mailbox. Among the credit card offers and political flyers, she found a personal letter, a rare occurrence.

Back in her apartment, she slit open the envelope and read the note from Francine inviting her to be a bridesmaid in her December wedding. Meredith couldn't help but chuckle. She hadn't seen Francine since high school. How like God to confirm His will. "All right, I'll go." She could leave next week and have time to research a possible Southern series before the wedding.

⁂

Two weeks later, Meredith stood at the public library desk in Natchez holding a stack of books. "You're saying I need proof of permanent residence to check out books? I'm researching for a novel, and I need these."

"We must have a recent utility statement with your address on it before we can give you a library card."

Meredith set the books on the counter and started to leave when the man behind her spoke. "Sylvia, what if I let her check out the books on my card?"

Meredith froze. Could it be? Gary Bishop, the boy she'd turned down for the senior banquet in high school. She turned to him, allowing him to see her.

"Meredith, I thought that might be you." He reached for her, and for a second, she thought he might hug her.

Before he could, she held out her hand to shake. "Gary, you're looking well."

"So are you." His voice held admiration. He handed the librarian his card and books then turned to her. "I haven't seen you since high school."

"Were you going to let just any stranger use your library card?"

"I wouldn't want to keep an aspiring historical writer from having good research materials."

So he knew she wrote historical fiction. "I appreciate this. I'm staying in Hap and Ellie Roberts's bed and breakfast, and that doesn't qualify as a permanent residence."

"How long will you be staying?"

"Long enough for Francine Green's wedding."

"I'm in that wedding." He took his card from the librarian.

"I'll be seeing you again, then." She picked up her books to leave, but he followed her.

"Meredith, do you have time to visit for a few minutes?"

"Uh. . .sure. Do you want to stay here?"

"It would seem like old times. We spent hours in the high school library, didn't we?" He laughed, shifted his books, and led her to a meeting room off to the side. "We can sit in here."

Meredith wasn't sure how to respond to his comment about the library. She couldn't tell him how those memories haunted her now. Instead, she pointed out the obvious. "I needed to go to the library. I had studying to do."

"That's why you became our valedictorian. You studied more than the rest of us."

"Yes, the nerdiest girl in the school." Would that phrase remind him of the senior banquet? Bobbi Lee Cox had told her that Gary accepted a dare from his friends to take the nerdiest girl. When he asked her, she turned him down cold, even though she wanted to go with him. How could she go to the biggest event at school knowing everyone was laughing at her?

"I wouldn't say nerdy, just intelligent. Meeting in the library before school helped me more than anything else to love history. You know, I'm a history teacher now."

"Are you? That's terrific. Where did you end up going to school?" He had mentioned Ole Miss and Mississippi State.

"I went to Mississippi College in Clinton. You went to University of Kansas, didn't you?"

"Yes, they gave me the best out-of-state scholarship."

"I remember. You wanted to get away so much. Do you still feel that way?"

"Well, I'm back now, aren't I? Speaking of studying, I need to get started on these books so I can get them finished before they're overdue. Thanks again for sharing your library card with me." She picked up the books and walked out.

Gary watched her retreating back with jumbled emotions, the most prominent, admiration. She looked every bit a bestselling author, with confidence and fashionable clothes, but clearly, whatever kept her from accepting his offer to the senior banquet still rankled her. He'd thought they had a good friendship, so why had she turned him down and hardly spoken to him since? He needed to know. Something about her bravado and vulnerability appealed to him, and he wanted to protect her now from whatever was making her unhappy.

On Tuesday nights, he ate dinner with his parents, often grading papers in his mom's kitchen till dinnertime. Tonight she welcomed him with a hug.

"We're having your favorite, chicken and dumplings. Your dad's washing up."

"Great!" Gary kissed her cheek below the silver halo of her hair.

After they gathered in the large dining room and Dad said the blessing, his mother started. "Okay, something's on your mind, and it isn't school. Spill the beans."

How did she always know? "I ran into Meredith Long at the library." Gary passed her the English peas.

"You're talking about that girl whose parents died in the tornado." His father dipped dumplings from the tureen.

"The poor girl. She's had a hard life."

"You wouldn't feel sorry for her if you saw her today, Mother. She looks incredible and she's a bestselling author."

"Yes, I know. She wrote those wonderful books you gave me. But I haven't forgotten what she did to you in high school."

Gary could sense his mother studying him as she said this. How could he explain to her how seeing Meredith affected him? "I know what you're thinking. You're afraid she'll hurt me again." He took a sip of his sweet tea to soothe the tightness in his throat.

"I've never seen you so hurt as that day she said she wouldn't go with you to the banquet."

He winced at the memory. "I was only in high school. A lot of time has passed since then. I'll be all right, Mother. You don't need to worry." Even as he said the words, he wished he could believe them himself.

"Are you going to see her while she's back in town?"

"Possibly. I'd like to talk to her about her historical research."

"Why don't you bring her home for a meal sometime while she's in town?"

"If the chance comes up."

His father wiped his mouth with his linen napkin. "Dinner with a bestselling author. That'll be a treat."

Chapter 2

Meredith worked late reading the books and fell into bed exhausted, no closer to a breakthrough idea for a novel. The morning sunlight and the mockingbirds singing outside her window woke her. She decided to go running. She donned sweats, feeling virtuous.

Outside, she took off down the street. This part of town was the same, and she hardly noticed where she was going until she saw her old elementary school ahead. The pine trees on the playground reminded her of playhouses she and her friends made by pushing pine needles together to create walls. Their imaginations provided everything else, along with a few twigs and pinecones.

She headed downtown, where the large church steeples and towers loomed over the streets and the courthouse stood surrounded by azalea bushes and magnolia trees. Turning a corner, she saw the school she had transferred to in fifth grade. Emotion threatened to engulf her. At that entrance, her daddy had dropped her off in his old beat-up pickup truck, the one he never replaced. A girl on the playground called out to her. "Hey, you're in the wrong place. Trailer trash goes to the other school." That first day of school taught her the world could be very cruel.

"Oh God. Why did I have to leave my friendly little school and come to this school to suffer?" She knew the answer—the scholarship to the gifted program. Her parents were so proud of her that she never told them what happened.

Meredith realized that she was staring at the school, clinging to the fence with tears running down her face. "See, God, I told you I had to move away. How else would I find out that not every place measures people by where they live or what they wear?"

She pried her tense fingers loose from the fence, then turned and jogged back to the bed and breakfast.

Mr. Roberts stood by the gate. "We wondered where you'd gone. Breakfast's ready."

Meredith teared up again at his Southern drawl, so homey sounding. "Thanks, Mr. Roberts. I'll come right back down after I get cleaned up." She went upstairs to her room to splash cold water in her face. How could she face three weeks of memories and encounters? With a sigh, she quickly showered and changed clothes.

The breakfast smells revived her appetite as she went downstairs. Mrs. Roberts appeared carrying a platter of sausage patties and homemade biscuits. "How do you like your eggs, honey?"

"Over hard or scrambled, whichever's easiest for you."

"No trouble either way. Would you like an omelet?"

"Scrambled's fine. These biscuits look marvelous." Meredith put some butter and homemade fig preserves on her biscuit. Closing her eyes, she savored every bite. Only her mother could make better biscuits than Miss Ellie.

Mr. Roberts came in then. "How are you, girl?" He set his coffee cup on the table and took the seat beside her. "Seems like you stay gone longer every time."

"It's been around four years, Mr. Hap." Quiet fell between them.

Finally, he sighed. "We miss your mom and dad. We sure do."

"Thanks, I do, too."

"I reckon our little church will go under soon. Just a handful of old-timers left."

"I'm so sorry. You've all taken care of me."

"We'll make do. But I'm worried about you. You got any young men interested?"

Meredith wanted to say, "None of your business," But she resorted to "I'm fine alone, Mr. Roberts."

"Humph, we'll see."

Miss Ellie came in with the scrambled eggs and fruit salad. "Now, Meredith, Hap and I won't eat dinner here tonight. We gotta watch our grandkids at their house for a few hours, but I left some food in the fridgedaire for you."

"Oh, Miss Ellie, you didn't have to do that. This is a bed and breakfast, not a full service restaurant."

"And you're our friend, not a customer. We'll see you after 'while."

After they left, Meredith went back up to her room. The

bed had been made and the bathroom cleared away. How did Miss Ellie find time to do that? She settled down beside her computer. She had to get some inspiration somehow. Looking at her e-mails, she remembered that she needed to get a gift for the co-ed wedding shower this Saturday night. Gary might attend. She sighed. This whole wedding business would be an emotional roller coaster.

She spent the day choosing a gift and getting it wrapped. The expensive silver platter reflected her desire to impress anyone at the shower who might still disdain her.

Alone at the bed and breakfast, she realized she hadn't eaten lunch, and now it was dinnertime. She opened the refrigerator door. Potato salad, pulled-pork barbecue, Jell-O salad, deviled eggs—what a treat. And on the top shelf chilled a full pitcher of sweet iced tea, exactly what she wanted. Miss Ellie must have worked for hours fixing all this.

Refreshed after a marvelous supper, she worked until late, polishing her Kansas manuscript.

On Saturday evening, she dressed in that studied casual look she liked, a lemon yellow T-shirt over khaki pants with a bronze jeans jacket and colorful accessories. She examined her reflection in the full-length mirror. The bronze jacket brought out the best of her brown hair and eyes. In high school, she had thick glasses, crooked teeth, hair pulled back in a ponytail. Book royalties could buy contacts, straight teeth, and good haircuts. Would the old crowd find her changed?

She had to park in front of Stanton Hall and walk down the street to the large home where the shower was taking place. A knot clenched in her stomach, she opened the doors into the crowded entryway. She might look sophisticated, but at this moment, she wanted to escape to the library and disappear behind a book.

"Meredith Long. I hoped you would make it. My, girl, I wouldn't have recognized you if I hadn't seen your Facebook picture. You got contacts, didn't you? Where've you been all these years?" The cheerful redhead behind the table loaded with wrapped gifts still looked the same, in spite of her advanced pregnancy.

"Joy, it's good to see you. When are you due?" Meredith set the package she carried on the table.

"Next month. This'll be our third. I married Bo Miller right after high school."

"That's right. I remember you two were dating." Other people pushed into the small entryway. Meredith moved on, looking around to see if she recognized anyone else. Most everyone arrived in couples. Then the bride-to-be came up to her. "Meredith, is that you? You look terrific."

"Francine. Thanks for asking me to your wedding. Now, tell me everything. Do I know Bill?"

"No. I met him at my job in Jackson. He has a landscaping business. Come meet him." Francine led her over to a buff-looking man. "This is Bill."

Meredith reached out to shake Bill's hand but noticed he was talking to Gary Bishop. Though seeing Gary rattled her, she managed to smile at Francine's groom. "Happy to meet you, Bill."

"Meredith hasn't told me yet what she's been up to for the last ten years," Francine said.

"She's too humble to say so, but I know what she's done." Gary moved closer. "How many books have you published now, ten?"

Bill whistled. "A published writer. That's impressive. What kind of books do you write?"

"Historical fiction," Meredith murmured.

"Really good stuff, too. I've read all I could find. I loved your pioneer series." Gary's praise sounded sweet to her.

"Thanks, Gary. How did you know?"

"Google. Best way to keep up with friends. You have more entries than anyone else I know."

"We'd better get in line if we want to eat." Francine pointed to the buffet. "They're having cajun-fried chicken and red beans and rice."

"This is more like a party than a shower. I can't remember the last time I had cajun," Meredith said, following Francine and Bill to the line.

"Where've you been, girl?"

"Lawrence, Kansas."

"You mean like *Little House on the Prairie* Kansas?"

"Her books are better even than those." Gary stood close enough his warm breath tickled her cheek. "Are you planning a series set in Natchez?"

"Yes, but I can't figure out where to start. I've never visited the mansions."

"Never?"

Meredith took a deep breath. "I guess I took the local sights for granted."

"I volunteer over at Longwood all the time. I'd be glad to

give you a personal tour."

Before she could answer, a woman's voice interrupted them.

"Gary, I told you I would save us some seats. I've already gotten your food."

"Bobbi Lee, you remember Meredith Long, don't you?"

Bobbi Lee's red lips stretched into a smile that didn't reach her eyes. "Oh, our class scholarship student. Good to see you. Come on, Gary."

Meredith watched them walk away together, as if they were a couple. Were they married? She hadn't thought to ask him. Her delight in reconnecting with old friends dissipated. Nothing had changed, not really. Bobbi Lee, at least, still saw her as the class nerd.

"We seem to have lost Gary." Francine nodded in their direction. "Bobbi Lee's after him again."

Meredith picked up a plate to serve herself and tried to sound casual. "Are they married?"

"Not them. Bobbi Lee was married to a casino manager. But that didn't last long. Now she's the school secretary. Gary's on the faculty at our old school, you know."

"I know he's a history teacher."

Francine put some beans and rice on her plate. "I hear the kids really like him."

"He always did like history."

"Yeah, I remember you two meeting before school in the library. I always thought he liked you. That's why I partnered you two in the wedding."

"You're kidding." Meredith forgot to serve her plate. Gary

partnered with her? A nudge behind her got her moving again. Why this unaccountable rise in spirits? Because Gary still wasn't married?

She found a place to sit down near Francine. Her food looked delicious with the spicy fried chicken and some mashed potatoes and gravy. Not since her mother died had she eaten as well as she had the last few days.

❧

Gary sat down next to Bobbi Lee, wanting to kick himself for agreeing to sit with her. He was missing his chance to visit with Meredith. She hadn't agreed yet to go with him through Longwood. She looked terrific, even better than the other day.

"You aren't listening to me." Bobbi Lee tapped his arm with a fire-engine red fingernail.

"I'm sorry, were you talking to me?"

"I said you would have to give the blessing tonight. You have some responsibilities as a groomsman, you know."

"If you insist." Gary didn't argue with her, but her bossiness sometimes got on his nerves. She thought being the school secretary made her responsible for everything, including the faculty. Joy Miller had organized the shower, but that didn't keep Bobbi Lee from taking charge.

"Hey, ya'll," Bobbie Lee said, tossing her sleek platinum blond hair back from her bronzed face and looking around the room. "It's so great that so many could make it tonight. I'm going to call on Gary Bishop to say our blessing."

Gary looked out over the room. Meredith gazed at him from her seat next to Francine. A gentle smile lit her face.

"Let's pray. Dear Lord, thank You for the food we're eating, for this chance to fellowship and help Francine and Bill celebrate, and most of all for the salvation You've provided through Jesus. Amen."

Back at the table, Bobbi Lee frowned. "Why did you have to mention Jesus? Some people may be atheists."

"I don't think I should have to deny my faith when I'm talking to the Lord."

"Yes, but nowadays we need to respect other people's beliefs and not offend them."

"If you don't like the way I pray, you can recruit someone else next time." Gary's exasperation threatened to overcome his good manners.

Bobbi Lee pouted by his side while he turned and engaged his old chemistry lab partner, John North, in conversation. "Did you see Meredith Long?"

"No, where is she?"

"Over there." Meredith sat near Francine, who was opening gifts with Bill while others stood around and watched.

"Man, she looks different. Where has she kept herself all these years?"

"Writing historical novels. She's published quite a few."

"Really, I didn't know that. She always acted like such a mouse in school. Brilliant, but a mouse." John drank some iced tea.

"She's the most intelligent woman I've ever known."

"Didn't she live in a trailer over north of town? I thought her father worked as a car mechanic."

Gary wondered how that related to her intelligence. "Her

father received the Purple Heart in Vietnam and came home disabled."

"Is she home visiting them?"

"Both her parents died in the tornado that blew through four years ago." Gary gazed at Meredith, wondering how anyone could go through all she had and still accomplish so much.

"Man, that's tough, but you know, trailers aren't the safest place in storms." John reached for his pecan pie.

"What is it with you and Meredith Long?" Bobbi Lee said, poking Gary's arm again. "I don't know what you're so excited about. So she wrote a few books."

"Have you read any, Bobbi Lee?"

"I don't have to. They're pulp fiction. I've got better taste than that."

"Then you wouldn't think much of my taste, because I've read them and liked them. She did thorough research and wrote interesting stories with great characters."

"Well, whatever. I won't argue with you. Anyway, Gary, I have an idea. After we eat, let's go down to the boats for a little fun."

Gary shook his head. "You know I don't gamble. Besides, I have some people I want to talk to here. I'll see you Monday at school."

"But Gary."

He didn't wait to see what she wanted, because Meredith had picked up her purse and started toward the door. "Meredith."

She turned. "Yes?"

"I wanted to catch up some more. Would you like to take a walk around Stanton Hall's grounds?"

"If you like."

They walked out into the cool air and up the street to Stanton Hall. "We can go hang out by the pool if you like."

"Can we?"

Her question surprised him. "My mother's a garden club member, so we're allowed to use the pool."

Meredith didn't say anything, but she followed him across the grounds. At the pool gate, he unlocked it with his key and held it open for her. The pool area glowed with twinkle lights on the umbrellas.

"They must be anticipating some Christmas weddings."

Meredith looked surprised. "Do many people have weddings here?"

"All the time. It's a major fund-raiser for the club. In fact, most of the houses have weddings. Francine and Bill's will be at Longwood." He led her to a table. "Speaking of Longwood, are you willing to go on a tour with me?"

Meredith sat in the chair he pulled out. "Do you have time?"

"I would consider it an honor. Longwood has a fascinating history, but I won't tell you anything yet."

"I should know more about the houses in Natchez, but I neglected local history."

"Yes, I remember. You wanted to study life in other places."

"Yes," Meredith said, staring off at the pool, "and now I'm back and making up for lost time."

"The successful author. Did you find what you were

looking for, Meredith?" Now why did he say that? She might consider it prying.

Instead, she answered. "I found some things. I got my education at Kansas, I've written some books, but. . ."

Gary leaned forward. "But not everything you hoped to find?"

"I didn't want to come back, but God told me to. I'm not sure why, but He has something to teach me here."

"It's so refreshing to hear you speak of God like that." Gary studied her face in the glowing pool lights. "So many people see church as a once-a-week obligation rather than a relationship with the Creator."

"I couldn't have made it without Him."

He touched her arm. "I'm so sorry about your parents."

"That was tough," Meredith said, shrugging, "but now I can say I'm glad they got to go together. I know I'll see them again."

Silence fell between them. Gary studied her face, looking for the girl he had known in this sophisticated woman. She had always attracted him, but now her style and accomplishments intimidated him. He wanted to understand her, to plumb the depths of her mind and thoughts, but he had no right. "You haven't told me when we can go to Longwood."

"You have school, don't you?"

"How about next Saturday? I'm down to lead tours until three. We could go through after that and maybe get some dinner somewhere."

When she hesitated, all the pain from her rejection in high school came back to him. Would she reject him again?

"Sure, I'll meet you there at three."

"Great."

They walked out to her car. Something still held her back from him, but at least she agreed to go out with him.

Chapter 3

Meredith spent the week revising her Kansas novel and trying to prepare a proposal for Linda to send out to the editors. When Saturday came, she wanted to cancel. What purpose would it serve to write novels set in the South? Those women didn't struggle the way the Midwestern women did. She couldn't identify with their wealth and power. How could she construct a believable heroine from one of them?

Nevertheless, she found herself on the dirt road to Longwood. Moss-draped trees shadowed the sunken road. It twisted around and finally emerged by a dark green pond. Above and surrounded by cultivated live oak trees reposed the five-story octagonal house, redbrick with white columns and arches, like something out of *Arabian Nights*. Those millionaire cotton plantation owners sure tried to outdo each other in grandeur.

Still following the signs, she rounded the house and pulled down into the graveled parking place beside the basement entrance. Gary met her before she got to the door. "Let's start you out in the gift shop in the basement."

Inside, he introduced her to the other volunteer workers. "I'm going to take Miss Long on a tour. She's a historical novelist looking for good ideas."

"By all means." The older woman who staffed the cash register beamed at Meredith.

Gary led her into a room furnished as a parlor. "The Nutts entertained here."

Meredith couldn't believe the tiny size. Why would the Nutts have entertained in such a small room in the basement? Why not up on the ground floor? Even though it contained several fine pieces of furniture, a piano, and an Oriental rug, she couldn't picture having more than a few people at a time in this room. She wanted to ask Gary, but he continued on with his facts, so she didn't.

"Building began in the late 1850s."

"Close to the beginning of the Civil War."

"Yes. At that time many millionaires in Natchez built big houses, each grander than the last. The Nutts already had a large home, but when the Stantons began building Stanton Hall, Mr. Nutt wanted something even larger, so he bought this forest and started building. Let me show you some other rooms."

Meredith followed him into a modest bedroom "Who slept here?"

"This was the master bedroom."

Again she wondered. The large mahogany four-poster bed and elegant chairs and portraits fit a master bedroom, but not the size. "How many children did the Nutts have?"

"Eleven, but only seven were living at the time they lived at Longwood." Gary led the way into another room. A sitting room, she guessed, by the simple chairs and the elegant fireplace. The room contained a modest circular staircase, plastered white with polished wooden rails, but they passed on into two rooms with several four-poster beds in each, one for boys and one for girls. Why had everyone lived in this basement? The elegant dining room, with its carved shoofly over the table for fanning guests and shooing flies impressed her. She could picture a family servant standing at the wall, pulling the cord to waft the large fan over the elegant table with its peach-colored china. Still the room felt cramped. Somehow she had expected more from a large mansion.

The center room struck her. It was round and contained no furniture at all. "What are those?" She pointed to the ceiling.

"Skylights." Gary had been strangely quiet, explaining only the rooms' functions but not their history as she expected. "Come with me. I want to show you something now."

He took her back into the small, informal sitting room, where he climbed up the circular stairs she had noticed before. As Meredith followed, she saw that the white plastering gave way to bare brick and wood. They came out on the ground floor into an entryway. The front doors opened onto a large wraparound porch overlooking the pond and the road. Brick walls and rough wood outlined the various unfinished rooms with their arched doorways. She had heard parts of Longwood had never been finished, but seeing it like this left her confused. What a waste.

"That would have been the master bedroom." Gary indicated a large space behind the stairs with an arched doorway and windows that looked out the front. Just as he had downstairs, Gary took her in a circle. She saw a large room that would have served as a reception room, the large main parlor with its doorways out onto the porch and its huge fireplace. A ladies' parlor was full of the packing rubbish of seventy years, all covered in thick dust. The dining room with banks of windows overlooking the porch and a huge oak tree beyond would have occupied one side of the floor. Finally, he took her into a center room, the match of the circular room in the basement. "Look straight up."

She did, and couldn't help gasping as the stories extended up and up above her to skylights in a dome.

"You can see that this would have been a huge house if finished, over thirty thousand square feet. Mr. Nutt planned a whole floor for the girls and one for the boys, with running water in the bathrooms. As it turned out, only the basement was finished, where Mrs. Nutt lived for thirty-three years."

Meredith's head swam from looking up. "What happened, Gary?"

"When the Yankee workmen heard the war had started, they left their tools and headed north." Gary pointed out some dusty buckets and tools with the rubbish in the ladies' parlor.

"And during the war?"

"First the Confederates burned over a million dollars of cotton so the Yankees wouldn't get it. The next year the Union army took the corn crop. Mr. Nutt died, and their other land was sold at sheriff's auction to pay taxes. All Mrs. Nutt had left was this property with the house."

Meredith stood speechless. This level of tragedy didn't fit with the life of a spoiled belle. Anyone would become very bitter after such trouble.

Gary showed her more details, all painting a picture of poverty and ruined hopes. "Would you like to see the auxiliary buildings now?"

"Yes, absolutely. This is fascinating, Gary. I appreciate your wanting to share this with me."

"It's my pleasure."

One auxiliary building housed a small museum of pictures and newspaper articles from the Nutts' years at Longwood. Meredith studied the pictures, absorbing the clothing, hairstyles, and activities of the period. An idea for a novel formed in her mind of a bitter, disillusioned woman getting what she deserved after an early life of indulgence and greed. Suddenly an article caught her eye. "Look at this, Gary."

"What?" He moved over close enough to see, and she smelled his aftershave, a scent that brought back memories of high school. How she had adored him then. That is, before the banquet.

She reached out to steady herself. "Look at this obituary. According to this, Mrs. Nutt lived her last few years as a productive and beloved member of Natchez society and her church."

"Why does that strike you?"

"I assumed after all that, she would become bitter and reclusive. I wonder what motivated her. I've got to do some more research, but this story's so amazing, it needs to be told."

She turned to look at him, realizing he stood so close that their faces weren't ten inches apart. His eyes held warmth and invitation. She started to move closer but caught herself. She wouldn't let him hurt her again.

As though nothing had happened between them, Gary guided her outside. "Let's go get some dinner. I've made reservations for us at the Castle Restaurant."

"Oh." The Castle. Only the elite went there. She looked down at her outfit, assessing its suitability for such a place.

"You look fine, but if you want to freshen up, I'll pick you up in an hour."

❧

Gary waited in the Roberts's parlor, thinking about the close encounter he and Meredith had had in the museum. Being so near Meredith brought back bittersweet memories of his crush on her from high school. If she had encouraged him at all, he would have kissed her. Did she know that?

Meredith came down the stairs dressed in a black sheath dress with a rope of pearls and black pumps. His first sight of her stunned him. "You look wonderful."

"Thank you, Gary. You look pretty good yourself." She eyed the blazer and tie he had added with approval.

He led her out to his polished and vacuumed Sentra. She accepted his help into the car without comment. She seemed hesitant to go with him. He still couldn't read her. "Dunleith isn't far. Have you ever eaten at the Castle?" He glanced at her and noticed her back stiffen.

"No, never."

"They have pretty good food, I think. I hope you enjoy it.

118

Of course, you've probably eaten at some nice places in your travels, haven't you?"

She appeared to thaw a notch. "Sometimes the writers' conference hotels have some really good places to eat. But I'm sure the Castle would rank above those."

"Why do you think that?" He made the turn onto Homochitto Street.

"I don't know. I always assumed that the upper-crust life of Natchez exceeds anything else. I suppose that doesn't make sense."

"What do you consider the upper crust of Natchez?"

"Oh, you know. The garden clubs and pilgrimage royalty. People who live in antebellum mansions with antiques and real silver."

"People who send their kids to private schools?"

"Especially those."

"Well, then that includes you, doesn't it?" He looked sidewise at her again.

"No. It doesn't include me."

He started to argue with her but decided not to. He turned in to Dunleith. The large mansion glowed in the spotlights shining on its white pillars and porches. Boughs of pine garlands decorated with red velvet bows hung on the doors and windows, and a Christmas tree covered in white lights sparkled like diamonds. He parked near the restaurant entrance and came around to open the door for her.

As she turned toward the restaurant, she suddenly grasped his arm. "Gary, you won't let me make a fool of myself, will you?"

Gary sensed the panic in her voice. "No, Meredith, I won't. You'll do fine. Perhaps I should be asking you not to let me make a fool of myself." If she understood the double meaning of his words, she didn't indicate it.

❦

Meredith realized how silly she had acted when they reached the door of the Castle. Gary was right. She had been to many nice restaurants because of her writing career. Why should she feel unnerved by this one? Taking a deep breath, she prayed for poise.

A waiter in formal clothes greeted them and led them to a secluded table. White tablecloths and candlelight, cloth napkins and good flatware—she had dined with these before. The unplastered brick walls caught her attention. What was the history of this building? Gary might know. "When was Dunleith built?"

"Before the Civil War, but this mansion is the second on this site. The first burned down from a lightning strike." Gary signaled the waiter. "What do you want, Meredith?"

"I'll have the pecan-encrusted chicken with mashed sweet potatoes and collard greens."

Gary handed the man the menus. "I'll have the surf and turf, medium rare, with loaded baked potato."

"Very good, sir."

After the waiter left, Meredith picked up the thread of their conversation. "What happened here during the Civil War?"

"A Mr. Davis still owned it then. It's said he hid some of his thoroughbred racing horses in the basement, under the dining room, and then invited the Yankees to dine with him.

He must have had a lot of nerve."

"I love stories like that."

"Do you remember studying about John Roy Lynch?"

Meredith nodded. "In Mississippi history. The first black secretary of state in Mississippi."

"Right. And congressman during Reconstruction. He mentioned the Davises in his autobiography. He had been Davis's slave."

"Do you mean at Dunleith?"

"At first, but his mistress had him sent to work in the fields in Louisiana because she thought he needed humbling."

"How sad for him. What did he do when the Yankees arrived?"

"He walked back to find his mother, but she had left, too. He said watching Mrs. Davis trying to fix a meal for her family without help touched him. The Davis family never again had wealth."

"You tell such good stories, Gary. I can practically picture people in these houses with all their pride and heartbreak."

"And you've always been my best audience. Not many people like history that much. Remember how we used to quiz each other before history exams in the library?"

Meredith toyed with her fork, not wanting to meet his gaze or answer his question. He couldn't seem to understand how he had poisoned those memories for her.

At last, Gary spoke again. "Every time I bring up the good times we had in high school, you clam up. Do you mind telling me why?"

The waiter came just then with their salads. Meredith

sighed in relief. Perhaps Gary would get distracted.

Instead, Gary continued to look at her after saying a blessing, not touching his salad. "Aren't you going to answer my question?"

"I hoped you'd let it go." She picked up her fork and stirred the salad to distribute the dressing. "Gary, I didn't have the same happy experience in school that you did. I hid out in the library because I got tired of the snide comments."

"Who? I never heard any."

"It didn't happen so much in high school, but I still felt their disdain."

Gary shook his head. "I don't know what may have happened to you earlier or who treated you like that in high school, but everyone I knew in high school admired your accomplishments."

"Really?"

"Yes. You know, I looked through the annual the other day."

"I never got an annual."

"Did you know that your picture appeared more times than anyone else's in the class?"

"No, I didn't know that. I assumed. . ."

"That since you weren't a pilgrimage princess or in the homecoming court, you were a nobody?"

Meredith stared at him, realizing for the first time that she had been somebody in high school: newspaper staff, honor society, drama, history club, valedictorian, academic team. "I didn't have a lot of friends."

"Francine thought of you as a friend, enough to track you down to be in her wedding. And I thought you were my friend, at least I hoped so. I've always believed that it's better to have one or two really good, deep friendships than to have a shallow popularity with everyone."

"I don't even have that now." She laid down her fork. "I'm completely alone in the world except for my agent."

Gary reached across the table and squeezed her hand. "You will always have a friend as long as I'm alive."

Meredith felt her heart contract at the expression on his face. How could she doubt such sincerity?

Their entrees came, and their conversation moved to other topics as they ate, but Meredith still felt the warmth of his hand on hers.

"I can't believe you ordered collard greens. I get those all the time at home. When I go out, I want a good steak." Gary grinned at her.

"So would I, in Kansas, but I haven't had any good collard greens since my mother died. Hers tasted better, although these are pretty good. You can't beat the ones pulled right out of the garden and cooked the same day."

"Your mother raised a big garden?"

"Yes. We had fresh tomatoes and melons, butter beans and okra right up into the fall. Then we ate her canned or frozen vegetables all winter. We didn't buy that much at the grocery store, but we always ate well."

"Tell me more about your parents."

"You know my father had a disability?"

Gary nodded. "He received a Purple Heart for Vietnam, didn't he?"

"Yes. He learned mechanics skills in the army, so that's how he supported us. We had a nice trailer. My mother kept it very clean, and she worked really hard in the garden and for the church. She always loved books, so she read to me a lot. That's where I got my love of reading." Meredith sat quietly, thinking about her parents, almost forgetting Gary.

"Have you been out to your home place since you came back?"

"No. After the funeral, I arranged for the remains of the trailer and furnishings to be hauled away. We didn't have any antiques or family heirlooms, just cheap, serviceable furniture. I kept what pictures and personal items I could find. Not much remained after the tornado. I still own the land, but it's going back to trees now."

The waiter brought the check, and Meredith reached for her purse, but Gary picked it up. "My idea, my treat. Don't even think about it."

"Are you sure?" He acted like they were dating.

"I'm sure." Gary rose and retrieved her coat. "This has been a pleasure for me. By the way, what are you doing for church tomorrow?"

"I hadn't really decided."

"Why don't you go with me and stay to lunch at my family's afterward?"

"Oh, I couldn't impose."

"My mother already told me to bring you. She loves your books."

That night as Meredith lay in bed, she remembered when Gary took her hand and assured her of his friendship. If he was her friend, why had he accepted that dare? This mystery baffled her.

Chapter 4

Church the next day refreshed Meredith. Her church in Kansas was so large that she could slip in and out without actually meeting anyone. Here many people who remembered her or her parents greeted her. During the sermon, Gary shared his Bible with her. Her fingers sensed his hand near hers. The sermon centered on Jesus' story of the unworthy servant whose master forgave him a huge debt, but he refused to forgive a fellow servant a small debt. That story always made Meredith uncomfortable for some reason, but she set her discomfort aside and praised God for sending Jesus to die for her sins.

After church, Gary took her to his parents' home. Mrs. Bishop came out in her apron to welcome Meredith. "Gary has told me so much about you through the years, and I've so enjoyed reading your books. Please come in and make yourself at home."

Meredith looked around the living room a bit awed. The antique furniture with its carved armrests and backs, the massive mirrors and worn Oriental rugs—no doubt his forebears had owned this house and passed it down. The painted portraits on the walls reminded her that Gary came from a long line of Natchez royalty. How could she make herself at home in a house so intimidating?

"Those are my great-grandparents, Samuel and Mary Galbraith Martin. Gary pointed at the portraits. She came from Pennsylvania to teach and met my grandfather here. My mother remembers her. You should ask her. I think my great-grandmother must have been a fascinating person and a very strong Christian."

Looking closer at her picture, Meredith could see the resemblance to Gary, the same intelligence and seriousness, but kindness, too. Suddenly Mary Galbraith Martin was more like a friend than an imposing ancestor. "What did your great-grandfather do?"

"Practiced law. My mother says he worked very hard to protect the rights of freedmen in the early twentieth century."

"You have a grand Christian heritage, Gary."

"My parents have always told me that God doesn't have grandchildren. Every generation has to enter into a relationship with God individually."

"My daddy told me the same thing. I think growing up with a Christian heritage sometimes clouds our understanding of our need for Christ." She turned from the pictures to sit gingerly on a chair.

"That's perceptive. I think I've had similar ideas, but I couldn't express it as well as you do."

Mrs. Bishop appeared at the door. "Dinner's ready. Come

this way, Meredith." She led her into the large dining room with its massive buffet and china cabinet filled with silver and delicate crystal. The table sparkled with lovely china and glassware.

Gary's father came in from the kitchen carrying a platter of roast beef with potatoes, carrots, and onions. "Welcome, Miss Long. We're honored to have you with us today."

"Thank you, Mr. Bishop. I appreciate the invitation."

Meredith watched Mr. Bishop set down the platter then turn to seat his wife. Suddenly she became aware that Gary stood right behind her, ready to help her as well. The intimacy of that action in this family setting unnerved her. She felt breathless when Mr. Bishop said his blessing. "God bless this food and this guest with us today. In Jesus' name, amen."

The dinner tasted marvelous, with butter beans and mashed potatoes to go with the roast and other vegetables. "Mrs. Bishop, this is the tenderest roast I've ever had. You're a wonderful cook."

"Thank you. I'm glad you like it."

Gary picked up the rolls and passed them. "Meredith is working on a new novel set at Longwood."

"Longwood? What period?" Mrs. Bishop buttered her roll.

"I'm not sure, but I wanted to include Mrs. Julia Nutt in it. She fascinates me. She went through so much but maintained her dignity until her death."

"My grandmother was Mrs. Nutt's friend."

Gary looked at his mother, surprise etched in his face. "You never told me that."

"It never came up before. My grandmother had just

married, and Mrs. Nutt was very near the end of her life, but they had a close relationship. I think they continued to correspond when Mrs. Nutt grew too old to get out and Grandmother began having babies.

"Did your grandmother tell you stories or talk about Mrs. Nutt?" Meredith leaned forward in her excitement.

"Not particularly, but I think I have something that might help you."

"Research must take a lot of time." Mr. Bishop smiled at Meredith.

"It does. That's why I often do a series, because I can use the same research to do more than one book."

"Could you do a series set in Natchez?" Gary wiped his mouth with his napkin. "I could help you look at other homes and dig up some more ideas."

His enthusiasm stirred something inside of Meredith. How lonely her life had been as a novelist. What would it be like to have someone helping her who sympathized? "You have so much to do with your teaching, Gary."

"Nothing would please me more than helping you." He said this with such warmth that Meredith capitulated.

"Then I accept. You've helped a lot already."

"Great."

Mrs. Bishop rose and removed the dishes from the table. Meredith followed suit. "No, you stay there," Mrs. Bishop gently ordered. "I'll be back in a moment with dessert."

Meredith sat down unwillingly. Much as she disliked doing dishes, the thought of Mrs. Bishop doing them alone bothered her more.

In a moment, the dessert arrived, a spice cake, still warm from the oven, topped with a dollop of whipped cream. Mr. Bishop offered everyone coffee to go with it.

"Now, Meredith. I don't want to keep you from your research, but I want to invite you to a meeting with me." Mrs. Bishop sat down and reached for her fork.

"At your church?"

"No, my garden club. We meet in Stanton Hall on Tuesdays at two. I'd be delighted if you'd be my guest."

Guest at the Natchez Pilgrimage Garden Club? She'd dreamed of such things but never thought it could happen to her. All her insecurity came back in a flash. "Mrs. Bishop, I'd be honored, if you're sure I wouldn't be in the way."

"They'll welcome you, my dear. Members bring guests all the time."

"Thank you. I'll come."

As soon as they had finished, Mrs. Bishop shooed them out to the living room. "You talk some more about those novels. I'll join you in a few minutes."

Gary offered her a seat. "If you like, I can come on Tuesday to Stanton Hall and give you a tour after your meeting. You might find something useful there. They have the best period furniture, if nothing else."

"All of you are so kind. I'm overwhelmed with your help."

"Miss Long, it isn't often this family has the opportunity to help a bestselling author"—Mr. Bishop laughed— "we're happy to do whatever we can, even if it's just listening."

"You don't know what that means to me." Meredith felt tears rise to the surface. "I've been alone for so long."

"I'll never forget your parents. I trusted your father with my car repairs. He always did quality work and charged fair prices."

"Thank you for saying that."

Gary reached across from the chair next to her and squeezed her hand, startling her into composure. "Do you think you could get anything from Dunleith?"

"Possibly. But let's keep looking for other ideas."

Mrs. Bishop came into the living room carrying a small package. "I thought I had these somewhere. These are the letters written from Mrs. Nutt to my grandmother."

"Oh, Mrs. Bishop. What a treasure! Are you sure you want me to take these?"

"Our family saved them all these years. I believe God preserved them for you to read, Meredith. Perhaps you'll find something for your novel in these."

"I don't know what to say but thank you." On impulse, Meredith hugged Mrs. Bishop, who patted her back softly.

"By the way, what are your plans for Thanksgiving?"

Meredith had forgotten about Thanksgiving. How could she answer this question without inviting herself?

Mrs. Bishop didn't wait for an answer. "If you don't have any plans, we'd really like to have you eat with us. Our older daughter and her husband are bringing our grandchildren."

"That's so kind. I couldn't insert myself into your family time."

"I'm inviting you. You aren't inserting yourself. Gary will pick you up around eleven on Thursday. Right, son?"

"Absolutely." His eyes twinkled at Meredith, as if to say, *Don't fight it.*

"Thank you. For everything." Meredith felt a little weepy again.

"You are most welcome. Well, Gary, your father and I are headed for our Sabbath rest, but you can visit as long as you like."

Gary grinned at her after his parents left the parlor. "They have always taken a nap on Sunday afternoon. They like to call it their Sabbath rest."

"I really like your parents. These letters will make all the difference. Nothing beats primary sources, but they're rare."

"I'm amazed at how much more I find out about my family when I bring someone home. I thought I knew everything."

Meredith wondered how many other young women Gary had brought home for his parents to meet. The thought made her restless. "If you don't mind, I think I want to have some of that Sabbath rest, too. Would you mind taking me back to the Roberts's?"

"Not at all."

❦

Back in her room, Meredith opened the neatly wrapped package. Inside were several yellowed and fragile envelopes carefully addressed to Mrs. Samuel Martin, but one letter was addressed to Miss Mary Galbraith at Stanton College. Curious, she opened it first.

Plantation Christmas *Weddings*

Mrs. Julia Nutt

Longwood

Dear Mary,

I enjoyed taking you on a tour of my house. You asked me how I could be so cheerful after all I'd been through, how I could be satisfied with what I had left after all the tragedies. I was miserable at the time. At times I gathered wild weeds and fed my children on them. We often went to bed hungry or lived on sour milk. My youngest was still a baby and my oldest only sixteen. I lashed out at God and the US government. I blamed them for my husband's death. I treated everyone, even those closest to me with anger and bitterness.

But just a few years ago, I changed. First, I thought how Jesus had suffered so much, worse things than I had, on that cross, and yet He said, "Father forgive them, for they know not what they do." Also, two other scriptures helped me, one about not letting bitterness take root, and one about being at peace with everyone. I understood that I had to forgive everyone who had hurt me.

So I made a list and put down what each one had done to me. Then I prayed and asked God to help me forgive. I didn't feel forgiving, but I said the words and burned the paper. When my bitterness left, I felt guilty for what I had done to hurt others even before all the tragedies. For the first time, I really understood that I needed God's forgiveness and the gift of salvation from sin that Jesus offers through His death on the cross.

Now you can understand why I can be content in my circumstances.

Come see me, my dear. You would be very welcome.

Sincerely,
Julia Nutt

Meredith laid the yellowed letters with their spidery script gently down on the desk. She knew what God was saying to her through these letters. She picked up her Bible and looked in the concordance. She found the verses in Hebrews 12. "Make every effort to live in peace with everyone and to be holy; without holiness no one will see the Lord. See to it that no one falls short of the grace of God and that no bitter root grows up to cause trouble and defile many."

She had let a bitter root grow up, and now she had trouble in all her relationships. Could she follow Mrs. Nutt's example? She took a piece of paper and listed all the hurts and pain she'd experienced. The list became very long:

I forgive the kids for calling me "trailer trash."
Bobbi Lee for not inviting me to her birthday party.
My parents for sending me to that school and dying and
*   leaving me.*
God for taking them, for putting me in a trailer instead
*   of a house.*
Gary Bishop. . .

She started to write, *for humiliating me by inviting me to the banquet,* but she knew the truth went deeper than that.

Gary for not loving me when I loved him so much, and
   for breaking my heart.

Just writing the truth down made her feel better. "Dear God, I need help to forgive all these hurts. I know that I can't have peace until I let go of my pain and let You have it, just as You took my sins on Yourself."

As she prayed, Meredith saw something she couldn't see before—that she was the prejudiced one. She had put everyone into classes and assumed, in some kind of backward pride, that her class was superior because all other classes discriminated against hers. But she had hated those other classes without really knowing anything about them. "We're all the same in Your eyes, aren't we? I'm no better than Bobbi Lee or Julia Nutt or Gary Bishop or anyone else. We all are sinners in need of Your grace. Please forgive me."

A feeling of such freedom came over her that she wanted to sing and dance in praise to God. She didn't have to prove anything to anyone. She could live to please God.

Chapter 5

The next morning during her prayer time, Meredith asked God for help to face the garden club meeting. "How like You, to give me this kind of challenge so soon after the blessing of forgiving. I'm trusting You to be with me and to keep me in perfect peace."

She tried on different outfits, rejecting most as too casual or too formal. At last, the look of a green wool dress with matching cashmere sweater struck the right note with her. Pumps and a pearl necklace completed her ensemble. The pearls recalled her to last Christmas—she'd had no one else to exchange gifts with, so she bought the pearls for herself.

Tuesday at two she found herself on the Stanton Hall porch, a little nervous but comforted by Mrs. Bishop's reassuring smile. The main hall inside ran all the way through the house, with massive oil paintings and chandeliers throughout. Mrs. Bishop led her into the main parlor where several women already gathered.

"This is my friend, Meredith Long. She graduated with

Gary," Mrs. Bishop said.

"Very nice to meet you, Meredith."

Meredith moved from woman to woman, murmuring greetings and smiling. To her surprise, she didn't feel at all intimidated by these women she had always seen as royalty. Instead, she saw normal people—grandmothers and wives, neighbors and friends—enjoying this break in their lives and some time to be with each other. In some eyes she saw pain, in others contentment, in some insecurity. God had changed her eyes to be like His, to see with compassion. What they thought of her didn't matter, only what God wanted to do in their lives through her. She wanted to share her elation with someone. Gary came to mind. Perhaps during the tour, she could tell him what God had done for her.

Mrs. Bishop found two seats together. The president went through the minutes and reports. The business related to the Christmas open houses and the regular house tours made Meredith see how much the garden clubs had helped the local economy.

Finally, the meeting's main business ended. "Before we have refreshments and some committees meet, I want to introduce any guests we have today."

Mrs. Bishop started to stand, but before she could, a voice behind them called out. "Meredith Long is here. I don't know if you remember her parents. Her father worked as a mechanic at Gus Rain's garage. They lived in a trailer off the Jackson road."

Meredith recognized Bobbi Lee Cox's voice. She trembled as she waited to see what would happen. Would they throw her out as an imposter?

Mrs. Bishop rose. "Meredith Long is my guest. She graduated from the University of Kansas. She's written several bestselling books that many of you have read and enjoyed as I have. The really good news is her plan to write a series set in Natchez, based around our pilgrimage homes. We should be very grateful for the wonderful publicity that will bring to our city."

Spontaneous applause burst out followed by excited chattering, until the president intervened. "Ladies, ladies, your attention please. What marvelous news. Miss Long, it is such an honor to have you here today. If we can do anything to help you with your research, please let me know. I'll be happy to personally arrange for it."

Meredith stood then, a little shaky, but elated. "Thank you so much for your gracious welcome. May I say that I have been impressed by the way you have unselfishly given of your homes, time, and work to improve the lives of everyone in Natchez. God bless you."

She sat down to more applause. The meeting dismissed, and she found herself surrounded by women, all chattering at once.

"I loved Lucy in *Prairie Firebrand*."

"I've read all your books."

"When is the next one coming out?"

"How long will you be here?"

"I'm so glad you're doing a Natchez series."

"Could you do a book signing here? We could arrange one in the library."

"Can I have a card with your contact information?"

"I'd love to have signed copies to give for Christmas presents."

Meredith fielded all these comments and questions as best she could. At last, Mrs. Bishop led her across the hall to the dining room, where plates of apple pie with candied pecans waited and a large urn dispensed fragrant spiced tea into delicate china cups.

Meredith picked up her dish and cup. Turning, she found herself face-to-face with Bobbi Lee. "I love your outfit, Bobbi Lee."

"Thanks. I always dress conservatively for garden club meetings." Bobbi Lee smoothed the pleated skirt of her tweed designer suit.

Meredith recognized the expression on Bobbi Lee's face, defensive and embarrassed. She tried to set her at ease. "Are you involved in the Christmas activities for the club?"

"Not really. I don't have time to lead tours or any of that. I'm a member because my grandmother is a charter member. She opens her house during the spring pilgrimage, you know."

"I didn't know. That's a lot of work for her. Do you help her?"

"My mother does, but I usually have things to do with the pageant. You know I was pilgrimage queen a few years ago."

"Congratulations. I'm sure you made a beautiful queen." Meredith did know this, because she had searched Gary's name on the Internet and found that he was king the same year. The picture of Gary and Bobbi Lee together as king and queen epitomized all that shut her out in Natchez society.

"I've never read your books. I don't like historical fiction."

Bobbi's unvarnished statement startled Meredith, but she knew not everyone liked her books. "I'm sorry to hear that. What do you like to read?"

"Nothing you would be interested in, I'm sure."

"Perhaps you're right, but I've met many other authors at writers meetings, and I'd be glad to get you a signed copy of your favorite, if you like."

Bobbi Lee's stony expression wavered a bit at this, but she changed the subject again. "How did you come to be Mrs. Bishop's guest?"

Meredith sipped her spiced tea before answering. "She invited me at her house Sunday. It seems she likes historical fiction."

"As do I." Gary's sudden appearance among all these ladies startled Meredith, though she expected him.

Bobbi Lee's sullen demeanor broke into a smile. "Gary. What are you doing here? You know only ladies come to these meetings."

"Normally, you'd be right, Bobbi Lee, but for Meredith's sake, I've come. I'm taking her on a tour."

"Oh, let me come, too. I've never heard one of your tour speeches. I'm sure it will be fascinating coming from you." Bobbi Lee possessed Gary's arm.

Meredith hadn't realized how she'd anticipated another private conversation with Gary until that moment. Seeing Bobbi Lee hanging on his arm shook her newfound peace. "Perhaps I should go on and find your mother, Gary. She may be waiting for me."

Gary moved away from Bobbi Lee. "You're riding home

with me. Mother and I discussed it."

"I'll just say good-bye to her, then."

Meredith found Mrs. Bishop in the hallway. "Thank you so much for inviting me. I've had a delightful time."

"You've been perfect, dear. I'm looking forward to Thanksgiving."

Gary and Bobbi Lee came from the dining room. Gary took Meredith's arm, leaving Bobbi Lee to tag along. "Let's start our tour in the library." A small library featured a huge gasolier made of medieval gargoyles, flails, balls and chains, and other weaponry. "Mr. Stanton designed this room as his personal office, but they were in the house only a few months when he died."

Meredith took out a small notebook from her purse and scribbled notes.

Bobbi Lee spoke up. "The other tour guides usually talk about the mirrors and furniture more."

"Would you like to hear more about the furniture, Meredith? I imagine you recognize some from your other research."

"You can point out pieces original to the house."

They crossed the hall to the front and back parlors. Gary pointed to the carved wooden supporting arch. "During the late 1800s, after Mrs. Stanton's death, the house became a school, Stanton College. Sheets hung from that arch to make two classrooms out of the parlor area. My great-grandmother taught here for a year."

Meredith stopped writing. "Mary Galbraith from Pennsylvania?"

"Yes. I'm surprised you remember."

Bobbi Lee sat down in an upholstered chair looking bored. "Shouldn't you be concentrating on the Stantons?"

Gary looked at Meredith with a question in his smile.

"You can tell me about both, but I'm really interested in this Yankee schoolteacher aspect. What would your mother think of my using her grandmother in a book?"

"We can ask her Thursday."

Bobbi Lee sat up. "What's happening Thursday?"

"Thanksgiving. Let me be the first to wish you a happy one." Gary led them across the hall to the enclosed staircase and bowed. "Ladies first."

"You must be getting quite chummy with the Bishops," Bobbi Lee whispered in Meredith's ear, "if you're eating Thanksgiving dinner with them."

"Where will you spend Thanksgiving?" Meredith asked, choosing not to address Bobbi Lee's comment.

"Oh, I'll probably go to my grandmother's."

"You don't sound excited."

"She's been really judgmental since my divorce. She didn't want me to marry in the first place. She should be happy now."

Meredith topped the stairs and entered the upstairs hallway. "Still, it's nice to have family during holidays." She smiled at Bobbi Lee before following Gary across to the bedrooms.

"All this furniture is period but not original to the house. The fireplaces are all Italian marble." Gary indicated the two four-poster beds next to the large windows overlooking oak trees.

"What role did these rooms play when Stanton Hall became a school?"

"Dormitory rooms. The teachers lived across the hall. I'll show you those next."

Meredith recorded data as fast as she could, noting details that would help her envision scenes in a book later. She could picture Mary Galbraith in a teacher bedroom, with the matching bedspreads, drapes, and large, comfortable chairs. But part of her brain marveled at how differently she saw Bobbi Lee today. She recognized Bobbi Lee's neediness, her bitterness at how life had turned out. She had been the same only a few days before, quick to criticize and judge because life had been tough. God's forgiveness changed everything.

Gary took them up the stairs leading to the third-floor game room and then to the fourth-floor observatory. "Normally these areas aren't part of a tour, but you get special treatment today."

Meredith noted the game room's large size and tiny dormer windows. "Would they have used this as a classroom?"

"Yes. Good guess. The arts and domestic science teacher used this space."

Bobbi Lee led the way to the stairs that went on up to the observatory. "I've always wanted to see from up here."

They entered a small room with arched windows and a view of Natchez that took Meredith's breath away. She had never seen her hometown in quite this way before. The winter sun had set in the west and left a glow that lit up the river far below them. The lights were coming on all over town.

Bobbi Lee pointed to the riverbanks far down below

them. "Look, the gambling boats. Do you want to try their buffet after this?" She turned to Gary, who shook his head. "Oh, that's right, you don't gamble. Never mind."

This exchange amused Meredith. Neither had asked her what she wanted because Gary correctly assumed she didn't gamble either, and Bobbi Lee didn't really want Meredith along.

Gary led them back down the stairs. "What do you think, Meredith? Did you get what you wanted?"

"Definitely. I'll need to do more research and talk to your mother some, but I have a good start."

"I'm starved. Let's at least go get something to eat. We could drop you off at your place on the way, Meredith." Bobbi Lee paused at the bottom of the stairs.

Gary helped Meredith down the last few steps. "Whoa, Bobbi Lee. Meredith and I already have plans for this evening. Perhaps we three could go out another time."

Bobbi Lee shrugged and turned to go. "In that case, I'll see you at school, Gary."

Meredith watched her go. Two days before, she would have been happy to see her so taken down. Bobbi Lee had been the worst in elementary school about calling her names. Revenge was not sweet. But Bobbi Lee wouldn't care that she'd had a change of heart about her. She turned to Gary. "What were these plans you mentioned?"

"Don't you want to discuss the books? I thought we could go out to a Chinese restaurant."

"All right, but only if you let me pay. All my costs while I'm doing research are business expense."

Gary shook his head. "No way. I'm still a Southern gentleman, and this is my idea."

Meredith respected his insistence, but she knew what teachers made.

Gary drove them across town to the restaurant. Inside, Chinese decorations and music gave the place a definite oriental flair. "You know, we didn't have a single restaurant like this in town ten years ago, and now we have several Chinese, Mexican, and even Japanese restaurants. Mississippi is changing."

Meredith ordered the cashew chicken with fried rice, but when Gary ordered the pepper steak, she couldn't help saying, "I almost ordered the pepper steak."

"Let's share entrees. I like cashew chicken, too." Gary sat quietly, studying her face. "Something's different about you today."

"In what way?"

"I'm not sure. You seem happier, more peaceful. Do you want to share?"

Meredith explained the impact Mrs. Nutt's letters had on her. "Even today, when I felt so intimidated, I saw everyone differently. My mother used to say we were just 'regular folks.' Today everyone I met looked like regular folk. Isn't God's power to change us amazing?"

"Have I told you how much I admire your faith?" Gary's gaze communicated a tenderness she couldn't interpret, but it made her heart race.

She forced herself to speak lightly. "You may have mentioned it."

Their food came then, and their talk turned to the novels. She explained how she loved the connection between Mrs. Nutt and Mary Galbraith. "I think I can write separate stories for them but tie them together in the series. If I can come up with a third story, connected in some way but in a different house, it would be perfect."

"I'll have to think about that some more." He picked up his fork. "I see you're using chopsticks."

"Sure, don't you?"

"Never tried."

Meredith held out her chopsticks. "Here, I'll show you." She demonstrated holding the lower stick and moving the top one with her index finger and thumb. He tried to pick up some food but lost it every time. Meredith reached across the table to help. When her fingers touched his, a powerful feeling went through her that made her fumble the chopsticks. He must have felt it, too, because the chopsticks dropped, forgotten as they looked at each other.

"Maybe you'd better stick with the fork."

After that, they ate quietly, but Meredith remembered that sensation long afterward.

Chapter 6

Thanksgiving morning dawned just cool enough that Meredith went for a run to help counteract all the calories she anticipated having later. She found herself outside the city limits, not far from her old home place. The weeds so obscured the turnoff that she almost missed it. On impulse, she went down the hill. She had been right about the trees. Pines grew, head tall, where her father's neatly mown lawn had been. A sob escaped her tight throat as she saw where the trailer had been. Only a few bricks from the foundation still remained.

She circled around to the back and found the garden plot, not as grown up as the lawn, but still containing weeds and trees. Then a flash of red caught her eye. Were those tomatoes? Yes, and green peppers, squash, even a small pumpkin. Volunteer plants had come up in the garden. Her mother was giving her a gift, even in death.

Meredith remembered seeing a plastic bag by the road. She retrieved it and filled it with as much produce as she could carry.

Gary drove up, right at eleven. He had been thinking about Bobbi Lee and the way she wanted to horn in on his time with Meredith. He had planned to invite Meredith to a basketball game the following Thursday evening at the school, but Bobbi Lee insisted that she needed to discuss the school Christmas bazaar during the game. That didn't make much sense to him, but he agreed to get her off his back and to make up for not taking her to eat after the garden club meeting. Honestly, she acted like a spoiled brat sometimes, but he tried to accommodate her because they had been classmates, and his mother would have been appalled if he told Bobbi Lee what he really thought.

When he knocked on the door, Meredith opened it. She had a basket of beautiful garden produce, all washed and polished. It looked like an improvised horn of plenty, a perfect hostess gift. "Wow, you must have hit up a produce stand."

"No, actually, I found this in my mother's garden."

"Really?" He took the basket and helped her out to the car. After she told her story, Gary's heart hurt for her. "That must have been emotionally wrenching."

"In some ways, but also strangely comforting. It's hard to explain."

As they got close to the house, Gary warned her. "My niece, Mary Elizabeth, and nephew, Samuel, are five and three. They're cute, but things get a little crazy when they're around." For the first time, Gary wondered if Meredith liked children.

In the entryway to the house, Gary made introductions.

"This is my sister, Rebecca, and her husband, Jim. And these are Mary Elizabeth and Samuel." He nodded at her. "My friend, Meredith Long."

"So happy to meet you all." Then Meredith knelt down on the children's level. "Happy Thanksgiving. Are you having a good time at your grandparents'?"

Mary Elizabeth nodded. "You should see the huge turkey Grandma is making."

"I'm looking forward to it."

Samuel pulled her hand. "Come see."

As Gary watched, Meredith made her way with the children to the living room and soon was stacking blocks. Gary sat down near Jim. "Well, I guess we'll watch the game this afternoon."

"Yes, it wouldn't be Thanksgiving without football."

Gary listened to Jim with only half his attention. He couldn't get over how quickly Meredith took to the children. When his niece begged Meredith to read her a book, he intervened. "Mary Elizabeth, let Miss Long alone."

"Now, Gary," said Meredith, "nothing's more important than teaching children to like books."

"She's training the next generation of fans," Gary said, and laughed with Jim. Meredith glanced up and caught his quick wink. He loved seeing her cheeks turn red as she ducked her head and kept reading *The Animals of Farmer Jones* to the children.

The smells coming from the kitchen made Gary's mouth water. "There's nothing like turkey roasting to wake up an appetite."

Jim nodded. "I wonder if my wife needs help in the kitchen."

"You can help the children wash their hands"—Rebecca poked her head in, smiling, a large platter of rolls in her hands—"and get settled at the table."

"Will do."

With the children and Jim gone, Gary had Meredith to himself for a moment. "Here, let me help you up."

"I'll just put these blocks back in their container."

He bent toward her, breathing in her perfume, and pulled her up, wanting to pull her on into his arms.

"Dinner's ready." His mother called from the dining room.

Reluctantly, he released her hands and followed her in just as his dad emerged from the kitchen with the golden turkey, which he set among the dishes of mashed potatoes, gravy, sweet potato casserole, green beans, cranberry sauce, broccoli salad, and fresh sliced garden tomatoes. Mother had not forgotten to put out Meredith's offering.

Meredith murmured, "I'm glad I got some exercise this morning."

After they were seated, his dad said, "Meredith, please join us in our family's tradition. We all tell something we're thankful for before the blessing." He smiled warmly. "I'll go first. This Thanksgiving Day, and every day, I'm thankful for God's salvation through Jesus Christ."

"Amen," several voices around the table said.

"I'm thankful for a beautiful wife," Jim said, "and two wonderful children."

"He means us, Samuel." Everyone laughed at Mary Elizabeth's comment.

Meredith's turn had come, and she choked a little. "I'm so grateful to be included in your family celebration. It's the first time since. . ."

Gary reached for her hand under the table—"I'm thankful to have my good friend Meredith back in my life." He squeezed her hand, and she squeezed back, thrilling him to his core.

After the blessing, the food made the rounds while everyone chattered and laughed at the funny things the children said or did. Meredith seemed a part of the family. Gary couldn't stop smiling.

Samuel's head drooped, so his mother scooped him up and took him and a protesting Mary Elizabeth off for afternoon naps. The dinner conversation became much quieter and more adult after that.

Gary's mother poured coffee to go with the pumpkin and pecan pie making the rounds. "Meredith, how are the novels coming?"

"I wanted to ask you something concerning that. You know my idea to do one about Mrs. Nutt? Well, what would you think of my doing one about your grandmother, Mary Galbraith Martin?"

"I think that sounds wonderful. I can tell you so many stories about my grandmother. She loved to tell me about her life when she lived with us. What time period?"

"The 1890s."

Rebecca had returned from settling the children. "You

should go see the photography exhibit at the Presbyterian church. They have some fascinating pictures from exactly that period."

"I'll try to go by there tomorrow. The ideas are starting to come together. I just need something for the third novel. Perhaps I can go to some pilgrimage houses for Christmas open house to get an idea. It would be nice if it connected somehow with the other two."

"Speaking of tomorrow, I was hoping you'd go with me to the Christmas tree lighting downtown," Gary said. "There'll be carols and businesses open. We could pick up a hamburger afterward."

"I may not be hungry before then." Gary liked the sound of Meredith's laughter. "I'd like that. What time?"

"I'll pick you up around five thirty."

"Harrumph." His dad cleared his throat. "It's my duty to remind you men of another Thanksgiving tradition—doing the dishes."

"Please, let me help. I didn't cook." Meredith rose to her feet.

Dad caved much quicker than Gary thought he would. "You and Gary do the washing and drying. Jim and I will clear the table and put the food away."

Gary found himself drying the dishes Meredith handed him after she washed them. "I want to go on record as saying this wasn't my idea."

"Many hands make light work. My mother's motto."

"Especially when she wanted you to do chores."

"Exactly." She lifted a stack of china plates and sunk them

in the hot, soapy water. "This is a lovely, big kitchen and very modern for an older home."

"Yes. My dad remodeled the old sitting room into a kitchen when he bought the house."

"Where was the kitchen before?"

"In a separate building. This house is antebellum, you know."

"No, I didn't. So your father bought this house for your mother?" She handed him another rinsed plate.

"Yes, she inherited the Victorian house built by her Grandfather Martin, but my dad knew she really wanted an antebellum home. This one had been neglected, but they worked hard to fix it up. The attic contains fascinating stuff. I didn't have much choice but to love history."

"Your parents seem to love each other very much."

Gary stacked the dried china plate. "Yes. It's a wonderful heritage and becoming rare to grow up in a loving home."

"My parents loved each other like that. I had them buried in the same coffin because they died in each other's arms. I couldn't bear to separate them." Meredith spoke matter-of-factly, but Gary saw tears falling into the dishwater.

He put his arm around her and squeezed. "I can't even imagine how I would feel if something happened to my mom and dad."

"I just wish. . ." He waited while she composed herself. "That I hadn't stayed away so much. I could have been with them more those last few years if I hadn't been so insecure."

Gary wanted to take her into his arms and hold her tight, but he knew she would be embarrassed. "You can't change the past, but your parents loved you and were proud of you."

Meredith took a deep breath. "Thank you, Gary." She picked up a casserole dish and scrubbed it.

After the dishes were done, Gary invited Meredith to sit beside him on the sofa in the living room to watch the football game. Her nearness beside him gave him both comfort and restlessness. At one point, he looked down because her head had slipped over to his shoulder and lay there. She looked adorable asleep. Not until the winning touchdown pass made Jim whoop did she look up and smile sheepishly. "I guess I drifted off."

"Football doesn't excite you?"

"Well, I could lie."

"That's all right. Thanks for sitting with me anyway."

"If you don't mind, I think I should get back to my work." Meredith stood and stretched delicately.

"I have something for you." Gary's mom left and returned with a brown paper sack. "These are some turkey sandwiches I made for your supper."

Meredith gave his mom a big hug. "Thank you so much, Mrs. Bishop. You don't know how much this afternoon has meant to me."

Gary smiled at his brother-in-law, who winked at him. Meredith had no idea how much this afternoon meant to him.

Chapter 7

The next morning, Meredith visited the Presbyterian Church's photography exhibit to study the fashions, buildings, and events of 1890s Natchez. She could picture her characters in those settings. The steamboats fascinated her. White tablecloths and napkins, china and chandeliers—those boats were floating mansions. In one room, she actually found a picture of some Stanton College students. What a rich resource. She must remember to thank Rebecca. She blushed when she realized she assumed they would meet again. Was she taking Gary's attentions for granted?

She worked all afternoon, studying her books, letters, and notes, writing down ideas for scenes. Before she knew it, the clock read four thirty, time to get ready for her evening with Gary. The high temperature that day had been in the seventies, but she knew it would be quite a bit cooler outside after sunset. She chose a sweater and corduroys, and topped them with a matching knitted beret.

Downtown bustled with people. Police had blocked off

Main Street to pedestrian traffic only. Gary led her down to the shops "I want you to see something." He entered a small bookstore. "I don't think this was open when you lived here before."

"Turning Pages. What a unique name for a bookstore. I think they had just opened then."

Inside, the manager came forward to greet them then froze. "It's you. You've come for our open house. See, your books." She pointed to a display of Meredith's books and a blown-up publicity photo. "Look, everyone, it's Meredith Long, bestselling author. Miss Long, could I get you to sign my personal copies of your books?"

Meredith looked at Gary, whose grin told her he enjoyed the scene. "Of course, I'd be happy to."

Once she started, a steady line came, asking for her signature. She'd done many book signings before, but never during a date. Where had that thought originated? Her face warmed at her presumption. Was Gary watching her? She glanced up and saw him standing by the display, discussing her books with potential customers. He was pushing her books. Affection swept over Meredith, and for a minute, she forgot the woman waiting for her to sign. "Oh, I'm so sorry. How do you spell your name?"

The crowd kept up until seven. The owner came back up to Meredith, smiling. "Thank you so much. How wonderful. We sold more books tonight in one hour than I can remember. You're welcome to come back anytime."

Meredith shook hands with her and followed Gary out onto the sidewalk. "Did you know that would happen?"

"No, I had no idea, but I found it exciting. You're probably used to book signings."

"I've done several, but not impromptu like this. I think you sold quite a few books for the store."

"I'm doing my part to keep you bestselling." Gary laughed.

"Thanks. Every book counts." The carolers' singing drew her attention. They were close enough now to see the dark outline of a tall Christmas tree in the center of Main Street. As she watched, the lights suddenly came on to gasps, cheers, and applause. Meredith stared at the glowing tree. Christmas had become such a sad time for her the last few years that she had forgotten the wonder, but standing with Gary, her heart sang with the carolers, "Joy to the world, the Lord is come."

With the crowd dispersing, Gary and Meredith decided to walk down the street and admire the Christmas displays in shop windows and listen to the Christmas carols that continued up and down the street. Gary pointed to a quaint restaurant decked out in holly and pine ahead.

"Let's eat there."

"Cotton Alley Café?" Inside, Meredith stared in surprise. "I thought you said a hamburger place."

"They have the best burgers in town."

"It's charming." A Christmas tree glowed next to the intimate table where the waiter seated them. She could see a lower floor with more tables below them. "I thought I'd never be hungry again after that dinner yesterday, but I'm famished now. I'll have the burger at your recommendation."

When the waiter brought their food, she eyed the humongous beef patty on its sourdough bun. "I don't know if

I can finish all this alone."

"A minute ago you said you were hungry."

"I am."

"You've put in an evening's work."

"Yes. That's all just part of it. You might be surprised at how much goes into being an author besides the research and writing."

"Do you mean like editing?"

"Yes, but also Facebook pages, blogs, websites, Twitter. All those take time to maintain, not to mention book signings, speaking engagements, and writers conferences."

"I get the picture."

"I've met very few writers who like all those things. Many are shy and would rather not meet people. I guess every job has aspects that aren't fun."

"Like grading papers."

"You don't like grading papers?"

"I don't know any teacher who likes grading." Gary studied her face, making her breath catch. "So what are your plans, next?"

"House tours tomorrow. I want to get that elusive idea for a third book. I don't suppose there has to be a connection between the books other than Natchez, but if I found one, it would be nice."

"I have an idea if you're game."

"What's your idea?"

"Brandon Hall only opens to the general public at spring pilgrimage and for the December open houses. What do you say to going up there with me tomorrow?"

Shouldn't she tell him not to give her so much of his time? He must have other things he needed to do, but somehow she didn't want to quit seeing him. "Sounds great. What time?"

"I'll pick you up around ten."

"Gary, I wish I could tell you how satisfying it's been to tell you my ideas. I haven't had that luxury. Before I came, I wanted to talk to someone one day, and I couldn't think of anyone except God. Not that He isn't enough, but human companionship is good. Thank you."

"Hey, I'm enjoying this, too."

"Do you remember how I told you that God made me come home for a reason? I think I see it, now. He knew I would read Mrs. Nutt's letters, and that would help me find peace. I needed that peace to get beyond myself to reach out to others. I never realized before what a selfish sin insecurity is."

"Once I was blind, but now I can see."

"Exactly. When I finally see something like this, it makes me wonder what else I'm blind to."

Gary didn't say anything to this, but he looked away with a pensive expression. Was she missing something about him?

Chapter 8

The next day dawned humid and hot for late November. Meredith changed the Christmasy outfit she had picked out for cooler slacks and a short-sleeved shirt.

The drive up the Natchez Trace Parkway calmed her spirits as it always did. She watched for deer and saw several other creatures scuttling into the underbrush. The trees flaunted colorful leaves and a few bare branches. "So Brandon Hall connects directly to the Trace?"

"Yes, look at this." He turned sharply off onto a dirt road that had steep banks on either side. "This is Old Trace."

"Really. I knew some sections remained, but I hadn't seen this stretch."

Gary paused at the gate, which stood open for the rare open house. "When the Brandons built the house, travelers could see it from the Trace as they headed north. I think they got many visitors."

The large multicolumned mansion stood on a hill above a pond and a parklike lawn. Soon they were following a hoop-skirted guide into the grand hall. She told them about the Brandon family, the many children who had died, and other tidbits that fascinated Meredith. "The oldest son, John, married Ella Stanton."

"Is that Stanton as of Stanton Hall?" Meredith whispered to Gary.

"Yes." His warm breath on her ear made her feel lightheaded.

"Did the John Brandons live here or at Stanton Hall?" asked Meredith when the guide called for questions.

"They lived here at Brandon Hall, even though many of the Stanton children continued to live with Mrs. Stanton after their marriages. John Brandon was the heir of Brandon Hall."

Outside, after the tour, Gary took her hand, and they walked down to the pond, their feet crunching on the dried pecan leaves. "Would you like to sit on the chairs by the pond?"

"Sure."

"You have an idea, don't you?"

She looked out at the live oaks that bordered the pond. "I think so. John Brandon would have been courting Ella Stanton during the time between Mrs. Nutt's story and Mary Galbraith's. I think I can tie all those together. I'll need to do more research."

"Here. Take my library card. You may need it."

"What if you need it?"

"I know where to find you." His voice caressed her. She wanted to say, *Please find me*, but she kept that thought to herself.

Gary pointed to the sky. "Just as I thought. This heat brought in a storm. No doubt some cooler weather will come behind that."

"I hope it isn't too cold for the wedding to be outside."

"Anything can happen this time of year. You know that."

A raindrop hit Meredith on the cheek, and she jumped up, pulling Gary up the hill. They ducked into Gary's car laughing, just beating the heavy rain. Gary took her back to the Roberts's, where she immediately got to work on the proposal. She worked steadily the rest of that day and sent it on to Linda late that night.

❧

Meredith hadn't seen Gary since church on Sunday. She knew school kept him busy. With her proposals in and the Kansas novel finished, the time pressure eased for her. This chilly December Thursday, she tried to plot the first Natchez novel, but her mind drifted back to Gary—how he grinned at her when he said something witty, how he reached for her hand when they sat together, the look in his eyes when he talked to her. She stared at the computer screen, aware that she hadn't typed anything for several minutes. What was wrong with her today?

She quit trying to work and lay on her bed staring at the ceiling, thinking about the last three weeks and how much had happened to her. "God, You've been faithful. I should have known that Your urging would bring something wonderful to my life. Learning to forgive is wonderful enough. Are You telling me that You brought me back to Natchez for Gary, to find not only healing but love?"

Hearing herself say the word *love* gave Meredith goose bumps. She hadn't dared to think it. Now she knew. She loved Gary, not just with a schoolgirl crush, but with a committed love. She loved the way his hair waved away from his forehead, the way he helped her in and out of the car, the way he understood and listened to her. She loved him—the person that he was.

So what did she do now? How did a girl let a guy know she would say yes if he asked? And what would she do if he didn't love her? Gary could have any girl in Natchez. He didn't have to settle for someone who grew up in a trailer. No, she wouldn't listen to her insecurities. She would trust God with her future.

Taking a deep breath, she went back to her computer and checked her e-mails. She had one from Bobbi Lee Cox. Strange, she'd never corresponded with her before. Bobbi invited her to a basketball game that evening at the school. Perhaps Bobbi Lee was offering her an olive branch at last.

Another e-mail from her agent said call ASAP. She picked up her cell phone and scrolled to Linda's number. "Linda? It's Meredith."

"Hey, Meredith. You aren't going to believe it, but the publishers have offered a contract."

"On the Natchez trio? Already? It's only been a few days."

"It seems they had marathon meetings to get everything wrapped up before Christmas. Our proposal fit into a niche they needed to fill, and your track record cinched it."

"How much?"

When Linda told her, Meredith squealed. "Wow, you're

a super agent, Linda."

"I know. Hey, you're my best client. I also negotiated the deadline to be May for the first draft. Can you make that?"

"I'm already plotting it."

Meredith sat stunned after the call ended. A three-book contract with an advance that would more than pay living expenses—she had to tell Gary. If she went to that game tonight with Bobbi Lee, he might be there. He'd be excited for her. Maybe she should move to Natchez from Kansas. Her lease would expire next month anyway, and living here would make research easier. Who would have thought she'd be excited about living in Natchez? She knew the reason. It was Gary.

That evening as she entered the gymnasium, the bright lights dazzled her eyes. When they adjusted, she scanned the stands. She spotted Gary. Bobbi Lee sat beside him, and as she watched, Bobbi Lee put her hand on Gary's knee, leaned over so the low-cut blouse she wore revealed even more, and whispered something in Gary's ear.

Meredith turned on her heel and fled the gym, hoping no one had seen her come in. A sob caught in her throat as she reached her SUV. All she had begun to hope for lay in ruins. She had just gotten the key in the door when she heard him.

"Meredith, wait." Gary sprinted toward her.

"Yes?" She turned her head so he wouldn't see the tears on her cheeks.

"I need to talk to you." His voice sounded breathless. "Please, can't we talk?"

"I should go. I can't. . ." Her words caught in her throat.

"Please, go with me to get something hot to drink. There's a coffee shop nearby."

"Don't you have a date with Bobbi Lee?"

"A date?"

His surprise confused Meredith. Hadn't she just seen them acting like a couple?

"We were discussing plans for the school Christmas bazaar."

"During a basketball game?" Meredith couldn't keep the skepticism out of her voice.

"You're right. It doesn't make sense." His frustration came through. "If you go with me for coffee, I'll explain."

Meredith hesitated, her hand on the door handle. She looked in his eyes. Even in the streetlight, she could see his anguish. "All right."

"My car's over here." He locked her door for her and took her by the hand. "Your hands are cold."

The warmth of his hand seeped into hers, just as the knowledge that he had left Bobbi Lee for her warmed her heart.

In the downtown coffee shop, a smattering of customers stood around. He led her to an out-of-the-way table. "What would you like?"

"Hot chocolate?"

"I'll be right back." He returned with her hot chocolate, topped with whipped cream, and a coffee for himself.

As they sipped their hot drinks, Meredith looked right at him. "So you're telling me that you and Bobbi Lee are not dating?"

"No. She keeps creating these reasons to corner me, like

setting me up to say the blessing at that shower or following us around at Stanton Hall. Tonight she said we needed to work on bazaar plans at the ball game."

"You looked pretty cozy when I looked in the gym."

"She didn't act that way until you got there. I can imagine what that looked like to you."

"You know, it was Bobbi Lee who mentioned the ball game and suggested I come to it." Was there a pattern here she hadn't seen before. "You don't think—"

"That she planned this to drive us apart? That's certainly possible."

A memory stirred, Bobbi Lee's catching her in the hallway between classes, telling her not to accept Gary's invitation to the senior banquet. "Gary, you took Bobbi Lee to the senior banquet, didn't you?"

"Yes, I did." For the first time, Meredith heard the pain in his voice that she had felt in her heart.

"Was it her idea or yours?"

"She suggested it after she heard that you had turned me down."

"How did she know that? Did you tell her?" Clarity dawned for Meredith.

"No. Didn't you?" Gary's look said he didn't understand.

"I never told anyone. After Bobbi Lee told me about the dare, I hurt too much."

"What dare?"

Meredith took a deep breath. "She told me that your friends had dared you to ask the nerdiest girl in school to the banquet."

"What? Never. I asked you to the banquet because I wanted to take you." He took her trembling hands in his. "Couldn't you tell that I liked you?"

"I wouldn't let myself believe that someone like you, a part of Natchez royalty, could ever care for me."

"So you believed someone like Bobbi Lee, who, it appears, is a habitual liar when it suits her purposes. Who used to call you names? Wasn't that Bobbi Lee, too?"

"I have some more items to forgive, it seems." Meredith sighed. "I need to ask you to forgive me for believing her instead of trusting you. I never thought I could hurt you."

"Consider yourself forgiven. Why didn't you think you could hurt me?"

"I wasn't much to give up, when you could take Bobbi Lee or any other girl in town."

"I didn't want any other girl. I wanted you." His gaze became more intense. "I still do."

"Why, Gary? I don't understand." Meredith looked at his face and read there the truth. Her heart beat faster and her mouth felt dry. Could she really believe that Gary cared for her?

"You're intelligent, a good conversationalist, a woman of deep faith, talented, passionate about your work, beautiful. . . I could go on."

"I don't know what to say. I'm overwhelmed."

"Just say that you like me a little."

"You've always been my ideal man." She smiled into his eyes. "Every hero in every book I've written is you."

"And your editors didn't object to that?" His voice held

such irony and repressed joy that she laughed aloud. "Let's get out of here." He reached for her hand and squeezed it as he led her out the door. Back at her car, he stood by her door. She looked up at him. Then her eyes closed and the lips of the man she loved were on hers.

"I love you, Meredith."

"Oh, Gary." Her arms went around him in a tight hug.

Chapter 9

The next day, Gary stopped by his parents' house on the way to the wedding rehearsal. "Mom?" he called as he came in the door.

"I'm here, Gary. What's up?" She came into the hallway from the kitchen.

"Do you remember your grandmother's rings? You promised I could have them when the right time came."

His mother hugged him. "I'm so happy for you. Are you absolutely sure?"

"I'm absolutely sure I'm going to ask her. I pray she'll accept."

"Do you doubt it?"

"You remember when I asked her to the senior banquet in high school, don't you?

"Yes."

"I was sure then that she would accept."

"I would hate to see you hurt."

"I understand now why she turned me down. We've

talked about it, but. . ."

"You're still nervous."

"Yes."

"I'll get the rings."

She left, and Gary paced. Meredith had achieved something he didn't aspire to—celebrity status. Would she be willing to marry a schoolteacher, a poorly paid one at that?"

His mother returned carrying the round leather jewelry box. "I had them cleaned last week. Things seemed headed in this direction."

"Mother, you're a wonder." Gary opened the box and examined the gold Victorian rings. One held a pearl surrounded by diamonds. Next to that, the plain gold band, inscribed inside with S.M. to M.G. "Do you think it will fit?"

"Ask her first. You can have it sized afterward, but I think the sizes are probably close. Your great-grandmother would love to see this."

Gary closed the box and pocketed it. "Well, here goes."

"Would you like to pray before you go?"

"Please."

"Dear Lord, Gary is going to ask a most important question. Thy will be done, Lord. Protect his heart from hurt, and give him the right words to say."

Gary's voice felt husky. "Thanks, Mother. I'll let you know how it turns out."

He drove out to Longwood, arriving before the five o'clock rehearsal. Meredith's SUV sat next to the wedding planner's. She must be around somewhere. He walked around the mansion and found Meredith looking at a copse of live oak trees with Spanish moss hanging down in the winter dusk. "You know about the Longwood ghosts, don't you?"

"Oh, Gary. You startled me."

Gary walked up and put his arms around her, holding her close. He could feel her heart racing. "Are you all right?"

"Mmm. I am now."

"Let's take a walk down by the pond."

Meredith walked along beside him, looking adorable in her red sweater and Christmassy beret. "Do you think the weather will be good for the wedding?"

Gary forced himself to focus on her words and not her presence. "No rain is predicted, and the temperatures should be in the seventies again."

"I'm so happy for Francine. She's been kind of frantic for a few days, but she really recommends this wedding planner, Wreath Anderson. Isn't that a great name, especially this time of year?"

"Yes, it is." A silence fell between them as Gary tried to think of a romantic way to approach her.

"Oh, I meant to tell you last night, but I forgot. I've gotten a three-book contract on the Natchez series. That's the fastest I've ever heard back from my agent. The advance is great. I'm so excited."

Gary's heart sank. She didn't really need him at all. Who was he to ask such a woman to be his wife? "That's great. I'm really happy for you."

Meredith paused in her stride. "Are you all right? You don't seem as thrilled as I thought you would be."

Gary looked out at the pond in the growing gloom, aware

that the wedding party was assembling above them and his time was short. "I am happy. It's just that, well, I guess you may be leaving Natchez now and going back to your life in Kansas."

Meredith stood right in front of him. "Gary, I can live anywhere I want to. I can write anywhere. What are you trying to say?"

Gary felt the box in this pocket. Did he dare? "What I'm trying to say is I want you to spend the rest of your life writing in Natchez, with me. Will you become my wife?" He held the jewelry box out to her.

He heard her gasp, and then her arms were around his neck. "Yes, oh yes, Gary." Then their lips met and lingered. "I love you."

"And I love you." He held her close, the leather box still held tight in his fist. In this euphoric state, Gary gradually realized that people were talking and getting closer.

"I know they arrived. I saw both their cars."

"Where could they have wandered off to?"

"I'll find them."

"Do you need help, Wreath?"

"We're here." Gary released Meredith with reluctance just as Wreath Anderson came within hailing distance.

"Come on you two. We need to get started while we still have a little light."

"Wait a minute, Wreath." Gary reached for Meredith's hand and squeezed it. She squeezed him back, which he took for assent. "We have a favor to ask."

"What's that?" Wreath paused.

"We need you to plan another wedding. Ours, actually." Gary looked at Meredith in the near dark. She smiled at him.

"I'd be happy to. I didn't know you were engaged."

"We weren't until five minutes ago." Meredith laughed.

"But don't tell anyone tonight. This is Francine and Bill's time," Gary said.

"Come by my office next week, and we'll begin making plans. Congratulations."

They headed up the hill together, Meredith's hand cradled in his. Gary couldn't remember when he'd been so happy.

The rehearsal went off without a problem under Wreath's supervision, though Gary caused some hilarity by talking the other groomsmen into carrying the groom in on their shoulders.

Meredith's dark brown hair and eyes sparkled in the rich glow of Longwood at Christmas—crystal lights twinkling in the galleries and trees, and hurricane lamps bathing the aisle in amber. Wreath's work impressed Gary. She'd created the perfect atmosphere for a romantic plantation Christmas wedding, and he couldn't wait to be the groom himself, since he'd found his bride. When they got to the Carriage House restaurant, Gary pulled out the ring box again and offered it to Meredith. "In all the excitement, I didn't give you this."

"This is an antique jewelry box, Gary. Where did you get it?"

"I hope you don't mind. These are family heirlooms. My great-grandfather Martin gave these rings to my great-grandmother over a hundred years ago." Gary watched with anxiety as Meredith opened the case.

"Oh, Gary, how stunning. And they're doubly precious to me because they were once worn by Mary Galbraith." She slipped the pearl and diamond engagement ring over her finger. "It fits perfectly. Thank you."

Gary leaned forward for a kiss, savoring the sweetness of her lips and the knowledge that she had accepted his proposal.

That whole evening, while others toasted the bride and groom and cracked jokes, Gary felt that he and Meredith were in a bubble of happiness. She would glance at her ring and then at him, her expression so full of delight, his heart felt near to bursting.

As soon as they could leave without being rude, they drove to his parents' house. Gary could read his mother's relief and satisfaction when she answered the door in her quilted robe and slippers and glimpsed their faces.

"I'm so, so glad, my dear girl." She enfolded Meredith in her arms and then embraced Gary. "You look so happy, son."

"I am, Mother."

Gary's dad grabbed them in a big bear hug. "We were expecting you, son. Mother's already got hot chocolate going in the kitchen. So how did you ask her?"

Gary laughed. "I don't know if Meredith knew how nervous I felt. When she told me about her new book contract, I almost chickened out."

"Why?" Meredith's voice held shock.

"Because I remembered how presumptuous it was for a poor schoolteacher to ask for the hand of a famous author."

"No more presumptuous than for a poor orphan girl to accept the proposal of a pilgrimage king from a wonderful family." Meredith took the mug from Gary's mom. "That's a wonderful part for me."

"Marrying a pilgrimage king?" Gary's dad asked.

"Having family again."

"You're one of us now. You'll come for Christmas, won't you?" His mom sat down across from them.

"I'll answer that. Yes. She'll be here for every holiday from now on." He put his arm around Meredith and hugged her. How good it felt to know where they stood.

"Where do you want to have the ceremony?" Mother asked.

"Longwood." They answered in unison. He looked at Meredith in amusement.

"Well, that's settled, then." Dad put down his empty mug. "I hate to break up this love fest, but it's after midnight."

"And tomorrow will keep us all busy," said Mother.

Gary stood and pulled Meredith up into his embrace. "I'll walk you out."

Chapter 10

Meredith woke the next morning and for a moment couldn't remember why she felt like singing. Gary loved her. He wanted to marry her. Was it only two days ago that she gave her future over to God? "I praise You, Lord. You are better to me than I deserve."

She rose and read her Bible. "Therefore, if you are offering your gift at the altar and there remember that your brother or sister has something against you, leave your gift there in front of the altar. First go and be reconciled to them; then come and offer your gift."

In her happiness, Meredith wanted to ignore the message of these verses. Why did she always find them so convicting? She didn't have to dig long to find someone who had something against her. Gary loved her, so Bobbi Lee would just have deal with it, right? Putting herself in Bobbi Lee's place, she knew she would feel angry and hurt. How could she go about being reconciled with her? "God, I understand that I need to do this, but I don't know how. If You'll set up the circumstances for me, I'll be obedient. I'm trusting You to give me the right words to say."

Uneasiness plagued her, as she knew it would until she settled this thing. Pulling on her exercise clothes, she went for a brisk jog in the chilly December morning, praising the Lord for the beautiful day, for His blessings in her life, for the gift of Gary.

When she came down to breakfast later, she caught Ellie as she came in with a platter of bacon, omelets, and muffins. "I have some news, Miss Ellie." She held out her left hand.

"Oh, my land, girl. Who's the lucky man? Is he from around here?" Ellie set down the platter to hug her.

"Gary Bishop. We went to high school together."

"Hap, look at what his girl's gone and done. She's engaged herself to John Bishop's son."

Hap gave her a hug, too. "Didn't I tell you? I told her, Ellie. She wouldn't be single long. And I was right." He chuckled.

After breakfast, Meredith wrote for a few hours then took out her bridesmaid dress. In flowing red velvet, she should be warm enough, even outside after sunset. She took her time getting ready, fixing her hair in a special french braid her hairdresser taught her. She got her dress and heels and drove to Longwood, arriving well before the time set.

She took her things out and carried them toward the place to dress. Wreath had arranged for the bridesmaids to dress in the redbrick building next to Longwood, which had housed the Nutt family for a time and had later been slave quarters, Meredith was startled but not surprised to see Bobbi Lee standing alone on the long porch looking pensive. Breathing a prayer for guidance, Meredith walked over to her. "Bobbi Lee, I have something important I need to say. Do you have a minute?"

"I suppose so. What is it?" Bobbi Lee's expression looked guarded.

"I've harbored a bad attitude toward you for years and haven't treated you the way God wants me to. I was wrong. Will you forgive me?"

Uncertainty and disbelief played across Bobbi Lee's face. She rubbed her hand across the back of the rocking chair in front of her then looked Meredith in the face. "You aren't the one who's done wrong. I have. I should be asking you to forgive me."

"I already have."

"You would." Bobbi Lee came around the chair and sat down. "For years I've hated you, and I don't know why. You always knew all the answers in class. Everyone talked about how smart you were."

"You made good grades in school." Meredith moved to sit in the chair across from her.

"Not enough to impress anyone. Your parents loved you and loved each other. I used to watch them during school assemblies when you got all the awards. They were so proud of you. My parents gave me everything I wanted except their time. They divorced when I was ten."

Meredith realized they were both ten when she came to their school. No wonder Bobbi Lee had been so mean. She was hurting. "I wish we had talked before now. I envied your beauty, your big house, and your popularity."

"I had stuff, but not what mattered—real love, real friendship, real accomplishment."

On impulse, Meredith went over to Bobbi Lee and hugged her. "I'll be your real friend. It looks like I'm going live in Natchez from now on."

Bobbi Lee returned the hug, almost fiercely. "Thank you, Meredith. I suppose Gary will marry you. You deserve him, and he never would have cared for me. I always knew that deep inside. I just wanted a fresh start."

"I know something about fresh starts. They come from a relationship with Jesus Christ. Do you know Him, Bobbi Lee?"

"Not like you or Gary. I want to know what you two have."

Meredith hugged her again. "I'd love to share."

Bobbi Lee smiled. "I wasn't going to tell you this, but I saw one of your books at my grandmother's house. Once I started it, I couldn't put it down. I stayed up all night reading it."

Meredith laughed and gave Bobbi Lee another hug. God provided a way to give her blessing upon blessing.

Wreath Anderson appeared in the doorway. "Bobbi Lee, you're coordinating the servers for the reception, right? Meredith, it's time to get dressed."

◆

Gary followed the other groomsmen across the grass to their place before the steps of Longwood. The congregation sat in rows out on the lawn. One by one, the bridesmaids came up the aisle; a string quartet played "Jesu, Joy of Man's Desiring." Then he saw Meredith. He'd thought her beautiful before, but in the red bridesmaid dress, she looked ravishing. Their eyes met, and her loving gaze made his heart pound. In just a few weeks, she would come down the aisle to unite with him. The thought overwhelmed him. How he loved her. He realized then that he had missed the bride's entrance while looking at Meredith. Perhaps no one noticed.

The lovely service lasted only a few minutes. Gary listened to the vows, honoring them in his heart. Now at last he had a woman he could say those words to without any reservation. "In sickness and in health till death do us part." Then he held out his arm to her and walked down the aisle with Meredith clinging to him, a sensation he liked very much. "You look stunning."

"I think the same about you. You make that tuxedo." Her breath on his ear as she spoke for him alone made his senses tingle.

"Did you think what I did during the ceremony?"

"That I wish this wedding were ours?"

They took their places in the receiving line inside the mansion. White Christmas lights and Christmas greenery had transformed the bare brick walls and unfinished wood. Gary murmured to Meredith, "The Nutts themselves would approve of how the old mansion has come alive."

"Wouldn't they?" She smiled into his eyes, making his knees feel weak with emotion. Then the crowd came in, and they greeted people they hadn't seen since high school, and parents of old schoolmates. Gary noticed that many people complimented Meredith on her books, and she responded graciously to every one. Finally, the crowd thinned. "I'll go get us some eats before they're all gone."

"Thank you, Gary. I'm famished."

They enjoyed a bit of a feast, discussing what they would want at their reception. Just then, Wreath Anderson came up to them. "Francine's going to throw her bouquet. Meredith, I think you should make every effort to catch it." She winked at Gary and walked away.

Curious, Gary followed Meredith out, where Francine stood on the top step looking down at the bridesmaids and other single women. As he watched, he could see them pushing Meredith toward the front and center. Francine didn't even turn around. She looked right at Meredith and threw the flowers to her. Then to his surprise, Francine called for everyone's attention. "I have it on good authority that Meredith really will marry next. Gary Bishop asked her, and she accepted."

Gary knew his role. He quickly moved up to Meredith's side and, to the sound of applause and congratulations, took her in his arms and looked deeply into her eyes, seeing his own joy reflected in them. Then his head went down to claim a kiss. Her response quickened his breath, and he deepened the kiss. Soon he would kiss her again, as his bride, on the steps of Longwood.

Christmas at Brandon Hall

Virginia Vaughan

Dedication

This story is dedicated to the memory of my father, JW Williamson, who always encouraged me to be a story-teller and never let me give up on my dream.

Chapter 1

Jackson, Mississippi
June

Sandra Brinks choked back the hot tears that stung her eyes. She trembled against the emotion pushing at her senses, waiting to burst through. But she couldn't break down now, not with Devon so close. She wouldn't let him see her fall apart.

She stole a quick look at her estranged husband standing beside her in the Wells Christian Academy auditorium. His attention was focused on the stage and the kids lined up to receive diplomas, among them their twins, Cara and Jacob.

Devon cheered, a big smile breaking his face as the headmaster called their names, first Cara's then Jacob's. His blue eyes sparkled as he looked her way.

Sandra shielded her face with her hand and turned away. She couldn't let this happen in front of him. She had to remain strong.

"Sandra, are you okay?"

She tried to match his smile, but the overwhelming

emotions of the day slipped through—joy, pride, excitement. Tears spilled down her face despite her internal protests. "I'm fine," she said, hastily swiping at the tears. She hated this display of emotion. She hated even more that Devon saw it.

"Excuse me." She brushed past him, making her way through the crowd toward the end of the aisle then through the auditorium doors.

Once in the hallway, she leaned against the wall and tried to regain her composure.

Crying was bad enough, but crying in front of Devon was inexcusable. Since their separation, she'd made it a point never to let him see her bend. She'd done well without him, and she'd promised herself never to give him reason to think she needed him. . .because she didn't.

The auditorium doors swung open, and Devon stepped through them, gazing up and down the hallway until he spotted her. Concern flitted through his gaze, but he kept an uneasy distance. They'd lost that close bond they used to share in the early days of their marriage. Most of the time she could forget how much she missed it, but today, having him so close to her, sitting elbow to elbow in the auditorium, she couldn't forget.

How had everything gone so wrong between them?

"Sandra, are you okay?"

She wiped her tears away. "Look, Devon, I know we were forced to sit together today because there are too many people and not enough seats, but that doesn't mean I need your pity."

"I was concerned about you."

"I'm fine. I don't even know why I'm crying. It's not a sad day."

He shortened the distance between them then leaned against the wall along beside her. He folded his arms as he casually shrugged his broad shoulders. "It's a little sad. Seeing them up there getting those diplomas makes me realize they're not babies anymore."

How could he be so composed when she was falling apart? "No, they're not. That part of their lives is over. In a few weeks, they'll be leaving for college. Then they'll be getting jobs and getting married. It seems to me like it was only yesterday I was rocking them to sleep. Now I'm watching them step out into the world." Her voice cracked, and another tear slipped from her eye then another and another.

Devon slipped his arm around her and pulled her close to him.

As she nestled her face on his shoulder, she couldn't remember all the petty stuff that had come between them.

"I don't know what's wrong with me," she said.

"It's all right to cry. It's normal."

The soothing tone of his voice calmed her, and she surrendered to the emotions of the moment, lost in a haze of tears and warmth mingled with the musky scent of his cologne.

With her tears spent, she stared up into his face. He smiled at her as he wiped away her tears his with thumb. Being in his embrace felt so good, so right, so natural. It was wrong to fight it. And she was surprised to find she didn't want to fight.

"Mom, Dad!" Jacob's voice called to them.

Sandra stiffened and pushed away. The auditorium doors were opening and people were streaming into the hall, the ceremony over. She wiped her face then pasted on a smile as the twins approached.

Talk about getting lost in someone's embrace.

"Check this out!" Cara exclaimed, holding out her diploma for them to see.

"Very impressive," Devon said, pulling her into a hug. "I'm proud of you." He hugged Jacob, too. "I'm proud of both of you."

"Mom, are you okay?" Jacob asked.

"I'm fine." But even as she spoke the words, she knew her voice sounded choked.

Both kids frowned.

Thankfully, Devon came to her rescue by changing the subject. "Hey, what do you say I take us all out for a celebratory dinner?"

"Mom, too?"

Devon turned to look at her. "Sure, Mom, too—if she wants to come."

Sandra nodded. "Sounds like fun, but I insist on paying for half." After such a weepy display of emotion, her sense of pride was returning.

"That's not necessary."

"Yes, it is." She didn't want Devon to get the wrong idea. She needed to remind him she was a strong, independent woman who could take care of herself. Not some weepy, emotional mess.

She pulled herself together and enjoyed the evening. They had plenty to celebrate. A chapter in their lives had just closed, but she knew another was opening.

Once through eating, the twins hugged their father then Sandra and the kids headed home. But once they disappeared into their bedrooms, Sandra had time to reflect on the day. She hated the way she'd broken down, but Devon's response to her plight had surprised her. . .and pleased her.

Her phone rang, and she noticed the number of her best friend, Paula.

"How was the ceremony?"

An embarrassed flush warmed her face as she told Paula about the incident with Devon.

"He hugged you? Did the kids see?"

"I don't think so," Sandra said. "I hope not. I would hate to give them the wrong idea about Devon and me."

Her friend hesitated then responded, "Would it be giving them the wrong idea?"

"What do you mean?"

"It's been six months, Sandra, and neither of you has filed for divorce. I'm just saying maybe this marriage isn't as over as you think."

"He left us, Paula. How can I ever forgive that?"

But later the empty side of their queen bed mocked her, and one memory of the day pushed its way to the forefront of her mind—the warmth of Devon's arms as they surrounded her.

Chapter 2

December

I

t's about time." Paula handed her an envelope containing the papers Sandra had asked her lawyer friend to draw up— divorce papers for her and Devon. "Now maybe you can get on with your life."

Sandra held them, pushing against the folds of the bulky papers as Paula cut into her salad. This lunch was more than a get-together between friends. Today they met to end the last twenty years of her life. These papers would forever change her life.

Suddenly lunch didn't seem like such a good idea.

"What do I do now?" Sandra asked.

"Sign where I've marked then give them to Devon to sign as well. Once he's signed them, he can forward them to his attorney. We'll file them with the court, and you'll finally be free of him."

Paula was right. It was time to move on. With the kids away at college, her link with Devon was forever broken. No use putting it off any longer. It had been over a year and a half since they'd called it quits on their marriage. It was time to make it legal.

After lunch Sandra pulled her car into the spacious two-car garage and cut the engine, remembering a time when the driveway and garage were full of cars—hers, Devon's, and one for each of the kids. It had been a long time since she'd needed so many parking spaces. With the kids now both away at school, the garage seemed too large for her single sedan.

She unloaded grocery bags from her trunk and carried them inside. Cara would be home in a few hours, and Sandra wanted to prepare a casserole dish for their evening together. Although her daughter had chosen a school only an hour and a half away, she rarely came home on weekends, so it had been several weeks since Sandra had last seen her. She was looking forward to spending a little mother-daughter time together before Cara left for her aunt's Christmas wedding in Natchez.

Sandra pulled the invitation she'd received to her sister-in-law's wedding from where she'd pinned it to the refrigerator with a magnet. Kim was having her wedding at Brandon Hall in Natchez and had reserved rooms for all the family to spend the week and enjoy Christmas together. Cara and Jacob would be attending, which meant Sandra would spend Christmas alone.

The back door opened then slammed shut, and Cara appeared in the kitchen doorway much sooner than Sandra had expected. She quickly returned the invitation to its place on the refrigerator.

Cara placed her purse on the table. "What were you doing?"

Sandra turned back to the casserole, away from her daughter's curious stare. "Nothing. I was just admiring the invitation—its beautiful design." Sandra and Kim had once been very good friends, as close as sisters, and Sandra realized she missed that relationship. In fact, she missed being part of that family. With her own parents gone, Devon's family had filled a void that had been missing in Sandra's life. But she'd not seen any of them since the separation.

"I've never been to Natchez. I wonder what it's like."

"Oh, it's beautiful, Cara. You'll love it."

"You've been there?"

"I have. In fact, that's where I first met your father."

"I never knew that. I always thought you and Dad met at a friend's wedding."

"We did. It took place in Natchez. When he looked at me across that four-tiered wedding cake"—she sighed at the memory of Devon's blue eyes on her. "I think I fell in love right then and there. We spent the weekend strolling hand in hand by the river and touring plantation homes. That place has such amazing history."

Cara smirked. "Apparently more than I ever knew."

"That reminds me. Help me remember to put the gifts I purchased in your car. I don't want you to forget them."

"You know, Mom, the room Aunt Kim reserved for me is plenty big enough for two people. Why don't you come? We could go sightseeing and do all the touristy stuff. You said yourself Natchez is pretty, and I'll bet it's even lovelier this time of year with all the Christmas decorations. Think of it as mom-daughter time."

"Honey, this is a family event, and I'm not a part of that family anymore."

"No one thinks that, Mom. Aunt Kim sent you an invitation. She wants you there. Everyone wants you there."

Nothing would please her more than to see Kim get married or spend time with the family. She realized it was her own pride that had kept her from it. Cara was right. No one had ever said a cross word to her about the breakup with Devon. In fact, sadness had been the prevailing emotion among his family, not anger.

She wanted to agree, started to agree, until a horrifying thought crossed her mind. What if Devon brought a date? "I can't, Cara. We'll do a mother-daughter thing another time."

"But why?"

How to explain her fears to her daughter without coming off petty? "I just don't think it's a good idea."

Cara sighed. "Fine. But my car has been making this really funny noise, so I'll need you to drive me to Brandon Hall."

"You can take my car."

"No way, Mom. I'm not going to leave you without a car for a whole week."

Sandra sighed then agreed. She couldn't let Cara make the two-hour drive if her car was acting up, especially on the Scenic Natchez Trace.

It looked like she was going to Natchez after all.

Devon typed up his report then e-mailed it to his boss, letting him know that installation of the new computer software at a medical clinic in Dallas was complete. His team of six was already packing to head home. They were anxious to be on the road, rushing back to their homes to be with their families.

Devon had once been one of them, rushing home to spend the holiday with Sandra and the kids, but no more.

He was in no particular rush to be anywhere this Christmas.

His cell phone rang, and he recognized his boss's number. "I have a piece of business to discuss with you," his boss said when Devon answered. "A promotion, effective January 1. It comes with a nice bump in salary as well as no more traveling."

Devon had been rallying for such a position for years, a job where he didn't have to travel, where he could be home for baseball games or recitals or just for supper more than once every few weeks. Only this offer came just a few years too late. The kids were away at college and he had no one now to rush home to.

He thanked his boss for the offer and promised to have an answer in a few days.

After hanging up, Devon opened a file on his computer and brought up a photograph of him and Sandra and the kids. What would this offer have meant to him years ago? More time spent with his family? The possibility of saving his marriage?

His phone rang again. Devon checked the caller ID and saw his son's name and number pop up.

"You are still coming, right, Dad?" Jacob's voice held a note of uncertainty that Devon didn't like.

"I said I'd be there, Jacob, and I will." If it had been anything but his sister's wedding, the choice of whether or not to go wouldn't have been difficult. He wouldn't miss watching Kim get married for the world, but spending four days that close to Sandra after what had happened between them at graduation—he wasn't sure he could handle that.

"Good, because it's not just the wedding. We're having Christmas there, too. Besides, Cara and I haven't seen you in months. You've been taking on more and more assignments since we graduated. We've hardly seen you since spring."

"Don't exaggerate. I was there to help you move into the dorms at school."

"And we haven't seen you since. It's like you don't want to come home. Does this have anything to do with Mom and what happened at graduation?"

For a young man, Jacob was keenly aware. Sandra had been on his mind daily since that moment he'd held her in his arms. They still ached for her. The scent of her hair, the feel of her petite frame in his arms. Seeing her that way had struck him. Since their separation, even before that, every time she'd been around him, she'd been on alert, stiff and unrelenting. How long had he prayed for a glimpse behind her armor? A crack in the tough shell she protected herself with. She'd been vulnerable that day, and although he was certain she saw it as weakness, Devon thought she'd been beautiful.

But there was no need to confuse the kids with the thought of a reconciliation that would never happen. Devon gritted his teeth. "Nothing happened at graduation."

"Dad, we saw you two hugging."

"It was nothing. Your mom was upset. I was comforting her. That's all it was." But the mention of Sandra brought up another question. "Look, Son, I might not be able to come for the whole week. There are some things I need to take care of at the office first. But I'm sure your mother—"

"Mom's not coming."

"I know Aunt Kim sent her an invitation."

"She did, but Mom said she can't make it. I talked to her a few days ago and couldn't change her mind. If you're not there, Cara and I will be alone for Christmas."

Even though that was an exaggeration—the kids always had grandparents and aunts and uncles to celebrate with—Devon felt wrong. He couldn't miss an opportunity to spend the holidays with his kids. He'd missed too much time with them already because of his job.

He faced the facts. He'd spent the past several months traveling, trying to get Sandra out of his mind. It wasn't working, and neither would staying away from his sister's wedding. And with Sandra not there, he didn't need an excuse to arrive late.

He smiled, pleased with the way things were turning around for him. This Christmas he would spend with his family.

Chapter 3

Is that what you're going to wear, Mother?" Cara dropped the suitcase in her hand at the doorway of Sandra's room and rushed inside.

"What's wrong with what I'm wearing?"

"You look like a mom." She opened the closet and began rummaging through Sandra's clothes. "You must have something nicer than that old T-shirt."

Sandra glanced down at her T-shirt bearing the name of Jacob's high school baseball team. She'd worn it to every game he played, and it was comfortable. "I'm not dressing up just to drive you to Natchez."

Cara pulled out a V-neck blouse and handed it to her. "Here, put this on instead. And where are those cute jeans I bought you? Never mind, you can borrow a pair of mine." She retrieved her suitcase, hoisted it onto the bed, then rummaged through her clothes until she found a pair of satisfactory jeans and handed them to Sandra.

"Is this really necessary?" Sandra asked her daughter.

"Mom, you're so pretty. You should look nice. You never know who you might run into."

Sandra carried the clothes into her adjoining bathroom to change. Maybe Cara was right. What if she saw Devon while dropping Cara off at Brandon Hall? She would want to look her best.

She stared at herself in the bathroom mirror. She had neglected her appearance of late. There always seemed to be so many things more important. And who did she have to look nice for anyway?

She thought of the legal papers in her purse. She could give them to Devon when she dropped Cara off. And of course she would want to look her best when she saw him, especially after the mess she'd been at graduation.

She pulled her long, dark hair from its ponytail and brushed it out. Devon used to like it when she wore it down.

"And put on some makeup while you're in there," Cara called from the bedroom.

Cara's suggestion made her stop and think. Was she really prettying herself up just to hand her husband divorce papers? Logically, it made no sense.

She reached for her makeup bag. It didn't matter if it made sense or not. Today Devon Brinks would see just what he'd given up.

❧

The Natchez Trace Parkway was a two-lane road commemorating the historical path used by travelers who brought their goods to Natchez down the Mississippi River then returned home on foot. Sandra chose this scenic route because it would take them directly into the city of Natchez, but it was also beautiful to see the changing colors of the fall foliage. The yellow and red leaves intermingled with the evergreens so common in Mississippi made for a beautiful landscape, unblemished by advertising billboards or businesses. The only buildings along the Trace were rest stops and markers signifying historic sites. Sandra would have enjoyed stopping to explore some of those sites, but there wasn't time today.

Despite living so close, she'd been to Natchez only once before—the friend's wedding where she'd met Devon. Kim was getting married at Brandon Hall Plantation, a place Sandra had never heard of. But she'd looked it up online. The pictures showed Brandon Hall to be a beautiful Greek Revival–style house off the Natchez Trace on forty acres of rolling hills. She couldn't wait to see it. If the pictures were any indication, it would be beautiful.

Kim and her fiancé, Mike Rogers, had reserved several rooms for her mother, Devon, and the twins to stay for the week. The nuptials would take place on December 21; then the family would stay and celebrate Christmas together. It sounded like a wonderful time, and Sandra was glad the kids were included.

She only wished she were.

Sandra found the turnoff for Brandon Hall, a sunken lane that used to be a part of the original Natchez Trace. Sandra let down her window at the gate at the end of the narrow path and punched in the access code Kim had written on the wedding invitation.

Cara's eyes widened as the gate swung open and Sandra pulled through it. Sitting atop a hill was Brandon Hall. The plantation home was two stories with white, stately columns and wraparound upper and lower porches that spanned the width of the home. The green shutters and brick smokestacks created a beautiful antebellum feel.

She'd been right. The pictures didn't do it justice.

She pulled into the curve at the front of the house and stopped the car. The front door opened as she and Cara reached the porch. The bride rushed out to greet them, her arms open wide. She hugged Sandra as several people followed her onto the porch.

"I'm so happy you came," Kim told Sandra.

Behind Kim, Lynn Brinks—Devon and Kim's mother and Sandra's former mother-in-law—pushed her way past and embraced Sandra.

"When Cara told us you'd agreed to bring her, we were all thrilled. It's so good to see you again, Sandra."

Overwhelmed by the greetings, Sandra smiled and hugged them all back. This was what she remembered, the overflowing love this family bestowed.

Kim reached for the man who was standing behind her. "Sandra, this is Mike Rogers, my fiancé."

Sandra was happy to see Kim getting married again. Her first husband had been an air force pilot, who'd died in an accident several years after Sandra and Devon had married. Since then, Kim had shown no interest in marrying again. . .until Mike came along, that is. "I'm pleased to meet you, Mike."

He shook her hand. "I've heard a lot about you, Sandra. We're glad you're here. I hope we get a chance to get to know one another over the next few days."

"Oh no, I'm not staying. I'm only here to drop off Cara."

"Sandra, please stay. You've already made the trip."

"Come on, Mom," Jacob said, "you should stay."

"Yes," Lynn interjected, "please stay."

"I really can't."

"You made other plans?" Lynn asked.

Sandra considered telling a tale. She wasn't looking forward to spending the week alone, and she would love to see Kim get married, but intruding on Devon's family at Christmas wasn't right. "I really can't."

Cara opened the trunk. "Why don't you stay, Mom? You've been looking at pictures of the plantation ever since we got the invitation. I'll bet you'd have fun."

"Yes," Kim insisted. "The grounds are lovely and Natchez is beautiful. There's shopping downtown, tours of historic homes, the Trace, and of course, my wedding. Please say you'll stay."

"I didn't bring anything."

Cara pulled her makeup bag from the trunk. "I packed for you."

"What? When did you do that?"

"I was hoping you would change your mind once you got here."

"Thank you for the invitation, Kim, but I don't think I should. Devon—"

"—isn't here. Something came up at work, and he had to drive to St. Louis."

"He's not coming to the wedding?" Hearing this frustrated her. It was typical of Devon. He always put his job over family.

"Hopefully, he will make it here before the wedding, but until then there is no reason you shouldn't stay."

Lynn patted her arm. "We've missed you, Sandra. We would love it if you would stay and be a part of this celebration."

Sandra felt an overwhelming love. She'd thought separating from Devon meant she wouldn't be welcomed by his family. It felt good to know she was wrong. And with Devon away, she had no other reason to resist. "I would love to stay."

⬦

Stepping into the massive foyer of Brandon Hall was like stepping back in time. The high ceiling held a beautiful chandelier, and she stepped onto a rug so thick her feet felt like bouncing. She spotted period furniture in the rooms off the foyer, including one with a beautiful piano.

Kim saw her notice it. "I would love it if you would play for us one night."

Sandra rejoiced at the idea of everyone sitting around the piano singing while she played Christmas music. It was the perfect setting for a Christmas family get-together. It reminded her of the days when she and Devon and the kids would sing carols while decorating the Christmas tree.

She smiled at the memory then remembered it wouldn't be the same even if he were here, because she and Devon weren't the same.

"We'll see"—was all the promise she could give.

Kim introduced Sandra to Rachel Garber, whose family currently owned and operated Brandon Hall. Rachel gave them a brief history of the plantation, including the fact it had once been a working cotton plantation owned by the son of one of Mississippi's first governors. Given its location on the Trace, travelers returning home would often come by Brandon Hall, exposing the family to diseases that claimed the lives of several Brandon children.

She led them through the men's and women's parlors, the library, and the elegant dining room at the end of the hall, pointing out interesting facts, such as the use of the jib windows in the house and the uses of the shoofly device in the dining room.

A curved staircase, its banister bathed in green garland, was tucked discretely into the back corner of the hallway, adjacent to the rear parlor. Kim hooked Sandra's arm as she started up the steps. "You and Cara will be sharing the Rachel Leigh room. Mother and I are staying downstairs in the Louise Suite until after the wedding, and then Mother will move in with you and Cara, if that's all right."

"Of course," Sandra said. "That's fine."

"The men are across the hall in the Rebecca Delaine room. Mike will be bunking with them until the wedding, and then he'll move into the Louise Suite with me."

Sandra entered their room and gasped. The luxurious four-poster bed took up one wall, and a twin bed sat nestled between two large windows. A lovely antique mirror hung over the fireplace, and four windows allowed light to enter the room and gave a stunning view of the grounds.

"It's so pretty," Cara said, her eyes wide as she took in her surroundings.

"This room has a private bath along with a dressing room that adjoins to the next suite."

Sandra turned to Kim and hugged her again. "It's lovely. Thank you so much for inviting me."

"We're happy you came, Sandra. This family hasn't seemed complete without you." Kim wiped away a few tears then turned to Cara. "I'm afraid I'll have to steal you away for a while. We need to go into town to do some fittings for the bridesmaid dresses."

"But what about Mom?" Cara looked at her mother. "What will you do?"

"I'm going to unpack your suitcase, and then I'm going to take a stroll. I'm anxious to do some exploring."

When they were gone, Sandra turned to their suitcases on the bed. Cara had picked out several dresses for the festivities. Seeing them reminded Sandra that she would need to purchase a dress for the wedding, as well as at least another change of clothing. She was really glad now she hadn't allowed Cara to convince her to wear those heels her daughter had tried to push on her. She'd seen online that Natchez offered a walking trail of historic sites. Sandra hoped to spend some time with her former family but knew details of the wedding would likely keep them busy. No worries. Although she hated the thought of sightseeing on her own, in a city like Natchez she knew she wouldn't get bored.

She pulled back the curtain and gazed out over the rolling hills and trees. Sunlight warmed her face, but she could feel the chill of the December afternoon air against the thick glass of the window. Sunset would be in a few hours, and then the temperature would quickly drop.

She grabbed her coat. Unpacking could wait until later. She wanted to enjoy the scenery before it got too cold outside.

She remained close to the house, beginning her exploration in the split-level gardens out back. Though no flowers bloomed this time of year, the green shrubbery and the redbrick walkways were beautiful. A gravel path led into a wisteria overhang, and the lapping water of the fountain in the center garden created a serene feel.

Sandra walked around to the front of the house, where large old oak trees towered. The front lawn gave way to the reflection pond, complete with a wooden dock. She chose to sit in the wooden swing hanging on the limbs of a large oak tree. How many kisses had happened under this old oak, she wondered? How many couples had it seen in its long life?

Her mind immediately went to Devon. What would it be like to snuggle with him on this swing, nestled in the bosom of the mighty oak? She sighed, realizing the futility of that particular train of thought. She was in a town and a home overflowing with rich, colorful history, but all she could think about was her own past with Devon.

That was not the history she'd come to Natchez to find.

Who was she kidding? Since the moment he'd first held her in his arms six months ago, her history with Devon was all she could think about.

A noise grabbed her attention, and she turned toward the gate as it swung open. A black SUV pulled into the driveway. Sandra shrank back, recognizing the vehicle and hoping its driver hadn't seen her hidden beneath the massive limbs of the mighty oak.

The worst had happened. Devon had arrived early.

Chapter 4

Devon parked beneath a large tree then turned off the car. Beside his SUV sat a blue Nissan sedan, identifiable as Sandra's by the tag. On the other side of her car was Jacob's old Chevy. Had Cara driven up in Sandra's car or—he caught his breath—was she here?

He grabbed his duffel bag and got out. When he entered the house, he heard familiar voices coming from the front room. He stuck his head in to see his mother, Kim and Mike, and the twins sitting around putting together rice bags for the wedding.

"Dad, you made it."

Both kids rushed to hug him, as did Kim and his mom. He shook hands with Mike. After explaining how he'd finished his project early, he turned to his daughter. "Cara, did you bring your mom's car?"

Everyone quieted at his question; then Jacob confessed. "Mom's here."

Devon stopped and turned to face his son. "You said she wasn't coming."

Jacob's face flushed with guilt, but his grandmother came to his rescue. "Don't fuss at the boy. This isn't his fault." She pulled Devon along the foyer and out into the back of the house for privacy. "I asked Cara to make sure Sandra came. She's been away from this family for far too long."

"That's not my fault, Mom. I never wanted that."

"I know you didn't. Sometimes that's just the way things work out. However, I think this weekend is the perfect time to change that. You and Sandra have two wonderful children together. There are going to be situations where you cannot continue to avoid one another, like the graduation. There will be weddings and birthdays and grandbabies. You should find a way to get along even if you're not together."

He remembered the way Sandra had felt in his arms. How could he be around her and not hold her? But his mother was right. He had to make the effort. "I'll try."

"I remember the first time I met Sandra, when you brought her home. She was so beautiful. I remember how her eyes twinkled when she smiled."

He nodded. "Yes, she was beautiful. She still is."

"Devon, I don't know how things went so wrong with you two, but this weekend is an opportunity. Don't run from what you want. Chase after it. Weddings are a time of joy and romance."

He shook his head. "It's too late for me and Sandra."

"It's never too late. Remember, nothing is impossible with the Lord."

She left him alone and went back inside. Devon walked to the gazebo and sat down, trying to clear to his head. It had been spinning ever since his mother first mentioned Sandra. He couldn't believe she was here. He'd spent months trying unsuccessfully to push her from his mind. Now she was here, invading more than just his fantasy—his physical realm as well.

He reached into his bag and pulled out his Bible. He'd stumbled upon the verse Malachi 2:14 during his time on the road, time spent praying day after day for God to push Sandra's memory from his mind if there was to be no chance for them. Instead, he'd found this verse stating that God was acting as a witness between him and the wife of his youth, the wife of his marriage covenant.

Sandra.

He'd prayed and prayed about what that verse meant for him and Sandra, until eventually his prayers had turned from asking God to help him forget Sandra to asking God to help him reunite with Sandra.

Was this God's response? Had He brought Sandra here for a second chance? Excitement burst through him. Was this the fulfillment of God's plan? The next verse seemed to give him his answer.

"Has not the Lord made them one? In flesh and spirit they are his."

"Father, forgive me of my weakness," he whispered. "I know it's Your will that Sandra and I reunite, so I ask You to go ahead of me, God. Give me the words to speak, and bend her heart to mine."

As always, he felt better after putting everything in God's hands. He would work it out the way He saw fit.

He glanced up at the sound of footsteps heading toward the house. *Sandra.* The nip in the air gave her cheeks a rosy red glow, and she pushed an errant strand of dark hair behind her ear as she walked. She didn't see him, but as he stood in the shadows and watched her, he was amazed at her beauty. This was truly God orchestrated.

⁂

Had she overheard right? Had Lynn just implied Devon still wanted her? And encouraged him to chase after her?

Her mind swam at the notion. So much had happened between her and Devon. Could it ever be undone? Was it possible for them to ever recapture what they'd once had?

She kept walking toward the house, uncertain now what to do. She'd thought she could make a clean getaway without being seen by sneaking around to the back of the house and up the staircase, but she'd been surprised to find Devon and Lynn having a conversation about her. She hadn't planned to listen, but she'd heard regardless.

But what should she do now? Should she leave? Or should she try to speak to Devon? She still wasn't sure. Ever since the graduation, something had changed in her when it came to him, something that made her uncomfortable being around him. The memory of that night, the feel of his arms surrounding her, still haunted her memory.

The gravel lane crunched beneath her feet as she moved toward the brick steps. Even as she walked, her mind contemplated which course of action to take. What should she do?

Oh Lord, how do I handle this?

"Sandra?"

She stopped, her foot on the bottom step. She knew that voice. Devon! A figure emerged from the shadows of the gazebo and approached her.

"Devon, hello." She pulled her jacket tighter around her, but it wasn't the nip in the air that chilled her as much as being so close to him. Had his eyes always been so blue? She tried to remember, but suddenly all the history she'd been unable to forget moments ago melted into the present and into his presence. It no longer mattered what they'd been through. It mattered only that he was there with her at this moment.

His eyes crinkled as he smiled, approaching her. "I heard you were here."

Panic gripped her. Had she overstepped her bounds? Did he consider her presence here an intrusion? She rushed to explain. "I thought you were working. I wouldn't have come if I'd known you were. I know this is a family event."

"You're right. This is a family event. But Sandra, you are family. You're Jacob and Cara's mother." He sat on the concrete bench at the edge of the walkway. "Besides, my mother and sister are thrilled that you're here. So are the kids."

She sat on the other end of the bench, leaving plenty of space between them. A cool wind rustled the trees. She decided to face this head on. Lynn was right. It was time they both acted like grown-ups. "Do you remember the night of the kids' graduation?" She dared to turn her head and glance at him.

A slow smile curved his lips. "I remember we were sitting a lot closer then than we are now."

The teasing glint in his eyes made her smile. "Yes, we were. We've been through a lot together—and apart."

The glint in his eyes vanished at her last words, and his body stiffened as if bracing for news. He leaned forward, elbows on knees. "I guess we have."

"The thing is, Devon, we can't continue to avoid one another. We need to find a way to be together without it being awkward for everyone."

"What do you suggest?"

"Let's make a pact that the past is the past. We can't change what happened between us, but we can put it behind us and move forward. No more anger over things we can't change, no more fights, no more hurt feelings. Just two people trying to get along as best they can."

He took a long, deep breath then straightened up. "I can do that."

"Good. Then it's settled. We'll be friends."

He nodded. "Friends."

He held out his hand for her to shake and seal the deal. She quickly shook his hand, ignoring the tingling sensation that traveled through her skin when they touched. At the moment, putting the fights and disagreements behind them wasn't nearly as difficult as putting away the memory of resting her head against his chest and feeling his arms close around her.

"Okay. I'll see you later, friend." She rushed away from the bench, up the stairs, and into the house, but felt his eyes boring into her back as she walked away. Despite what she'd said, she would need the safety of distance if she was going to make it through this weekend without making a complete fool of herself by gushing over him.

Chapter 5

Biscuit & Blues was crowded as Devon and Jacob entered. The server greeted them.

"A table for two please," Devon said.

"Make that for four," Jacob interrupted.

As the server led them toward a table, Devon glanced at his son. "Are we expecting someone else?"

Jacob grinned slyly. "No, I just. . .I just thought we might want the extra space."

The kid was up to something.

They both ordered iced tea to drink. Devon didn't need to scour the menu. He ordered a pulled-pork sandwich with the fixings. However, when it came Jacob's turn to order, he hesitated, glancing at the doorway and pretending to study the menu.

"I'm not sure what I want yet. Can we have another few minutes?"

The waitress obliged and walked off.

Devon stared at his son. Yep, he was definitely up to

something. "Do you want to tell me what's going on?"

Jacob glanced at the doorway again then gave his father his best innocent expression. "I don't know what you're talking about."

He glanced back at the doorway then leaped to his feet and waved.

Devon followed his son's glance. Sandra and Cara stood by the door, shedding their jackets.

"Over here!" Jacob hollered.

Cara grabbed her mother's hand, pulling her along as she moved toward their table.

"Hey you two, what a coincidence."

The smug look that passed between Jacob and Cara assured Devon this was no coincidence.

"This place is busy tonight. I hope we can get a table."

"Why don't you join us?" Jacob suggested.

"Great idea." Cara turned to Sandra. "Isn't that a great idea, Mom?"

Sandra glanced his way. It was obvious this was not a great idea in her mind. However, instead of coming to her rescue and chastising the kids for this blatant attempt to bring them together, he stood and agreed.

"I think that's a terrific idea. Join us, please."

"Great." Cara took the seat beside Jacob, leaving only the one next to Devon for her mother. He pushed back the chair for Sandra.

"Have a seat."

She hung her jacket over the back and slid into the chair. Devon sat down, gently brushing her shoulder.

She jumped, obviously startled by his unexpected touch. Suddenly hyperaware of his hands and what do with them, he awkwardly fiddled with his napkin. Every longing inside of him wanted to reach out and touch her, aware of how close she sat to him. The wall prevented him from moving farther away from her to a safer distance.

He glanced at the kids, noticing the smug looks on their faces as they studied their menus.

Despite the crowd and the noise, the low lighting and the man on stage playing the acoustic guitar and singing gave the room an intimate feel. On another night, at a different time, this might have been a pleasant family outing.

"So, Jacob, tell me about school. How is it going?" Sandra asked.

"Good. I like it."

"Really? I went online and checked out your grades for the semester. I noticed you withdrew from Algebra."

Jacob shrugged. "I can take it again in the spring semester."

"But why did you need to drop it in the first place?"

"It's no big deal, Mom. I had trouble understanding Algebra. I've already signed up for next semester with a different teacher. I'm sure that'll solve the problem."

"Perhaps it's that girl you've been seeing. Did she distract you?"

"Jacob has a girlfriend?" Devon directed his question to Jacob. His son hadn't mentioned a girl to him.

"How did you know about her, Mom?"

"I'm sorry, Jacob." Cara sunk farther into her seat.

"Thanks a lot," Jacob said.

213

"Jacob, you're so young and college is about more than having fun. Don't let some girl distract you from your studies."

"She's not some girl, Mom. Don't call her that. Her name is Maggie. She's majoring in early education and she hopes to be a teacher one day."

Jacob's eyes betrayed his defensiveness, despite his outward bravado. The boy was lovesick. How had he not noticed that before? He remembered that feeling from his own young love days. He especially remembered it with Sandra. When he was a young man, loving Sandra had been easy. All his mind could comprehend was the sound of her voice and the way his arms ached to hold her. He'd breathed her in with every breath and focused on little else but her.

Is that what the verse meant by "wife of your youth"?

He stole a look at her now. They sat so close yet were so far apart. They had been for so long.

God, help me to reach her.

He ignored the awkwardness of his hands and slid one behind her chair. He smiled at Jacob.

"Maggie sounds nice. I can't wait to meet her."

Jacob and Cara hurried ahead when they left the restaurant, enjoying the excitement and energy of downtown Natchez. The streetlights were lit, and Christmas decorations adorned most of the shops along Main Street. Crowds of people bustled in and out of shops or gathered to talk with friends while waiting in line for admittance to restaurants.

"You could have backed me on that with Jacob," Sandra stated.

Devon looked surprised by her statement. "Alienating Jacob is not the way to develop trust."

"And letting him get away with dropping out of college isn't either."

"Who said he was dropping out of college?"

"I know where this is headed. Cara says he and this Maggie are getting serious. I don't want to see him throw his life away over some girl." She slipped her arm into her coat to block out the evening's chill then struggled to find the other sleeve.

Devon reached to help her, his hand brushing her neck. "Maybe she's not just some girl. Maybe she's the one he's meant to be with."

She shot him an annoyed look. "He's too young to know what true love is."

"We were his age when we first met."

"Exactly, and we were married within six months. I got pregnant. You dropped out of college. And look how we turned out."

"We didn't do too badly. We have two great kids and we built a nice life together"—he shrugged then continued—"except, of course, for the separation."

"I don't want Jacob to wake up at forty years old and have regrets. I want him to experience life."

He stopped walking and turned to look at her. "Do you have regrets about us?"

She sighed. Was he really going to play that game? "Look how everything has turned out between us, Devon. How can I not have regrets?"

The kids reached the River Walk and called back to them. Sandra hurried to catch up, joining them at the edge of the bluffs overlooking the Mississippi River. Devon didn't join them until a few moments later.

The majesty of the river amazed Sandra, reminding her why this body of water was called the mighty Mississippi. A riverboat was docked upstream, a replica of the ones that used to navigate these waters a hundred years ago. She breathed in the smell of the river. How many generations had watched this same water rush by from this bluff? How much of history had unfolded on its banks?

"We're going to walk down to the docks," Jacob said then rushed away with his sister following.

"Be careful," Sandra called after them.

She glanced at Devon, who seemed deep in thought as he leaned against the guardrail, obviously pondering the same questions as she and soaking in the beauty of the river. Sandra walked toward a gazebo in the center of the park and then climbed its steps. The wood floor creaked beneath her feet, but the view of the river was much better from this perch. The floor creaked again, revealing another person stepping inside the gazebo.

She turned to see Devon staring at her, his eyes blue rivers of their own, pouring himself into her. He reached out and caressed her face, his voice deep and husky when he spoke. "I don't regret one moment of our life together," he said. "Not one moment since the day we met. In fact, I would do it all over again, everything the same."

She pulled in a deep breath and closed her eyes, fighting

against the flood of emotion that tore at her at his statement. Did he really mean that? Every moment since their first meeting was seared into her mind. She replayed every kiss, every smile, every heartfelt "I love you." But then the last few years of their life together rushed back to her, reminding her that rosy memories have little to do with cold, hard reality.

She stiffened her stance and locked eyes with him. "Does that include walking out on your family?"

❧

The night air chilled at her words, matching the intensity of her stare.

Devon heaved a heavy sigh. He'd spent months trying to get past his own behavior and wondering how and why he could ever leave his family. He knew the truth. God had already convicted him of his behavior. He would make no excuses for how he behaved. He couldn't take it back. All he could do was ask forgiveness and hope Sandra could find a way to forgive him.

"No," he answered her. "You're right. That is one thing I wouldn't do the same." He walked to the edge of the gazebo and leaned against the railing as he stared out at the view. The sun was down but the sky still glowed in shades of orange and purple, reflecting off the water. He looked out at the water because it was warmer than her eyes. "If I could go back in time and change that, I would, but I can't go back, Sandra. All I can do is ask your forgiveness and pray that you can find it in your heart to forgive me."

Her eyes narrowed as a confused expression clouded her face. "You want me to forgive you for ending our marriage?"

Hearing her say those words cut into his heart. He bit his tongue before harsh words fell from his mouth. His leaving had been more of a symptom of their marriage ending than the end of it. But God had convicted him that he'd given up too soon. Saying such things to Sandra, however, would only cause an argument.

He chose his words carefully. "It doesn't have to end, Sandra, not if you'll give me another chance."

"Is that what you want? Another chance?"

"Yes." He moved toward her. "I shouldn't have left. I know now it was a mistake to give up so soon. I've spent the past months crying out to God to show me a way to bridge this chasm between us. And now we're here together tonight in this romantic setting. I think it's God's way of telling us we belong together. If you'll agree, I promise I'll work harder to make you happy."

His finger caressed her lips. He felt her give beneath his touch, and all the fight drained from her. Their lips touched, and life surged back into him. He could see the future again clearly, a future with her.

She pulled away from his grasp. "No, stop. We're talking about our marriage, not some job. It shouldn't be work."

She marched off the gazebo and headed back toward town.

His throat burned as she walked away. He'd done what he was supposed to do. He'd shouldered the blame without bringing up her role in sabotaging their relationship. Still, her heart hadn't been moved.

This wasn't going to be easy.

Sandra touched her lips as she walked back to her car. Her head was still spinning. Had that just really happened? Had Devon said he wanted to make their marriage work?

She unlocked the car and slid into the driver's seat, still trying to catch the breath he'd stolen with that kiss. How easily she could have fallen into his arms and stayed there forever.

But one kiss didn't change their circumstances, and a moment of regret from him didn't guarantee he wouldn't once again change his mind and leave. She was certain she couldn't live through that kind of heartbreak again.

She drove back toward Brandon Hall, her mind never far away from that kiss. How would she concentrate on anything else? And how would she be around Devon without becoming flustered by the memory? She couldn't let the kids notice either. Cara—

"Cara!"

She'd forgotten all about her daughter, left her at the bluffs when she'd run from Devon.

She hit the button on her car phone and dialed Cara's cell number. No answer. She tried Jacob's. Again, no answer. Finally, desperate, "Call Devon's cell."

He answered after the first ring.

"Hey, Sandra."

"I cannot believe I did this, but I left without Cara. Can she ride back to Brandon Hall with you and Jacob?"

"Don't worry. I've got her. She's already heading to the car with us. I told her you weren't feeling well but didn't want to disrupt their evening. They were fine with it."

Relief flooded her. Devon wouldn't let anything happen to Cara. He'd always been good about looking out for the kids. And he'd covered for her with them. Heat rose to her face. But how could she have let a simple kiss cause her to forget her own daughter? She couldn't let it happen again.

She heard the amusement in his voice. "Glad to know my kiss can still affect you so much."

She gasped. "Am I on the speaker phone? Why would you say that in front of the kids?"

"Don't worry. We're not to the car yet. They didn't hear me."

"This is all some big joke to you, isn't it?"

"Not at all. I meant what I said. I want you back."

She sighed. She couldn't get into this again, especially not on the telephone. "Just make sure the kids get back safely. Good night."

She made it back to Brandon Hall then walked up to her room, bypassing the rest of Devon's family. She opened her purse and pulled out the divorce papers Paula had given her. Why hadn't she presented them to him tonight? He'd given her the perfect opening to do so.

She unfolded them and read the cause—irreconcilable differences. That summed up their marriage. It didn't matter that her knees still went weak when he kissed her or that he mentioned wanting to reconcile. No matter what residual feelings they still had for one another, it didn't change the fact that they hadn't been able to make things work out between them. They still had all those irreconcilable differences standing in their way.

She put away the papers. Better not to give him the wrong idea. They would all be better off if she just stayed away from Devon for the rest of the weekend.

Chapter 6

Sandra found Kim curled up in a rocking chair on the massive front porch. A tray with hot coffee and several mugs sat on the table before her.

"Good morning," Kim said.

"Good morning." Sandra helped herself to a cup of coffee. She noticed the photo album in Kim's hand as she sat down. "What have you got there?"

Kim opened the album, revealing a family photo of herself and her first husband. "I was reminiscing."

It struck Sandra as odd that she would spend the morning before her wedding thinking about her first husband. "Is everything okay?"

"Yes. Some days I miss him more than others." Sandra must not have hidden her surprise very well. "Does it seem odd to you that I'm thinking about Kevin the day before I'm going to marry Mike? I suppose I will always miss him. I'm so thankful, however, that God has given me a second chance with Mike. He's a good man, a godly man, and I love him dearly. I only hope I can make him a good wife."

"Kim, you'll be a wonderful wife. You're already experienced at it."

"My marriage to Kevin wasn't always smooth. We were both so young and so wrapped up in ourselves. When I look back now, I'm saddened by what we could have had if only we'd given our marriage over to the Lord."

Sandra sipped her coffee. It was better that she didn't speak. Her sister-in-law's wistfulness caught her off guard. Kim had no idea what a difficult relationship looked like. She had no idea how much it hurt to watch your husband walk out the door.

"It breaks my heart what's happened between you and Devon. To see you both throw away twenty years of marriage."

Sandra replaced her coffee cup. "Sometimes things just don't work out."

"Few things in life just work out, Sandra. More often than not, you have to fight for it."

This conversation was getting too personal. Was Kim actually telling her she and Devon needed to work harder to make their marriage work? She had no idea what they'd been through. No idea how badly Devon had hurt her and the kids.

"I've been alone for a long time now, Sandra, and what I've come to realize is it's not better to be alone. I struggled for years with sadness and loneliness. I know you and my brother have your problems, but I wonder how you would feel if you lost the chance to ever forgive him. I pray you'll never have to find out." She set down her cup and the photo album then stood. "I'd better go and wake up Mike. We've got to meet with Wreath about the rehearsal dinner arrangements."

"Wreath? Is that a person?"

"Yes. Wreath Anderson. She's my wedding planner. A very sweet woman with a tragic story. She was left at the altar several years ago."

"Really? And she still plans weddings? It must be difficult to watch other people get married after her day was ruined."

"I imagine it is, but she has a very sweet disposition. I don't know what I would do without her." Kim placed a hand on Sandra's shoulder. "Think about what I said. It's not too late for you and Devon."

Sandra finished off her cup of coffee. She'd been unprepared for Kim's emotional plea for her and Devon. She'd been so caught up in seeing everyone again that she hadn't been prepared for what it felt like to belong to this family again, to belong with Devon.

She reached for the coffeepot. Kim had left the photo album opened to a familiar photo. Sandra pulled the book to her. She and Devon on their wedding day. She sucked in a breath at how happy they looked. She ached at the memory. They had been happy. But what had happened to the passion these two young lovebirds had shared?

She sighed, knowing the answer. Life had happened. So many things had gotten in the way—work, kids, chores, bills. But mostly frustration and indifference had killed their relationship.

Kim's question echoed in her mind. How would she feel if Devon were lost to her forever? If she could never say sorry for how messed up things became? Or tell him how much their life together had meant to her? A sense of urgency pressed at her. Was Kim right? Should they have fought harder to save their marriage? Could they have fought harder? She knew the answer to that. They'd hardly fought at all, just given up on their dreams and on their relationship. She'd been so tired of the drama and of arguing. Giving up had seemed easier. But as she stared at the photograph of the love shining from the faces of two young people on the page and she remembered the loneliness of the past months since the kids had left for college, she had to wonder if she'd really made the better choice.

❧

Lynn pulled the car into a parking space downtown, and she, Sandra, and Cara got out. Sandra was glad for the outing. She needed to find a nice dress and shoes for the wedding, as well as an extra change of clothes.

"We should be able to find what you need at Darby's," Lynn told her. "They have some very cute outfits. Oh, and we must get some of their fudge. They're famous for their fudge."

Darby's was a charming shop with accessories and gifts. They also had an appealing selection of clothes, and Cara was quick to point out cute tops that might please Sandra.

She pulled down a red jacket. "Mom, you should get this. It's so nice."

The red color and the cut appealed to Sandra, but she still shook her head. "I have a jacket. I don't really need another one."

Cara held it up against her. "But, Mom, it's so cute and

you look so good in this color."

Lynn joined Cara in her encouragement. "Yes, you should get it, Sandra. It's lovely."

"Okay." Sandra finally caved, slipping off her old coat and handing it to Cara so she could try on the red. She slipped it on and loved the texture and cut.

"It looks terrific," Cara exclaimed. "And you should totally get these earrings, too." She presented a pair of dangly earrings for Sandra to try on. "They'll look great with your hair down like that. In fact, you should wear them now." She tore them off the paper and handed them to Sandra to put on.

Despite her daughter's pushiness, Sandra liked the items she'd chosen. She picked out two more blouses and carried them, the coat, and the earrings to the cashier. All in all, she was pleased with her purchases. "I still need to pick out a dress and shoes for the wedding."

Cara's phone beeped and she glanced at it then smiled. "While you do that, Grandma and I are going to walk one street over to the bookstore. There's this new novel I've been dying to get. Want to come with me, Grandma?"

"Yes, I think I will," Lynn said.

"Great. Mom, we'll meet you down at Cotton Alley Restaurant at the end of the street in about a half hour. Okay? Bye." Cara made a beeline for the door, followed closely by her grandmother.

Lynn stopped and turned back to her before she left. "Don't forget to try the fudge. It's delicious."

Sandra watched them leave, stumped by their abrupt departure. What could be so important about a book that it couldn't wait while she tried on a few dresses?

The dress she picked out had flecks of red in the pattern that would match her new red coat. It would be the perfect thing to wear to the wedding. She also picked out a lovely picture frame as a wedding gift.

"Anything else today, ma'am?" the lady at the counter asked.

Sandra shrugged and nodded. "I'll take some fudge."

❧

Satisfied with her day's purchases, she headed to Cotton Alley to meet Lynn and Cara. She found the restaurant toward the end of Main Street. She stepped inside, surprised to find an elegant feel to the establishment. Charming and quaint with cozy corners, cloth tablecloths, and wind chimes intermingled with plants and lovely paintings. The manager greeted her at the door, and just as Sandra said she was meeting her daughter, a familiar voice called her name.

She spotted Devon sitting at a table tucked into the corner by the window. He waved her over.

"Devon, what a surprise. Are you here alone?"

"I was supposed to meet Jacob here, but it seems I've been stood up."

"What do you mean? Where did he go?"

"He was heading to the bookstore to buy a book on the history of Natchez."

She frowned. "Since when has Jacob been interested in history? Or reading?" Lately, all that seemed to be on their son's mind was girls, not schoolwork.

"I was suspicious, too. But apparently he met up with Cara and my mom at the bookstore, right about the time they all got called back to Brandon Hall to meet with the photographer. He rode back with them."

"They left?" Without her? Sandra sighed. Had she been forgotten?

"They asked me to make sure you got back." He held out a chair. "But why don't we eat first?"

She set down her bags then slid into the chair Devon held out for her. This wasn't a good idea. After his comments last night, being alone with him wasn't smart. She wanted to ask him about it, demand to know if he'd been serious or if some fanciful romantic notion had hit him because of his sister's wedding. But she didn't dare open her mouth about what he'd said.

What if he told her, in the light of day, that he'd changed his mind?

"You look great," Devon said. "Is that a new coat?"

Sandra fingered the red coat she'd been forced to wear from the store after her daughter had absentmindedly walked out with her old one. "I just bought it."

"The color is great on you, matches the warmth of your eyes."

When the waiter came to take their orders, Sandra ordered a chicken salad while he ordered the burger. They both ordered iced tea with lemon.

"So what were yours and Cara's plans for today? I see you already did some shopping."

"Yes, I needed a dress for Kim's wedding. Then we were going to Longwood to take the tour. I hear it's amazing."

"That's the octagonal shaped house, right?"

"It is. They say only the basement floor was ever completed.

The remaining floors are still unfinished to this day."

"Jacob and I had plans to go out to the city cemetery. I hear there's a man there who was buried sitting straight up."

She giggled at the notion. "Really? How strange."

He rattled the ice in his glass. "Why don't we go together? I'll go with you to Longwood and you come with me to the cemetery. It'll be fun."

"Together?"

"Why not?"

She could think of a million reasons why she shouldn't go, but they all had to do with putting her heart at risk again. "We don't want to give anyone the wrong idea."

"The wrong idea about what?"

"All children of divorce want to see their parents get back together. I don't want to give them unrealistic hope."

"Who says it's unrealistic?"

"Devon, we've done this. We've gone this route. We couldn't make it work before. Why would this time be any different?"

"Look, I'm not asking you to marry me under the old oak tree. I'd just like us to spend some time together, have some fun. We used to have fun, remember?"

He looked like a little kid, begging for another ice cream cone, and her heart melted. How could she resist him? "Fine, but this doesn't mean anything. We're just two friends spending the day together. Agreed?"

"Agreed."

But the grin that spread across his face told her the truth—this definitely meant something.

Chapter 7

Armed with brochures from the convention center, they toured several plantation homes, including Stanton Hall, Rosalie, and Melrose. Sandra loved seeing the old furnishings and the large old curtains hanging over the windows. She also enjoyed hearing the history of the historic homes and imagining how it must have been to live there.

Longwood touched her most. The octagonal home was six stories, but only the basement level was complete. From the second floor, she could look up to see four more levels of only structure and the promise of what might have been. The wooden floors remained unfinished, the window spaces unglassed, and Sandra could see evidence of birds living right at the base of the finial.

Devon stared into one of the side rooms, and she followed his gaze to unopened crates of furniture tucked into a corner, still bearing the original owner's name. Stacks of wood remained unused, and equipment lay covered in layers of dust.

"Construction was halted on Longwood at the start of the

Civil War," the tour guide explained. "The builder brought his own workers in from Philadelphia, and when the war broke out, they dropped everything to return home, not wanting to get caught behind the lines. Because of blockades, most of the furniture and materials that had been purchased to finish the home were seized by the Union army and therefore never made it to Longwood. The war also took a toll on the family's wealth, as they were unable to move their shipments of cotton. By the time the war ended, the family was financially unable to complete the building of Longwood, and so it remains unfinished to this day."

The guide's explanation touched a sentimental place inside her. The toll of that war could still be seen here in this house and in the history of this family. "It's so sad," she said. "They dropped everything because of the war. They left their lives, their livelihoods."

"War has a way of disrupting lives." Devon looked at her then away. "Any kind of war."

His words seemed more profound than their surface meaning, and she was sure he meant them to be. Somehow she got the feeling he was talking about them, about the war between them, the war that had come into their lives, a war of wills that had devastated everything between them.

Though they were beautiful, Sandra was no longer interested in touring the grounds of Longwood. She was ready to get away from the reminder of how this unfinished home mirrored their lives. She pulled the brochures from her purse and thumbed through them. "Why don't we go see the graveyard next?" Natchez was known for its city cemetery, with generations in family plots and unusual history. She'd read online that during the pilgrimages, townsfolk would dress up as their ancestors and recount the stories of those buried there.

At the car, Devon opened the door for her. Sandra slipped inside then watched him close it and head around to the driver's side. How long had it been since anyone had opened a car door for her? He used to do such things in the early days of their marriage, but somehow that habit had fallen away. That he remembered to do it now touched her heart. But was it just an act of kindness, or was he, too, remembering the war that had stolen their marriage away from them?

✧

The words of Ecclesiastes ran through Devon's mind as he drove toward the cemetery. A time to live, a time to die, a time to love, and a time to fight. Seeing those tools and crates lying unused at Longwood had set his mind on life and all the interruptions that happened. Sandra had commented on how sad it was to see the house unfinished. She was right. It was sad, but not nearly as sad as seeing a life, a marriage, unfinished.

They toured the graveyard and saw innumerable tomb-stones bearing names of husbands and wives buried side-by-side. The history of this place overwhelmed him. How would it feel to live and love with someone for so many years, to be devoted to one another long enough to reach eternity together? He stared at Sandra. He wanted her by his side even at the end of life and the words immortalized, "husband and wife."

She stood beside him, where he was concentrating on the headstone, and read the names. "That's lovely," she stated. "They must have loved one another very much."

"Yes. Do you think they always got along?"

"What kind of question is that?"

"These two people were married for thirty years, Sandra. They built a life together, so much so that someone, presumably their children, kept them together even in death. It couldn't have been easy. Their lives wouldn't have been nearly as easy as ours are. They probably had to fight for every year they were together. But they stuck it out together."

"You don't know—maybe they hated each other. Maybe they never got along and they lived out their lives miserable with each other until the very end."

"Or maybe they found a way to get along, to find the good in each other. Maybe they loved and laughed and lived all those years together with joy and thanksgiving."

She laughed a nervous laugh. "Devon, you can't possibly be comparing our lives to the lives of these people."

"Why not? Marriage was meant to last for a lifetime, like these people did."

"It was a different time. Things were different."

"Yes, they were. Our grandchildren's grandchildren probably won't be able to find a headstone with the name of a husband and wife that lasted more than a few years."

"It's the way the world is changing."

"It doesn't have to be. It shouldn't be. God intended marriage to be for a lifetime. Whatever happened to that?"

She stiffened. "Well it's difficult to make a marriage last a lifetime when one of the parties walks out."

The bitterness in her cold stare ripped through his heart. The way she crossed her arms and stiffened left little doubt they were back to talking about their lives, their marriage.

"I would take it back in a moment if I could. Leaving you and the kids was the worst mistake I've ever made. I wish I had never done it."

"But you did, Devon. You can't change the past."

"No, but I thought we were forgetting the past. Isn't that what we agreed to? Putting the past behind us and moving forward. That's what you said yesterday."

"I only said that for the benefit of the children. I didn't want them to see us fighting all weekend."

"Don't you think they would benefit more knowing their parents were trying to work things out?"

"Is that really what you want. . .to work things out between us?"

"When I see all this history, it makes me sad to think history will remember us as separate individuals, not as husband and wife. The thing I regret most is that we didn't fight to save our marriage. Aren't you tired, Sandra? Aren't you tired of the bitterness and the anger between us? I'm exhausted. I almost missed my sister's wedding because I was worried about being around you."

"Devon, think about what you're saying. We've been apart for a long while, and you're only remembering the good things about our life together."

"No, I remember it all, Sandra. I acted out of anger and selfishness. I behaved like a single man instead of a husband.

I thought only about myself instead of about our family. And I'm ashamed of myself. I can't change what happened. All I can do is ask your forgiveness. Will you forgive me, Sandra?"

She turned away. "You have no right to ask me that. You hurt me, Devon, me and the kids."

He bit back a slew of excuses that came to his mind, reasons he did the things he did, shifting the blame to her behavior. He said none of it. God gently reminded him this wasn't about him. It was about restoring his marriage. When Jesus was persecuted on the cross, he didn't fire back. Devon couldn't either if he truly wanted to reconcile with Sandra. He would have to be the bad guy, the guy who had walked out. He would accept that blame without argument.

He touched her shoulders and felt her shiver under his touch. That was a good sign. "Isn't there anything in you that still wants what we had? I felt it that night at the graduation. I haven't been able to stop thinking about it."

She stepped back away from his touch and shook her head. "I can't. I'm not ready for this. I just got used to the notion that perhaps we can be friends."

"I don't want to be your friend, Sandra. I want to be your husband."

"Why do you have to do this? Why do you always have to ruin a good moment?"

"I ruined the moment by telling you I want you back? Most women would melt at that kind of romantic gesture."

She jutted her chin. "I'm not most women, Devon."

"No, you're not most women. You're my wife. The woman who is supposed to stand beside me through thick and thin."

"Well it's hard to stand beside someone who is walking out the door."

Anger bit at him, deeply rooted in past hurts and past transgressions. This time he didn't bite them back. "Why shouldn't I have left? What did I have to come home to besides a cold, controlling woman who wanted to plan my every mood and emotion?"

"So now it's my fault you walked out on your family? I did everything I could to make a nice home for our kids."

"If you had lavished as much love and attention on me as you did on our kids, we would still be together."

She marched toward the car. "I knew this was a mistake. Take me back to the house."

"Gladly."

She didn't even give him a chance to open the door for her this time. Beating him to the car, she got in and slammed the door.

He slid into the driver's seat, his blood still boiling with anger. He started the car and headed back toward Brandon Hall with gusto.

"Slow down before you kill us," Sandra quipped as he darted between traffic.

He knew she was right. He shouldn't be letting his emotions control his driving, but the fact that she'd pointed it out. . . "So now you're trying to control how I drive?"

"Someone should."

He sped up just to irritate her, taking the curve that put them back on the Natchez Trace at a speed that would have thrown her into his lap had she not been buckled up.

"You're a maniac," she shouted.

He slammed on the accelerator, speeding up on the open stretch of road.

She gripped the dashboard. "You're going to get us both killed."

He glanced at her, enjoying the panic in her voice and on her face. At least she felt something for him.

Suddenly her eyes widened in fear. "Deer!" she screamed.

He jerked his head back toward the road in time to see a herd of deer darting across the asphalt. He hit the brakes and jerked the wheel, causing the car to skid sideways. It narrowly missed the deer, who bounded away. The car nearly went off the road.

His focus went immediately to Sandra, making certain she was unhurt, but when he looked at her, the expression of contempt on her face threw him right back into retreat.

Her words were quick and full of resentment. "Take me back now."

Devon jammed the SUV into gear as he continued toward Brandon Hall, waiting for the inevitable I-told-you-so from Sandra.

She was out of the car the moment he pulled up to the house. "I cannot believe you. I should have known better than to think you would ever change."

He jumped out, too, and followed her. "Why should I change? You're the one with all the lists and the plans. You think you can control everything and everyone? Well, you can't control feelings."

He was only vaguely aware that the front door had opened

and the family was spilling out onto the porch.

"You certainly can't control yours. One minute you still love me and the next you're trying to drive us into a ravine."

"I should have. At least that would put us both out of our misery."

"Yes, and it would be a lot cheaper than a divorce, wouldn't it?" She reached into her purse then threw a stack of papers at his chest. "Consider yourself served."

His mother marched between them. "Stop this, both of you! Think about the children."

He looked at Cara and Jacob standing on the porch. Jacob's face was sullen, and Cara's face was planted in Kim's shoulder as tears shook her.

His anger began to dissipate.

He'd done it again. He'd hurt his family.

God, why can't I get this right?

Chapter 8

Don't worry, Lynn. It won't happen again. I'll be leaving in the morning. I see now it was a mistake to come." Sandra marched up the steps, stopping only momentarily to shoot Devon an angry look. She looked at Kim. "I'm sorry if we ruined your wedding."

His mother turned to him once Sandra disappeared into the house. "What happened between you two?"

He pulled his hands through his hair and let out a resigned sigh. How had things spiraled so out of control between them? One moment he was telling her he wanted her back, and the next she was accusing him of trying to kill them both with his driving.

He brushed off his mother's question. "It's complicated."

"Well then, uncomplicate it."

"She thinks I'm jealous of my own children."

"Are you?"

"What? No, of course not. I love Jacob and Cara."

"That wasn't the question. Are you jealous of the kids' relationship with Sandra?"

He struggled for an answer. Why didn't "no" slip easily from his lips?

"Sandra was right about one thing. You do need to learn to control your emotions." She walked back onto the porch and went inside. Kim and Cara followed behind her. Jacob stayed behind, standing on the porch. His face was full of disappointment.

Shame filled Devon at his son's disdainful stare. "Jacob—"

"You did it again, Dad. You blew it." He walked back into the house, shutting the front door behind him.

Devon couldn't face the family inside yet, so he walked down by the pond. The evening air was beginning to grow cold, but not nearly as cold as his family would be. He picked up a rock and tossed it over the water. Overhead the sky was clear and cloudless. Stars began to appear in the night sky.

He sat on the ground and stared up. The big question loomed. Was he jealous of his own children?

Ashamedly, he was.

Jealous of the love and attention and affection Sandra showered on them. He didn't begrudge them that, but he wanted some of it for himself, too.

He closed his eyes and aimed his prayers toward heaven. "God, I've messed up again. I thought I could do this. I thought I could shoulder the blame and the rejection, but I can't. I need Your help. I need You to fix this mess I've made."

❧

Sandra stared at her reflection in the mirror. She'd tried to hide the tears from Cara, but even looking at herself now she knew she hadn't been successful. Devon's words cut like a knife into her heart. He'd tried to blame her for the failure of their marriage. He was the one who'd given up. He was the one who'd walked away.

For one fleeting moment, she'd had the hope that he was serious about reconciling. But his behavior, his out-of-control emotions, had ruined that. She should have known better than to pin such hope on him. He was a man controlled by his feelings. He wanted to be with her only because they were in a romantic setting and she was close by. But if he couldn't even stick to the plan of being friends for one day, what hope would their marriage ever have? They would be right back where they were within a matter of months, at one another's throats playing the blame game.

She switched off the bathroom light but stood in the doorway watching her daughter sleep. She should never have allowed Cara to convince her to stay. It had been a mistake. Now they had ruined Kim's wedding getaway with their bickering.

Tears pushed at her eyes. The truth was it was more than the fighting that upset her. It was the fact that the one fleeting moment of hope she'd had came crashing to the ground. Why had she allowed herself even that brief glimpse into what their futures could hold? Why had she allowed Devon the control to raise her expectations and then shatter them to pieces?

She tried to sleep, but it wouldn't come, so she finally pushed back the covers and got up. Perhaps she could sneak into the kitchen for a glass of warm milk or take a walk to release some of the energy that would not allow her brain to shut off.

She put on her slippers then grabbed her coat, deciding a brisk walk might be just what she needed. She was quiet as she moved about the room then opened the closed the door, careful not to awaken her daughter.

She stopped as she approached the stairs and saw Devon's familiar frame sitting on the steps.

He turned when he heard her.

"What are you doing out here? It's late."

"Actually, it's early. It's 4 a.m."

She was surprised at the time. Had she spent all night crying over him?

"Actually, I was waiting for you. Will you take a walk with me? There's something I want you to see." He pulled a flashlight from his coat pocket.

She tried to keep the tremor from her near emotional break from showing. "What is it?"

"Please, Sandra, come with me."

She slipped into her coat and followed him outside. As he headed toward the edge of the drive, he flipped on his light.

Sandra stopped when he moved into the woods. "What are you doing?"

"It's safe. I promise." He held out his hand for her to take.

Reluctantly, she took it and followed him through the woods. Her feet crunched leaves and fallen sticks, and every now and then something else crunched loudly beneath her feet.

Devon moved the flashlight to the ground. "It's pecans. Rachel says they're all over the place." He continued walking, and Sandra followed.

They came to a clearing, but it was only the absence of the crunch beneath her feet that alerted her. The night was so dark she could see only what was illuminated in the beam of light in Devon's hand. She held tightly to his arm as he walked.

"Are you certain you know where we're going?"

"Absolutely." He shined the light on a group of trees then headed for them. "We're here."

Through the trees, Sandra saw an old iron gate and tombstones inside. "Another cemetery, Devon?"

"This one is special. Rachel told me about it. It's the Brandon's family plot, the original Brandons who built the house. Only six of their thirteen kids survived past the age of eighteen. The rest were buried here." He scanned the light over the large oaks surrounding them. "Mrs. Brandon planted thirteen trees, one for each of her children. They surround this place, protecting her children."

He scanned the light over small markers. Sandra noticed some had only initials. Some were bigger than others. She knelt beside one that indicated a one-year-old was buried there. "This is so sad. Some of these were just babies."

"I know."

"I don't know what I would do if something ever happened to Jacob or Cara." She leaned back into the comfort of his arm that surrounded her, and his breath tickled her ear as he spoke.

"When Rachel told me this story, it reminded me of us."

"Why?"

"They suffered so much loss in their lives, yet they didn't

give up. They kept on going"—he stared down into her eyes—"together. Sandra, you and I have no idea what it means to suffer like that, yet we gave up. After the war, Mr. Brandon fled with his slaves because he was going to have to pay them freedman wages. Yet when he heard about the death of one of his children, he immediately returned, unconcerned about what it would cost him, to be with his wife in her grief. I want to be like that, Sandra. I want to be that kind of husband. One who will drop everything when you need me. I promise you, that's the kind of man I'll forever strive to be. And I have a surprise. No more traveling. I'm off the road for good. They offered me a new position, and I'm going to take it. I want to be home with you, with my family, as much as possible from now on.

"You were right about me. I am jealous of the kids. I see the way you fuss over them. It's been a long time since you fussed over me that way."

So they were back to blaming her.

"I know I should have said something. I should have opened my mouth and told you straight out how I felt, but there was a time when I didn't have to do that. When you fussed over just me, when you made me feel special. I miss that. I miss you. I don't want you to go, Sandra."

"I think it would be the best thing."

"No, it won't. It won't be the best for anyone." He grabbed her hand and pulled her close to him. "Please stay. Give me one more chance. Give me tomorrow. Take the plunge with me, Sandra. If you won't do it for yourself, then do it for the kids."

She cringed. It was unfair of him to use the kids against her. She would never intentionally do anything to hurt the kids.

He pulled her hand to his lips then kissed the other one, too. "Think about it," he whispered.

As they followed the path back through the woods, Sandra's mind was awhirl with what Devon had just said. He'd seemed so sincere, but did she dare get her hopes up again?

Her foot slipped on a pecan, and she lost her balance. Devon caught her before her feet went completely out from under her. His strong arms surrounded her now, just as they had months ago at the graduation.

"I've got you," he whispered, his voice lingering in the darkness. The dim light from the house and the beam from the flashlight he'd dropped wasn't enough for her to see his face, but she felt his hot breath on her skin and the desire to kiss her. As his lips touched hers, a shiver rushed through her, not caused by the chill in the air but by the warmth and familiarity of the man beside her.

"Oh, Sandra," he whispered. "Please say you'll give me another chance. I want to prove I can get it right this time."

She pushed away from him and rushed ahead toward the light of the house. She didn't slow down even when she heard the familiar crunch of the gravel driveway beneath her feet. She rushed toward the back of the house, her mind awhirl with Devon and all he'd had to say.

Did she owe it to the kids to give her marriage another try? Did she owe it to Devon? To herself?

And what was the worst that would happen if she took the chance?

She stopped running when she heard a voice. As she got closer, she recognized Jacob's voice then spotted him sitting on the brick steps, his cell phone to his ear.

"I love you, too," he said into the phone. "Good night, Maggie."

He hung up, slid his phone into his pocket, then turned back toward the house. "Mom, what are you doing up?"

"I could ask you the same thing."

"I was just talking to Maggie."

"It's cold out."

"I wanted some privacy." He took a deep breath. "Did you hear what I said?"

"Yes."

"I know you think I'm too young to fall in love, Mom, but I'm not. I love Maggie, and I want to marry her."

She closed her eyes and sat down, uncertain how to handle this situation.

"That's why I'm so worried about you, Mom."

"Jacob, you're worried about me?"

"Sure. With me and Cara away at college, you must be lonely."

"I'm the parent. I'm supposed to worry about you. Not the other way around."

"I can't help it, Mom. I love you. I don't want you to be alone. Me and Cara both want you to be happy."

"Cara and I," she corrected.

"Both of us. We just don't want you to be lonely." Jacob

kissed her cheek. "Good night, Mom."

"Good night, sweetheart."

She watched Jacob walk back into the house. His words stayed with her. He and Cara were moving on with their lives, just as children should. Devon's accusations flowed back to her mind. Was he right? Had she given so much of herself to the kids that she'd had nothing left for him? For the first time, she realized she had. She'd given them everything she'd had, leaving nothing for her husband—or for God.

She went to church every week, but it had become more about habit and duty than about praising the Lord. And since Devon left, she'd thrown herself even more into serving at the church instead of taking time out to listen and learn. She knew why now. If she kept busy, she could suppress the anger and heartache of allowing her marriage to falter.

And she had allowed it.

Loving the children had been easy. They'd relied on her. Now she realized Devon had needed her, too. He'd needed her support, her encouragement, and mostly, her attention. But did she even know how to be a wife again? And did he know how to be a husband?

Sandra sat on the steps and watched the water flow up through the fountain then rain back down. A verse from a Sunday school lesson in Ezekiel came to mind. *I will give you a new heart and put a new spirit in you.* One of her friends had admitted to using the promise of this verse to change her attitude toward her husband and learn to be more loving. Her words and this verse had stuck with Sandra, though she hadn't known before exactly why.

She stared up at the night sky through the branches of the mighty oak. Had God orchestrated this weekend to bring her and Devon back together? He had certainly opened her eyes to her own shortcomings in the marriage.

Months ago, her friend Paula had asked her if it was really over between her and Devon. Sandra had been sure then that it was. Now she wasn't so sure.

With God's help she was sure she could learn to be more loving toward Devon. She wanted to learn. But what if she took the chance and he broke her heart again? Could she take that?

Tears stung her eyes as confusion mounted. She was scared, scared of being hurt again, scared of taking another chance on what she truly wanted. But she wouldn't let fear and pride continue to hold her back.

She bowed her head and asked God to give her a new heart like He promised in Ezekiel, a heart for her husband. She wanted to be the wife Devon deserved.

Chapter 9

When Devon came down for breakfast, he was freshly showered and clean shaven. Sandra enjoyed the way his aftershave tingled her senses. She missed the intimacy of seeing him this way. He was still half asleep until he had his morning coffee. She longed to reach out her hand and caress the smoothness of his freshly shaven face, knowing full well that by afternoon it would no longer be smooth, replaced with a prickly patch of stubble. His hair, still wet, curled a bit at the ends, but once dried would be straight and thick as the day they'd met. She knew his left knee was stiff in the morning, especially cold mornings, but would loosen up soon with the activities of the day.

And he still wants me.

She pushed back her chair and walked over to his. Her knees shook as she moved. Was she really doing this? Had she really just decided to give Devon and their marriage another try?

A grin spread across his face as she approached him. "Morning, Sandra."

"Good morning. Can we talk?"

"Sure." He placed his cup on the table, but before they had a chance to speak, Kim entered with a young dark-haired woman she introduced as Wreath Anderson. The wedding coordinator came into the room and began handing out duties.

"Devon, will you drive Mike into town to pick up the tuxes?" She turned to Sandra. "And if you'll help make sure the bride and bridesmaids have everything they need?"

"Certainly." She shrugged at Devon. "We'll talk later?"

"I can't wait."

Sandra smiled. Neither could she.

❧

Mike drummed his fingers against the car door as Devon drove them into town to pick up the tuxes.

"Nervous?" Devon asked him.

Mike grinned. "Nervous? Yes. But excited, too. I love Kim so much."

"I'm glad to hear you say that."

"I understand you're trying to get back with your wife."

"Where did you hear that?"

"Kim told me. She and your mom and your kids have been planning for weeks to get you two together this week." He flushed. "And now that I say it, I believe that was supposed to be a secret. I hope I haven't messed anything up."

"Don't worry about it, Mike. I had a pretty good idea, anyway, they were up to something."

He pulled the car through the gates of Brandon Hall. On the hill at the front of the house, chairs had been lined up and lights strung. Flowers were being hung, and an arch stood at the entrance to the lawn.

When they stopped, Mike grabbed his tux and headed inside. Devon walked toward the activity.

Wreath Anderson rushed about making sure details were settled as the family gathered on the front lawn. The nip in the air made Devon wonder if an outside wedding was the best choice.

He stopped and questioned Wreath about the cold temperatures.

"It's what your sister wants, Mr. Brinks. Besides, the ceremony will be short, and then the reception will be inside. But if it's too chilly, we have heat lamps to warm things up."

His mother took his elbow. "Devon, we need someone to stand in for the groom during the rehearsal. Would you mind taking over that role?"

"No problem." It made sense for him to do it. He didn't have an official role in the wedding.

Wreath led him toward where the altar stood and planted him in position then gathered everyone around and called for the stand-in bride. He was stunned to see Sandra step forward and move to the bride's position.

Wreath gave instruction. "Kim will ride in on the horse-drawn carriage. It will stop at the foot of the lawn, where she'll disembark. Bridesmaids will be here waiting. Then the music will begin." She made a motion with her hand, and the wedding march sounded.

The three bridesmaids, including Cara, marched up the lawn, followed by Sandra.

Wreath began explaining how the ceremony would go. As Sandra walked toward the altar, Devon's heart lurched. She was so beautiful. Time had only enhanced her beauty. The way her eyes crinkled when she smiled, the slope of her neck, the way her chin jutted out when she was determined. He knew her, every inch of her, and his arms ached to reach out and hold her.

When she reached him, she held out her hand, and he took it. He enjoyed the way her dress hugged the curves of her body as she approached. The aroma of her shampoo floated over him as the wind blew her hair. Her hand was soft and delicate inside his. The sun bounced off her rosy cheeks as she stared up at him, igniting every molecule inside of him, awakened with the memory of the feel of her wrapped in his arms. She took his breath away.

How did I ever walk away from this woman?

Wreath went on with her directions then turned toward them. "Then the preacher will read the vows and ask, 'Do you?'"

"I do." The words were on his lips before he meant them to be.

Wreath moved on, without a beat. "Then he'll ask the bride the same question," she said, turning to Sandra.

Sandra stared up into his eyes and smiled before saying, "I do."

He realized his heart had stopped beating until she said those words. They meant nothing in the context of his sister's moment, but had she meant them for him? Or was she just repeating lines? He kept his eyes locked on hers, and she jutted her chin, determined not to be the first to look away. He could just as easily have swept her into his arms and kissed her.

His skin was on fire. Every hair was on end with excitement, and his muscles twitched as if he would jump right out of his skin. He'd felt like this on the first day he'd married her—that overwhelming urge to lift her into his arms and spin with glee, shouting the triumphs of something so immeasurable that his body couldn't contain it.

When he imagined his future, he imagined it with her. When he imagined holding someone's hand, it was always hers, kissing someone's lips, hers. The connection they shared was something bigger than he'd ever realized. His body ached for hers. His soul longed for her.

He wanted his wife back.

Chapter 10

Devon's hand grew heavy and tight on hers, matching the longing stare in his blue eyes. She sighed. She could easily get lost in those eyes. He stepped closer, shortening the distance between them as Wreath neared the part about kissing the bride. Her heart raced with excitement. How long had it been since she'd seen such passion in him?

Years since she'd stirred any such feeling from him.

It was strange how God kept throwing them together this weekend. Was it His will that they reunite?

It didn't seem so unrealistic anymore.

His fingers entwined with hers. She only vaguely heard what Wreath was saying over the pounding of her own heart. She'd happily given him her hand when she'd arrived at the altar. And the spark she'd seen ignite inside of him matched her own. This was her husband, her soul mate, the man God had given her to love. And she wanted another chance to prove to him that she understood now, that she wanted to fight for him, that she was willing to make him a priority in her life.

Wreath thanked everyone, and the rehearsal ended. The others began walking away. It was over. Nothing had happened between her and Devon, yet everything had changed between them. With one touch a thousand memories came to life.

He tightened his hand on hers, reaffirming in her that the feeling hadn't been one-sided. He'd felt it, too. She moved closer and touched his arm. His muscles were tense and tight beneath his jacket.

"Were you serious?" she whispered the question. "Were you serious about us?"

He squeezed her hand tightly, reassuringly, and leaned close. "Absolutely."

"Then okay."

She watched a big smile spread across his face.

❧

"Have you told anyone?" Sandra asked, helping Devon tie his tie.

"No. I was waiting for your lead."

"This is Kim's day. I don't want to take away her spotlight."

He covered her hand in his. "This is a good thing, Sandra. I know everyone will be thrilled for us." His brow creased. "You're not having second thoughts about us, are you?"

"No." She smoothed his tie. "I suppose I'm just uneasy about having everyone know. They'll all be watching us, waiting to see if we can make it work this time."

"Hey, this is a good thing. They'll be happy for us."

"I know. Still, I don't think we should tell anyone until after the wedding. I don't want to upstage the bride and groom."

He held her hand then pulled her into his arms and kissed her, gently at first. Then he deepened it, pulling her close. "Fine, but come tomorrow morning, I'm shouting it to the world. I love you, Sandra, and I want the world to know it."

He kissed her again then smiled sheepishly when she pulled away from him. "I'd better go and check on the bride and the bridesmaids. Make sure they have everything they need."

"Okay. I'll see you at the altar."

She smiled then nodded. "I'll see you at the altar."

Sandra stopped to catch her breath as she closed the door behind her. Would everyone notice the flush of love on her face? How could they not? She couldn't quit smiling, and she was certain she was much too happy to attribute it to Kim's wedding day. Someone was sure to notice.

"How is everything?" she asked, entering the bridal suite. Cara and the other two bridesmaids looked cute as buttons in their flamingo-pink dresses and heels.

Cara reached out to her mother for help clasping a string of pearls around her neck. "Mom, I need your help."

When Kim entered, Sandra cheered along with the others. She looked beautiful, and the glow of radiance on her face only intensified her beauty.

A knock sounded, and then Wreath peeked around the door. "The carriage is downstairs and the groomsmen have already left the house. Are we ready in here?"

Kim took a deep breath then blew it out as she looked at her wedding party. "I'm ready." She picked up her bouquet and followed as everyone else walked out the door.

Sandra watched while Kim and her bridesmaids got into the horse-drawn carriage. She waved as it pulled away with the wedding party inside. Then she walked back to the front lawn with Wreath.

"Everything looks so beautiful," she said. "You've done a lovely job, Wreath."

"Thank you."

Lynn waved her over to sit beside her. Minutes later Devon took the next chair. He slid his hand into hers, and she clasped it, smiling at the secret encounter between them.

The carriage stopped at the edge of the lawn. Sandra watched as they disembarked and walked toward the crowd. The guests all stood as music began to play. At the end of the aisle, Jacob took Cara's arm and escorted her down the aisle, followed by two more groomsmen and bridesmaids. Sandra glowed at how lovely her children looked. She was so proud of the young adults they were becoming. She glanced at Devon and saw the same look of pride on his face.

Kim was radiant as she walked down the aisle to meet her groom at the altar. Sandra watched her glow with happiness and felt it with her. Who would have dreamed someone else's wedding day could bring her such joy? But when she looked into the faces of Kim and Mike and saw the love shining from them, she knew it was a lasting kind of love. They shared not only a love for each other, but a love for the Lord as well.

She listened as the preacher spoke about love and devotion and commitment. Devon had promised such things to her last night.

When the happy couple kissed and the preacher announced

the newly married Kim and Mike, Sandra cheered. All the same happy faces would surround her and Devon, too, when news of their reconciliation was known. She thanked God for each and every one of them, for those who'd had a hand in bringing her and Devon back together.

Thank You, Lord, for Cara's car trouble. Otherwise she never would have come to Brandon Hall, such a romantic setting for her and Devon to rediscover their love.

She stopped as a realization hit her. She was nestled in the bosom of her former family, holding Devon's hand, and no one seemed surprised. She scanned the crowd. Surely they were all concentrating on the bride and groom, but she caught Cara's stare then noticed the way she nudged Jacob and the slow, smug grin that spread across his face.

Suddenly the pieces began to fall into place. She'd only come because of Cara's car trouble. She'd only stayed at Lynn's encouragement. Kim had softened her up with photographs and encouraging words, while Cara and Jacob arranged for her and Devon to be thrown together. And Devon—

She looked up at his handsome face. He'd swooped in and swept her right off her feet.

And just as they'd planned, she'd fallen right into his arms.

Chapter 11

How foolish she must seem to everyone. How easily she'd been so swayed by Devon's good looks and words of woo.

The crowd began to move toward the reception area at the back of the house, but Sandra didn't join them.

Devon turned to her and put his hand on her back. He stared at her. "Are you okay?"

She looked into his eyes, and all she saw was betrayal. He'd betrayed her again.

"I have to leave." She headed the opposite way, toward her car. Thankfully, her keys were in the pocket of her coat. . .the coat Cara had insisted she had to have! Another piece of the deception.

Devon followed her. "Sandra, what happened? What's going on? Where are you going?"

"Home."

"What happened?"

She stopped at her car and turned to him, willing her gaze to convey the anger bubbling inside of her. "You lied to me. You manipulated me. All this—you planned all this, didn't you?"

"I didn't plan anything."

"Really? So it was just a coincidence that Cara's car wouldn't start and I would have to drive her and then your mother and sister told me you were working and then you showed up an hour later? And I guess it wasn't part of your plan for my own kids to leave me stranded in downtown Natchez with you? I can't believe how gullible I've been this entire week. I thought God was drawing us together. Turns out it was just my own family manipulating me."

"Sandra, wait. Now, I'll admit there has been some plotting going on this weekend to push us back together, but that wasn't my doing."

She spun on him with a ferocity she hadn't felt since the last days of their marriage. "I can't believe I'm such a fool. I see it now. All the coy smiles and heartfelt talks. Your entire family was playing me for a first-class idiot."

"No, that isn't what this was about."

"And I can't believe I fell for you hook, line, and sinker. You must think I'm so easy. All you had to do was flash your smile and turn on the old charm and Sandra would come running back into your arms. Well, it worked. I hope you're happy, Devon, because you won."

"This isn't a competition."

"Are you going to stand there and tell me you didn't know what they were doing? What they were planning? That this entire weekend was nothing but one big trap to push us back together?"

"I didn't know, Sandra. I mean, I did know. I figured it out. Our kids are not that subtle."

"You should have told me what was going on."

"I know I should have, but I was afraid if you knew that you would leave, and I meant what I said last night, Sandra. I want to be with you. I love you. I've known for months that leaving you was a monumental mistake. I didn't want to risk losing you again."

"So you lied to me."

"I didn't lie. I played along."

"You let me fall into their trap."

"I fell with you."

"I feel like such a fool. I can never face them again. I can never face any of them again." She walked toward her car. "I have to leave."

"No, wait! Don't run away from this, from us. Yes, maybe our family set a trap for us, but they did it because they want to see us back together. They know how much we belong together, Sandra. Don't let your foolish pride tear us apart again."

"My pride? I'm not the one who walked out on our marriage."

"You're the one who pushed me out. You had nothing for me, Sandra. You gave everything you had to those kids."

"So I'm being accused of being a good mother? That's my crime?"

"You are a great mother, Sandra, but you were a lousy wife. I did everything I could to reach you, but you shut down on me a long time ago. Over the past years, you've gotten more and more controlling, and everything is your way or nothing."

"The kids needed me."

"I needed you! I wanted a wife, not just a mother for my children. I wanted you, Sandra. I have since the moment I met you. But you can't imagine what it's like to feel like a stranger in your own home. You lavished your love on Jacob and Cara, but you had nothing left for me. I know I wasn't the man I should have been. I should have spoken up, I should have told you how I felt, I should have been more of a leader in my house, and for that I'm so sorry. I can't change what I did, but I want to fix it."

She pushed him away and got into her car.

He held the door. "Sandra, please don't do this."

She ignored his plea and started the engine.

"Fine. If you want to leave, go ahead, but think on this: the trap only works if you still love me."

She jammed the car into gear and drove away before his pleas could penetrate the anger soaring through her. She had to hold on to that to keep from breaking down. How could she have been so blind, so naive, all this time?

She glanced in the rearview mirror. She could see Devon still standing in the driveway watching as she drove away.

This time it was truly over.

∽

"Devon, we're so sorry!"

He turned to find his mother, sister, and kids standing on the porch, watching him with sadness.

"We had no idea she would react so badly," Kim said. "I really thought she wanted to get back together with you. I just hated so much to see you both so unhappy when I was so happy."

Jacob stepped forward. "Dad, go after her."

Cara followed. "Yes, Daddy, go. Make her see reason. Tell her we didn't mean any harm."

He hugged the twins to him. The sadness and guilt lining their faces spoke volumes. "Your mom knows you love her and only want what's best for her."

Kim lifted the hem of her wedding dress and stepped off the porch. "What are you going to do?"

He stared around at his family and sighed. "What else? I'm going to fight for her."

Chapter 12

The tears started even before she'd left Natchez. Sandra aimed her car toward the Trace and raced for home, her anger dissipating and being replaced by profound sadness. An hour ago, everything in her life had seemed perfect. Now everything was in shambles.

Had everyone in her life set out to betray her? Her own kids had turned against her. She replayed moments from the weekend over in her mind, seeing things from a different perspective now. What a fool she'd been to fall so easily for Devon's charms.

Lord, what should I do?

In the rearview mirror, she spotted a vehicle approaching behind her at great speed. As it grew closer, she recognized the familiar black SUV. She gripped the steering wheel as he pulled alongside her. Was he trying to get them both killed?

She let down the window and shouted at him. "What are you doing? You're driving like a crazy person."

"Pull over," he called. When she didn't respond, he laid on

the horn. "Pull over, Sandra."

She jumped, startled by the sudden noise. He was crazy and was going to get them both killed. Still, she didn't stop.

Devon sped up and cut in front of her, stopping suddenly and causing her to slam on her brakes and skid to a stop.

He jumped from his SUV and headed toward her car.

She got out and confronted him. "What do you think you're doing? Are you trying to get us both killed?"

"I'm not giving up on us, Sandra."

"I can't have this discussion now."

"Why? Because our family loves us enough to fight for us? Did you get your ego bruised? Yes, they planned this. They wanted this to happen. It doesn't change the fact that it did." He reached for her arm. "Sandra, I love you. I can't lose you again. I won't. You can get back into your car and drive home, but that won't be the end of us. I'll continue to fight for you, for us. That's a promise."

"You can't make that kind of promise, Devon. You can't know what will happen in a few weeks or a few months. What if I mess up again? What if you leave again? I don't think I could handle losing you twice."

He stroked her hair. "That will never happen."

"Why would this time be different?"

"Because I'm different. We're different. We fell apart because we were trying to make this work on our own. We were two people trying to have our own ways. This time we'll let God have His way with our marriage, and that means what God has joined together, no one can pull apart." He reached into his jacket and pulled out a folded blue paper.

Sandra recognized it as the divorce documents. "I'm taking the D-word off the table. It's not an option anymore." He ripped them. "It will never be an option again. You're stuck with me, and this time I mean for life."

She so much wanted to fall into his arms and believe him, yet she hesitated, looking up at him with vulnerability. "I'm scared, but I want this. I want us."

"We'll make it, Sandra. We'll make it together."

Love warmed her heart and soul, and she couldn't contain the smile that spread across her face. When their lips met, she melted into his embrace, feeling alive and safe for the first time in years. God had truly made all her dreams come true.

Chapter 13

The reflection pond glowed amber with candles and torchlight. Christmas lights hung from the oak trees and evergreens, creating a canopy of lights in the evening sky. The stars shone bright on Christmas Eve as Sandra walked toward the old oak tree where Devon waited for her. The ground had been cleared of leaves and pecans for the event.

Big smiles stretched across the faces of the family, her family, now and forever. The twins, Mike and Kim, and Lynn. The only person present that wasn't family was the preacher Rachel had secured for them on short notice.

She reached Devon, and he took her hands. As she placed her hands in his and the family gathered around for the renewal of their vows, Devon smiled. Brandon Hall would forever be in her mind the place where dreams came true and love rekindled, the place where Sandra and Devon were forever joined under the old oak tree.

How many kisses had taken place under this old oak tree? Sandra knew of at least one, when the preacher pronounced them, forevermore, husband and wife.

Christmas at Monmouth

Lorraine Beatty

Dedication

To the special ladies of Monmouth Historic Inn, Nancy Reuther and Carol Jones, whose help and kindness made this story possible. God bless you and the entire Monmouth family.

Chapter 1

November

Wreath Anderson strolled through the hall of Monmouth Plantation, her gaze resting admiringly on the antique furniture, the curved staircase, and the colorful mural wallpaper. Of all the antebellum homes in Natchez, Monmouth was her favorite. The early nineteenth-century Greek Revival with its large portico, broad zigzag railing, and four massive square pillars across the front epitomized the image of a Southern estate. Situated on twenty-six acres of beautifully landscaped gardens, the historic property had evolved over the years into a five-star boutique hotel.

Chilling winter air rushed around her ankles as she stepped outside, sending a shiver all the way up to her neck and hastening her steps across the courtyard of the historic inn. Winter in Natchez, Mississippi, was always unpredictable. One day's balmy, spring-like weather could become a blustery sweater-and-boots day the next. Today had been a combination of both—warm in the morning and cold and windy by the afternoon.

As soon as she checked in with sales manager and event planner Helen Fletcher at the office, she'd head home, fix a pot of raspberry tea, and snuggle up on the couch. But first she had a few wedding details to go over. Her business, Wedding Wreath Bridal and Event Planning, was exceptionally busy this Christmas season. The next three weekends were packed full of luncheons, parties, a special benefit dinner, and a small wedding at one of the historic plantations. But it was the wedding at the end of the month here at Monmouth that was churning up the past and keeping her off balance. The bride, Grace Donovan, had chosen an antebellum theme for her wedding, complete with period uniforms and hoopskirts—the same theme and the same venue as Wreath's wedding six years ago. The wedding that never happened.

A gust of wind lifted her hair from her shoulders, chasing her inside the brick building that had once been the historic home's kitchen but now served as the main offices and gift shop. If this cold spell lingered too long, it would make for a very uncomfortable wedding ceremony for Grace Donovan and Brian Blair. Outdoor weddings in December, even in southern Mississippi, could fall prey to bad weather. And when the wedding was for the daughter of a state senator, bad weather could ruin the day for a lot of important people.

"I think the cold front has arrived." Wreath smiled at the woman standing behind the registrations counter. An attractive woman in her fifties, Helen had been the property's sales manager and event planner for years, and her love and passion for the property gave the inn its heart.

Helen frowned and shook her head. "It's going to get

down into the fifties tonight. I really don't like cold weather."

Wreath laughed, planting her hands on her hips. "You're a Yankee. You should be used to cold weather."

"I might have been raised in the North, but I've lived in the South too long. Anything below sixty is too cold for me." Helen led her through the gift shop to her office in the back, originally the plantation's warming room where food was placed for the head butler to carry to the main house. She handed Wreath the folder she'd lifted from her desk. "Here's the final menu for the Donovan-Blair wedding dinner. There are a few changes. You may want to run it by your bride again. I know how upset they can get when they don't get everything they want."

Wreath scanned the list of sumptuous foods. "Not Grace Donovan. I have never had an easier bride to work with." A fact for which she was grateful. This wedding was unearthing enough pain as it was. A difficult bride would have made it unbearable. She closed the folder. "It's kind of strange, actually."

Helen peered at her over glasses. "Don't look a gift horse in the mouth. A wedding as large and unique as this one is hard enough to coordinate. Having an easygoing bride is a blessing. Plus it'll make the new manager look good. It never hurts to make the boss happy. And I want to keep this man happy." Helen smiled and fanned her face with her hands. "He's a looker. And when he smiles, I just want to melt. Wait until you see him."

Wreath followed Helen into the small alcove that held the copy machine and leaned against the doorjamb as she watched the woman work. "Oh really? I meant to ask you about him."

Helen tapped the small stack of paper on the top of the copier to even up the sheets. "Well, he's from Nashville, and apparently he's some hotshot wonder boy making a name for himself in the hospitality industry."

"What's his name?"

"Micah Broussard," a man's deep voice responded.

Wreath spun around—she knew that name, but it couldn't be the man she remembered. Her gaze landed on a tall sable-haired man with sparkling blue eyes and a charming lopsided smile. Her memory faltered briefly, adjusting to the fully matured version of the man she remembered. His hair was darker, the face more sculpted and with deep character lines in his cheeks and a sharper angle to the jawline. The broad shoulders and muscular chest showed off his expertly tailored dark gray suit to perfection. He could have posed for the cover of *GQ* on the spot. Six years had only improved on a good thing. "Micah. I can't believe it's you. The last time I saw you. . ." She stopped, her heart chilling as old, painful memories burst to the surface. This wedding was difficult enough to work on without having a very physical reminder of her greatest humiliation. She folded her lips together, struggling to maintain her composure.

"It's good to see you again, Wreath."

Before she realized it, Micah had opened his arms and pulled her into a friendly hug. It was over in an instant but left her with a sense of warm strength and the scent of peppermint. She stepped back, disconcerted. "You're the new manager?"

"I prefer *innkeeper*. It fits the antebellum surroundings better, don't you think?" He smiled, brushing back his suit coat and resting his hands on his lean hips. "Helen, here, has been giving me a crash course. I understand we have a big wedding coming up at the end of December."

Wreath lost her voice. The knot in her stomach tightened. The last time she'd seen Micah was at her wedding. She rarely thought about that horrible day six years ago when her fiancé, Jack Mason, had abandoned her at the altar. "It's the event of the year. We've got it under control."

Micah studied her a moment, his blue eyes probing, searching for something. She looked away. She wasn't sure she liked the idea of working with Micah. Normally she'd only interact with the hotel manager in a minor capacity. Mostly she worked with Helen when the Wedding Wreath was planning an event at the inn, but the Donovan-Blair wedding was too big a deal. She'd have to coordinate with everyone to pull it off. But having Micah around, her ex-fiancé's best friend and the man who had introduced her to Jack, would play havoc with her already tattered peace of mind.

"I have every confidence in you, Wreath. I remember your strong sense of commitment to whatever you set your mind to."

"Thank you. I'll need it."

Helen clutched a folder to her chest and smiled at each of them in turn. "So how do you two know each other?"

Micah looked a bit taken aback by the blunt and nosey question. Wreath smiled. Helen wasn't shy about expressing her curiosity. "We worked together several years ago in Memphis at one of the Hancock Hotels." Maybe she could keep the explanation focused on an old friendship and skip the part about the wedding and Jack. "It was my first job, right out of college. Micah was my trainer."

"And now you're together again. Only this time, Wreath, you can be his trainer."

"What do you mean?"

Helen lifted one shoulder. "Well, you may not work for Monmouth, but as many weddings and events you've held here, you know as much about the hotel as I do."

Micah smiled down at her. "That's good to know. Between you and Helen, I should be an expert in short order."

Helen slipped her glasses in place and looked down at her desk. "Why don't you two go get reacquainted. I've got work to do, and I can't do it with this reunion going on."

Micah shrugged and, gently taking Wreath's arm, steered her toward the stairway at the back.

Upstairs he stopped at the first door, opened it, and stepped back to allow her to enter first. Her heart skipped a beat as she brushed past him, inhaling the scent of peppermint again. She used to tease him about always having the candy in his pockets. He'd explained how the sweet had helped him stop smoking years ago. The habit had stuck. She glanced over at him to find him staring, an appreciative glint in his blue eyes. "You haven't changed a bit. Still as lovely as ever."

The compliment sent heat rushing to her cheeks and tightened her throat. She searched for a response. "And you look taller." She cringed.

Micah laughed out loud. "No, I'm still standing right at

six feet, but you seem taller than I remember." He glanced down at her five-inch heels, cocking one eyebrow.

"Oh. Yes, well, I had a meeting with a vendor and I had to dress the part. I'm still five feet five."

"And a half."

"What?"

Micah leaned closer, holding her gaze. "Five feet five and one-half inch."

He was right, but she never added that half inch. "How did you remember that?"

"I never forget important things." He gestured her to be seated in one of the chairs opposite his desk.

She sat down, anticipating his sitting in his desk chair. Instead, he took the chair beside her, which only sent her nerves quivering again. Seeing Micah had unleashed a wave of memories she didn't want to revisit, and she regretted coming to his office. She should have claimed her busy schedule as an excuse to leave. Now it was too late. She inhaled, willing her nerves to calm down.

He crossed his long legs and gazed at her with a warm and tender expression. "So tell me about this big wedding you're coordinating. Helen said it's an antebellum theme like yours. . . ." He exhaled, setting his jaw and rubbing his forehead. "Sorry, Wreath. I didn't mean to bring that up."

Wreath forced a smile, swallowing past the lump in her throat. "No problem. That was a long time ago."

Micah leaned forward, forearms resting on his knees, peering into her eyes as if trying to communicate something of importance. "Yes. It was. A very long time ago." He leaned back in the chair again, smiling. "I'm looking forward to working together again."

Wreath wanted to say the same, but in the short time she'd been with Micah, the undertow of old pain and hurts were dragging her under. He'd introduced her to Jack. They'd been best buddies. He should have warned her about what kind of person Jack was. A twinge of guilt pricked her. She was being petty and childish. Micah had never done anything to her except be a friend. "It's good to see you, too. I schedule a lot of events here, so we should see a lot of each other."

"Good. And I hope you know that I'm available to help in any way I can. Don't hesitate to ask."

Wreath relaxed at the calm, friendly tone in his voice. "Thank you. I will, but you have to know that your staff is the best I've ever worked with. They'll make your job easy."

"I'm glad to hear that."

She searched for something to say. "So where are you staying?"

Micah chuckled and tugged on his ear. "Uh. Room 26."

Her eyes widened, and she swallowed a laugh. "You mean the small suite up in the rafters of the main house?"

"Technically it's the third floor, but yes, that would be the place."

"Are you comfortable in there?"

"Sure. It has everything I need. It's quiet and makes for an easy commute to work." His cell phone chirped. "Excuse me a minute." He stood and moved to the end of the room.

Now was her chance to make her escape. Quickly, she rose and started to the door, intending to wave good-bye and leave. But he ended his call and hurried to her side before she reached the door.

"Leaving so soon?"

"I have an appointment with a bride." She turned and smiled at him, a funny little skip in her heart when she looked up into his clear blue eyes.

He nodded, one corner of his mouth lifting slightly. "Wreath, I'm new here—Natchez is a small city, but I've been too busy to even look for an apartment, let alone search out the best restaurants. Have dinner with me tonight? Pick your favorite place. It'll give us a chance to catch up."

Wreath took a moment to consider his request. She'd dated Micah for several weeks before he'd introduced her to Jack. She'd liked him. He'd been a nice, thoughtful guy. But now he was a reminder of her past, of the most painful time in her life. "I'm sorry. I'm so busy I barely take time to eat. Maybe after Thanksgiving." She thought she saw disappointment in his eyes but dismissed it as her imagination.

"I understand." He touched her arm. "But I won't let you avoid me forever."

Was she that obvious? "I'd better go." She turned to leave, but the question that had been hanging in the back of her mind couldn't be contained any longer. She glanced at Micah. He was staring at her, his blue eyes intense and probing, and she knew he was aware of her thoughts. "Do you ever talk to him?"

A muscle in Micah's jaw flexed, and he glanced away briefly before answering. "No. I ran into him about a year ago at the airport in Atlanta."

"How did he look?"

"The same. He's been married a couple of times and has a child who lives with the mother. He said he just couldn't be tied down. Too much fun to be had. And no, he didn't ask about you."

The harsh tone in Micah's voice tore through her like a dull knife opening an old wound. Her heart burned, as if Jack had left her again. What was wrong with her? The man walked out on her at her wedding. How could she even harbor a thought about him? She turned and hurried down the stairs, tossing a quick good-bye to Helen before leaving the building.

Outside, the cold brisk wind helped clear her mind and settle her nerves. A quick glance at her watch told her she'd be late for her appointment with Grace to go over the music for the ceremony. She shifted her focus away from the sight of Micah and the memories his presence had unearthed. It was too much to deal with right now. She'd have to avoid him as much as possible until this wedding was over. Maybe then she could put it behind her once and for all.

Chapter 2

Micah shut the door to his office, dragging a hand along his jaw. Taking a small peppermint candy from the jar on his desk, he unwrapped it and popped it into his mouth then stood by the window that looked out over the courtyard and fountain in the rose garden. He wished his office window overlooked the parking lot so he could watch Wreath leaving.

The sight of her had hit him like a fist in the gut. She was even lovelier than he'd remembered. Still slender, her curves were those of a grown woman now. Her once long, dark brown hair was cut shorter, brushing her shoulders in fluid strands. Her cinnamon-brown eyes with their long lashes gave her a wide-eyed innocent look, though the sparkle he remembered was missing.

He turned from the window and moved back to his desk. His gaze landed on the chair where Wreath had sat. She was part of his past. He'd been in love with her then, and he'd kicked himself a thousand times for allowing Jack to swoop in and steal her away. He'd been furious when the jerk had left her standing at the altar heartbroken and crushed. But there was nothing he could do. Wreath loved Jack. Not him. Even after all this time, her primary thought was for Jack.

He opened his laptop and pulled up the files he needed to go over before his meeting with the hotel's owner tomorrow. He looked forward to working at Monmouth. He'd been blessed to land such a prestigious position. The property had garnered numerous awards and industry recognition; named one of the "top 50 U.S. Inns & B&Bs" and one of the "top 100 small luxury hotels" in the world. He intended to maintain those rankings.

With a grunt of disgust, Micah leaned back in his chair. If he could keep his mind on his job and not Wreath Anderson— The sight of her had unleashed feelings he thought long buried. From the moment she'd turned to face him, his heart had exploded in his chest. The narrow skirt and ridiculous spiked heels emphasized her slender legs. The softly draped top in royal blue, the bold necklace resting against her delicate throat, had called attention to her dark hair and warm brown eyes. He'd thought his feelings for Wreath were long gone, but now he had to acknowledge the truth. Whatever he'd felt for Wreath wasn't dead. It was very much alive.

❧

It was dark when Wreath pulled her car into the Wedding Wreath's parking lot, even though it was only four thirty in the afternoon. She was a sunshine person, and she always had difficulty adjusting to the loss of daylight savings time and the early onset of darkness that made the nights seem long and lonely.

She gathered her materials from the backseat and started toward the 120-year-old church that housed her wedding consultant business. The building stood on the corner of two downtown streets and had served as the Community Church for decades. When the congregation outgrew the building and put it up for sale, Wreath's aunt and uncle had bought it and turned it into an event facility.

The motion detector blinked on as she took the steps, illuminating the weathered old brick. Even in the dark, the building was beautiful with its stained-glass windows and tall brick-and-wood bell tower with gabled roof. She loved her job, and she thanked God every day for the opportunity to organize and plan lovely events and fantasy weddings for her clients. She liked to think the people who celebrated here enjoyed a little leftover grace from when it was a house of worship.

Inside the reception area, the fragrance of fresh flowers and old wood welcomed her back, along with the wave and smile from her close friend and assistant, Bonnie Coleman. Wreath stopped at Bonnie's desk in the anteroom outside her office, waiting for an update. Bonnie was always on top of everything at the Wedding Wreath. The business couldn't run without her.

"About time you showed up. What kept you?"

"Sorry. I got sidetracked at Monmouth. Turns out the new manager is an old friend of mine, so we took a few moments to catch up."

Bonnie stared, wide-eyed. "Broussard?" A smile slowly spread across her pretty face. "Oh my. I wish I could say he was a friend of mine." She exhaled a heartfelt sigh.

"You've met him?"

"Not officially, but I saw him the other day when I was there. That guy is delicious. I seriously thought about quitting this job and going to work for Helen just so I could look at him every day."

Wreath tilted her head and smiled. "Bonnie."

"So how do you know him, and why didn't you ever tell me about this guy?"

"It was a long time ago. He was my trainer when I went to work for the Hancock hotel chain in Memphis. I haven't seen him in years."

Bonnie leaned forward over the desk. "Did you date?"

Wreath thought about Micah's compliment. He'd always been one to notice what she was wearing. "Briefly."

"And you let him go? Why?"

Wreath sat down in the armchair in front of Bonnie's desk and slipped off her heels, using the time to decide what to tell her friend. Bonnie was one of the few people who knew about her wedding humiliation, so there was no point in trying to hide the truth. "Bonnie, Micah is the one who introduced me to Jack."

Bonnie's expression shifted quickly from curious anticipation to a sad realization. "Oh, Wreath." She sat back in her chair and shook her head. "Well, I'm going to write him off my hunk-of-the-month list. I don't want him introducing me to any of his friends."

An unexpected wave of defensiveness rose in Wreath's chest. "It wasn't his fault. Not really. Micah is a great guy.

A nice guy. He was always thoughtful and considerate. Very attentive when we were together, and he has a great sense of humor."

Bonnie raised her eyebrows. "Okay, so were you happy to see him again or not?"

That was the million-dollar question. Wreath stood and picked up her shoes and purse. "Are Grace and Brian here?"

"They arrived right before you did. They're waiting in your office. Are you not going to answer me?"

"I don't have an answer yet." Turning, she dismissed the disturbing question and walked to her office. She needed to tell Grace about the change in the wedding menu. Hopefully she would take the news with the same easy attitude she had other obstacles in the planning. Wreath walked down the short hall to her office, putting a regretful smile on her face. "I'm so sorry I'm late."

Grace waved off her concern. "We haven't been here long. Do you realize we're only four weeks away from the big day?" She exchanged a happy smile with Brian, her groom.

Wreath sat behind her desk and pulled up their file on her computer. "Oh believe me, I'm fully aware of that, and I'm working around the clock to get it all done in time."

Grace's beaming smile dimmed a shade. "Oh, I'm sorry. I get so excited I forget how hard you have to work to make this all happen."

"Please don't worry about that. It's my job, and I love the challenge. Pulling everything together is fun for me." Wreath picked up the menu Helen had given her earlier. "I'm afraid I have some bad news about the wedding dinner. We'll have to make some adjustments on the dessert." She explained the reason behind the change and pointed out the options. Bride and groom made their choice, and Wreath logged it into her computer. "Sorry for the change, but as you've discovered, nothing ever goes exactly as planned."

Grace smiled and waved off her concerns. "It's not a big deal. The only important thing about that day is that Brian and I will be married, and our friends and family will be there to celebrate."

Wreath couldn't help but smile at the sentiment. If only all her clients were this easy. "All right. Now about the music."

Brian pulled his smartphone from his pocket and glanced at the screen. "It's the jeweler. The groom's gifts are ready. Why don't I let you ladies sort out the music, and I'll come back and pick you up later."

He kissed Grace good-bye and left. The ladies went into the next room, where a piano and sound equipment were set up. Brides appreciated having a place to listen to the CDs or hear music played before making their decisions. Wreath laid out the CDs Grace had requested, plus a few suggestions of her own. "Have you thought about the tone you'd like to set for the first song? A hymn, a romantic ballad, or a solo?"

"I want the music to be reverent but joyful. We're not being married in a church, but I want the church feel. My friend Paula has agreed to sing. We're going to talk about the songs this weekend when she comes to town. I know I want, Pachelbel's Canon in D, and some version of the Lord's Prayer."

Wreath pointed out the songs she thought would be

appropriate and stepped away to give her time to listen. With Brian and Grace only in town for Thanksgiving week, they were trying to solidify as many details of the wedding as possible. Long-distance wedding planning was always a juggling act. Thankfully, Grace and Brian lived in New Orleans and were able to make weekend trips to Natchez. During the week they relied on tweets, texts, and video chats.

The biggest blessing with these clients was their easygoing approach to every challenge. Grace had never become irritated or angry at any of the many adjustments and changes that occurred.

Wreath glanced over at Grace, who was removing the headphones. Maybe this was a good time to ask the question that had plagued her for the ten months they'd been planning the wedding. "Grace, why are you so calm about this wedding? Most brides I assist are obsessed with every detail. They fly into a rage or burst into tears when things don't go as planned."

Grace smiled. "Obsessing over the details is a waste of time. I want the wedding to be romantic, to reflect our interests. That's why I chose the antebellum theme. Brian and I love history. Brian is a reenactor. The hooped skirts and the uniforms reflect our interests and make it special. But the wedding is about us. Brian and me pledging our lives to one another in front of God. Saying those vows is a sacred covenant that we don't take lightly. All the rest is just glitter."

Wreath had never heard any of her brides comment on the vows. It was always about the dress and the napkins and the glitter. "That's lovely, Grace. And I can honestly say this is the most enjoyable wedding I've ever planned."

"I love everything you're doing." She gave her a hug. "It's going to be beautiful."

Wreath thought about Grace's comment later that night as she prepared for bed. Micah Broussard's unexpected presence in her life had stirred more memories of her failed wedding. It had been her fantasy wedding, held at Monmouth Plantation in the spring with the azaleas in bloom, the wisteria hanging in thick clumps over the pergola. The groomsmen were resplendent in historic uniforms, with gold braid, epaulets, and swords at their sides. The bridesmaids wore pink-and-white period gowns and wide-brimmed hats. Her dress was a vision in white alençon lace, tulle, and satin. It was still hanging in the storage closet at her shop, preserved for no reason. She'd simply been unable to let go of it. She still wanted that wedding someday.

She wanted to repeat those vows.

Wreath slipped under the covers. Grace had said they mattered more than anything else. She'd never considered that before. She could recite them by heart. She believed in the sanctity of marriage and the joining of man and woman according to God's design. But she'd been too preoccupied with the wedding—the glitter—not the words she would say to her groom.

The groom who never showed.

She rolled over, hugging her pillow closer. But the best man had been there. Micah Broussard. He'd been the one who had taken charge, who had calmed the waters. She'd found out later from her maid of honor that he had acted as de facto host during the reception while her aunt had handled other details. Her mother had dissolved into tears. Wreath had been too numb to do more than sit in her elegantly appointed antebellum room in the main house and stare out the window.

Micah had been waiting when she'd finally changed from her gown and faced the few friends remaining. He'd driven her back to her aunt's home, sitting silently behind the wheel while she struggled to make sense of what happened. He'd held her hand, squeezing it tightly in a gesture of comfort before she pulled away and ran inside to hide.

She hadn't seen him again until today. Funny how she'd forgotten how kind and dependable he'd been. A true friend. Even her mother and her Aunt Julia had commented on his kindness.

How had she forgotten something so important?

Chapter 3

Thanksgiving Day dawned bright, clear, and cool, with no pressing business to intrude on Wreath's holiday. She took advantage of the freedom to sleep late and indulge in a big pot of coffee. The last few days had been hectic. She'd put out fires for two stressed brides and handled a last-minute rescheduling of a sorority reunion brunch at Linden Hall. Next weekend she had a wedding at Dunleith, a brunch at the shop on Sunday afternoon, and meetings with a couple of new clients planning spring weddings. With the ongoing details for Grace and Brian's antebellum event, her days were filled. She liked it that way. But she also liked the fact that, for the next few days at least, she had some time to herself.

Today she planned on hibernating in her cozy townhouse and shutting out the world. She would ignore the fact that it was Thanksgiving and she had no family to celebrate with. Normally she and Bonnie spent the day together, but this year her friend had gone home to Hattiesburg to be with her family.

As the day wore on, her mood downshifted from contentment and slid steeply toward an all-out pity party. Micah Broussard kept intruding into her thoughts, bringing with him memories of the humiliation of her abandonment at the altar and the painful similarities between her wedding and Grace's.

Disgusted with herself, she checked out restaurant sites online. Maybe treating herself to a Thanksgiving dinner later would lift her spirits. But the thought of dining alone was less appealing than eating a microwave turkey dinner. Micah's invitation to dinner came to mind. He would be alone today, too. She'd turned him down because he'd reminded her too much of Jack. But now she regretted her selfish response. He'd reached out to her in friendship and she'd figuratively batted his hand away. Not the kind of Southern hospitality she wanted to convey.

She was still marveling at the change in him. Had his smile always been that unsettling? Had the twinkle in his blue eyes been so charming? The man he was today was disarmingly attractive. The kind of confident, self-assured man who would turn female heads. Females like her. She'd been unable to get him off her mind. She hadn't thought to ask him if he was married, though she had noticed he wasn't wearing a ring.

What did matter was that he was an old friend who might welcome a kindly gesture on a holiday. She reached for her phone only to have doubts crop up. Knowing Micah and his dedication to his job, he was probably working today, allowing the married employees to spend time with their families. And come to think of it, the restaurant at Monmouth served a gourmet Thanksgiving dinner, so he'd probably eat there. Which meant he wouldn't be alone, so she could stop worrying.

Satisfied with her decision, she picked up the new DVD she'd bought of season two of her favorite detective series and wrestled off the clear plastic from the case. She had a rare day. She needed to take full advantage of it. There was no reason whatsoever to feel sorry for herself. The opening bars of "Hark! the Herald Angels Sing" pulled her attention to her phone and away from loading the DVD. She glanced at the screen. Micah. "Hello."

"Happy Thanksgiving. I hope I wasn't interrupting anything."

The sound of his deep voice sent a tickle of warmth along her nerves. "No. I was just enjoying a quiet day. What about you? Are you working?"

"Yes, but I'm done for the day. Which is why I'm calling. The restaurant will be closing shortly and the chef has promised me my own personal Thanksgiving dinner. There's only one problem."

"What's that?"

"I don't want to eat alone. I know it's short notice, but I'd be eternally grateful. This is a family holiday, and since neither one of us have family here, I was hoping you'd take pity on me and join me."

Refusal touched the tip of her tongue, but for some reason she clamped her mouth shut. She'd been given a second chance to make Micah feel welcome. And the 1818 Restaurant at Monmouth served the most elegant, exquisite feast in the

South. But spending time with Micah would only dredge up more painful memories.

"Did I mention that we'll be served in the study off the Quitman Lounge? It'll be just the two of us. I could really use some downtime with a friend."

She'd worked in the hospitality industry long enough to know that feeling. Constant activity, always putting out fires, being "on" for the guests, then suddenly it was over and you were left feeling lost and forgotten. But Thanksgiving with a friend did sound inviting. "All right. What time?"

"Half hour, and wear something comfortable. I want this to be relaxing for both of us. I'll see you soon."

Nervousness and regret churned in Wreath's stomach as she made her way up the sloping walk from the parking lot to the two-story brick office building. She'd talked herself out of coming twice since she'd talked to Micah. Picked up the phone three times. She looked forward to a sumptuous meal at Monmouth, but dining alone with Micah seemed too intimate and romantic.

Micah stepped from the door of the office building as she came near. He must have been watching for her. He looked elegantly handsome in dark gray slacks, a cream-colored crew neck sweater over a light blue shirt. One glance at him eased her concerns. She had nothing to fear from Micah. He was a nice, comfortable man.

"Thanks for coming, Wreath. I hope you won't be disappointed."

"That would be impossible. I have tasted Chef Ruth's food many times."

"Then let's go." He held out his hand and smiled.

Wreath hesitated a moment at the look in his eyes. It was admiring. Surely she'd imagined that. It was simply gratitude for dining with him. She slipped her hand into his and started toward the east wing of the house, across the courtyard, aware of a strange tingling in her fingers. Micah's hand was firm and strong, a hand you could depend on.

"You look lovely."

Wreath glanced down at her attire. "You said dress casual. I hope jeans and a sweater are all right."

"Perfect. Lavender is my favorite color."

Chef Ruth met them at the door. "Good evening, Micah. Wreath. I have everything ready for you."

Wreath glanced at Micah. "So formal." He laughed. The deep-throated sound skittered along her nerves. She remembered his laugh. It had been one of the things she'd found attractive about him. The chef ushered them into the small, elegant room to a single table by the fireplace, set with white linen, crystal goblets, and fine china. Micah pulled out her chair then seated himself.

Wreath smiled at him. Always the perfect gentleman. She felt her tension ease, replaced with an unfamiliar sense of peace. "I think this is exactly what I needed, Micah. A quiet dinner with a friend. Thank you." She saw a small shadow pass across his face.

"I appreciate you coming to my rescue. I love what I do, but the odd hours can take a toll. Especially on holidays when you're new in town."

The first of their courses arrived: gumbo with duck,

andouille sausage, and basmati rice. They ate in companionable silence, enjoying the elegant atmosphere.

Micah uttered a soft, appreciative moan when he took a bite of the main course. Cajun fried turkey with cranberry chutney. He smiled over at her. "Not exactly Mom's but still delicious."

"I'll bet your family misses you. I remember how close y'all were." She searched her memory. "Two brothers, one sister, right?"

Micah smiled. "Right. They were disappointed, but I promised I'd make it home for Groundhog Day."

A giggle escaped her throat before she could stop it. "Are you serious? Nobody celebrates that day."

"Exactly. That's why we try and get together then. With all our different schedules and responsibilities, the only way to get time off is to pick an odd day. We try and cram that weekend full of family time. It's like Thanksgiving, Christmas, and birthdays all rolled into one."

Wreath chuckled. She'd forgotten how funny Micah could be. "Sounds like fun."

"It is. I'd love to take you with me, let you experience it for yourself."

Was he inviting her home to meet his family? Surely not. She focused on her meal, ignoring his comment. "I'm sure they'll be glad to see you whenever you come home."

"What about your family, Wreath?"

She speared a bite of her green-bean casserole, uneasy with the topic. "My mom died a few years ago. My Aunt Julia and Uncle Bob retired to the Florida Keys."

"So you're all alone. That's tough."

"I'm used to it. Besides, running my own business keeps me too busy to think about much else." That wasn't exactly true. Lately she'd been feeling the loneliness more than usual, and she wasn't sure why. Nothing had changed, but she'd found herself wanting more than work and her church activities.

"So no boyfriend in the picture?"

Wreath met Micah's blue gaze. She thought she saw a glint of anticipation there. She shook her head. "My almost-wedding cured me of any romantic ideas. Love and romance is for my clients. God has given me so much more than I ever dreamed. I don't want to be greedy and ask for more."

He looked at her over his glass. "God doesn't ration His blessings, Wreath. Don't shortchange yourself. He has many more blessings He's waiting to give you. As for the romance, you'll find it again."

"Not likely." She masked her discomfort by taking a sip of her sweet tea. "How about you? No fiancée, girlfriend?"

"Not at the moment. So how did you end up being a wedding consultant? It seems an unlikely career path, considering."

"I suppose so. My Aunt Julia started the business. I was named for her company. The Wedding Wreath. She came up with a design using the wreath, the symbol of forever, making it out of white material and using it in the wedding ceremony. It was quite innovative for its time. Now it's become the symbol of the business."

"So you took over the business when they retired?"

"Yes, but I worked with them for a year before that learning the ropes. The timing was perfect. I needed a new direction for my life after. . .well, after you know. . .and my aunt and uncle wanted to retire, so it was the perfect solution for everyone." Time to redirect the questions to Micah. "So how did you end up here in Natchez?"

Micah took a sip of his drink and leaned back. "I was working in Nashville with the Gaylord organization."

"That must have been exciting. I remember when you and Jack and I were working for the Hancock hotels. We dreamed of working with one of the resort chains. I used to think I wanted to work in a big hotel."

"It was exciting, but also long hours, lots of stress, and little time for personal life. The job was wearing me down. I realized I was more comfortable managing the smaller hotels. Monmouth came open, and I jumped at the chance."

"I think you'll like working here. The people are wonderful. Hardworking, dedicated. They all have a deep love for the home and its history. Have you met Hal and Roosevelt?"

Micah nodded, a smile lighting his eyes. "I have. Those men have forgotten more about Monmouth than I'll ever know. The knowledge and experience they possess are invaluable to this inn." He leaned forward slightly, looking into her eyes. "Having a friend here in town makes it even better."

The soft, intimate tone in his voice stole her breath. She tried to interpret his words. Did he want their friendship to become more? Or was she simply experiencing leftover pangs of self-pity and reading more into his words than intended?

"So, I understand that Natchez during the holidays is quite unique." Micah leaned back and cut a piece of deep-fried turkey into a bite-size piece.

Wreath's tension eased somewhat. "Oh yes. Starting tomorrow the city turns into a Christmas wonderland. Next to spring pilgrimage, Christmas is my favorite time of the year."

"Helen told me the staff will begin putting up the decorations tomorrow. She assured me, by Monday the entire plantation will be dressed for the holidays."

"Not only Monmouth but the entire city. The antebellum homes, the downtown streets, the park along the bluffs overlooking the Mississippi River, everything will be lit and draped for the holiday. It's magical." Embarrassed by her obvious passion for her city, she looked down at her plate, tucking her hair behind her ear. He probably thought she was silly.

"You love this city a lot, don't you?"

The quiet tone of his voice drew her gaze to his. "I do. I wasn't raised here. I grew up in Madison, Mississippi, but we visited my aunt and uncle frequently, and I fell in love with Natchez."

Micah laid his hand on hers. "I'm glad to know you're happy and that you're all right after what Jack did."

"I'm fine. It was hard at first, but I found my new career and I reconnected with my faith. I'd wandered too far away. So now I'm at peace and I'm happy."

"I'm glad, Wreath. You deserve to be happy." He removed his hand as plates of white chocolate bread pudding with praline sauce were placed in front of them, along with a silver coffeepot.

"Wreath, I'm sorry."

"For what?

"I feel responsible for what happened. It was never my intention to introduce you to Jack. In fact, I'd avoided it the entire time you and I dated. But that night at the party, he swooped in and took over like he always did, and there wasn't much I could do about it. I should have tried harder to protect you."

His caring words touched her deeply. "You couldn't help what happened. I went with him willingly. But it would have been nice to know what kind of a guy he was before I got so involved."

"Would you have believed me if I had told you?"

Wreath thought back to those days. Her feelings for Jack had blocked out everything else in her life. "No. Probably not."

Micah stared at his plate a long moment and then said, "I wanted to warn you at first, but you two hit it off. And Jack stayed with you longer than he had any other woman he'd known. I'd hoped it was the real thing."

Mistakes of her past blurred her vision. "I didn't see it at the time. Later I could see the signs, all the indications that our relationship wasn't going to work, but I didn't want to acknowledge it. I thought once we were married he'd change."

"I still feel responsible."

"I did blame you for a long time. It was easier than admitting I was an idiot."

"You weren't an idiot. You were a woman in love."

She stiffened at the words, holding her head high. "I won't make that mistake again. Ever."

Chapter 4

Micah surfed through the television channels for the third time, but nothing had changed. The ball game was too lopsided to care about, the rest of his choices couldn't hold his attention. His small suite on the third floor of the nearly two-hundred-year-old mansion was cozy and convenient, allowing him to be available at a moment's notice. But he could see that it wouldn't be long before the rooms would start to feel cramped. He'd have to find a place to live soon before he developed claustrophobia.

In the tiny alcove kitchenette, he opened the small fridge and pulled out a can of cola. Who was he kidding? This restlessness he felt had nothing to do with him and everything to do with Wreath. He couldn't get her off his mind. It broke his heart to hear her say she no longer believed in love. If Jack were here, he'd punch Jack's lights out. Jack had not only broken her heart and left her humiliated at the altar, but he'd stolen her dreams. His callous treatment had caused Wreath to lock away her heart. Now she lived through her clients, the brides who dreamed of a fantasy wedding, and giving them the dream she'd been denied.

He wanted a second chance to win her heart, but first he had to get around her barriers. Had to find a stronger reason for her to agree to spend time with him. He wanted to restore her belief in romance. He stretched out on the sofa. Maybe there was a way to give it to her as a Christmas gift. And maybe he could convince Wreath Anderson that there was a man in her life who would cherish her and promise her romance every day of her life. That was his dream. But first he had to get her to see him as a man and not a good friend. He'd set his plan into motion first thing tomorrow.

❧

Wreath pulled into the Monmouth parking lot the next day at the same time as Grace Donovan. The weather had turned warm again, at least for the next few days. The forecast for the month of December called for above-average temperatures and little rain, a blessing Wreath was grateful for. More than anything she wanted Grace and Brian's wedding day to be as perfect as she could possibly make it.

Grace waited on the sidewalk, her ever-present smile brightening her face. "You'll be happy to know that I've decided to follow your suggestions on the placement of the cakes. The wedding cake will be in the front parlor under that gorgeous Waterford chandelier, and the groom's cake will be in the back parlor."

"Wonderful. Have you decided where you want to hold your ceremony?"

She nodded, taking Wreath's arm and starting across the

brick courtyard. "The pergola. I can see it draped with winter greenery and lights, Christmas bows maybe, or ornaments. What do you think?"

Wreath's heart squeezed inside her chest. She hadn't realized she'd stopped walking until Grace turned and stared at her.

"Wreath, is something wrong?"

Forcing a smile she didn't feel, she moved forward, trying to wipe away the mental image of the pergola at Monmouth in the height of spring, thick with lavender wisteria, white tulle, and large white wreaths. The gardens bursting with pink azaleas. "No. I'm fine."

Grace reached out and touched her arm. "No you're not. I've seen that look on your face before, and it's usually when I'm making a decision about this ceremony. What is it? You can tell me. Am I doing something to upset you?"

A rush of shame and regret washed through her. "Oh no, Grace. It's not you. It's just that—well, I didn't want to say anything, but maybe it's time I explained. I held my wedding here six years ago. It was an antebellum theme like yours, and we staged the ceremony at the pergola."

Grace stared at her intently a long moment. "I thought you said you were single. What happened?"

Wreath wrapped her arms at her waist, wondering if the words would ever be easier to say. "The groom never showed up."

The look of horror on Grace's face brought tears to Wreath's eyes. She blinked, hoping to chase them away but failing. "I'm sorry. I never meant to tell you."

"Oh, Wreath." Grace pulled her into a tight hug. "You

should have. I could have chosen a different theme. We still can. I don't want to cause you any pain."

"Nonsense. This is your wedding. I'm being silly. It's just bringing up old memories, and then when Micah showed up. . ."

"Micah?"

"The new manager here."

As if on cue, Micah stepped from the office and joined them in the courtyard. Wreath quickly composed herself and smiled. He looked handsome as ever in his dark suit, crisp white shirt, and patterned tie. But he'd looked better last night in the casual sweater and slacks. "Good morning. Micah, I'd like you to meet Grace Donovan. Grace, this is Micah Broussard, the new innkeeper of Monmouth. Grace and Brian are the couple I told you about with the big Christmas wedding."

Micah shook Grace's hand. "Donovan. Yes, of course. We're pleased to be hosting your special event here at Monmouth. Please don't hesitate to call me with any questions or concerns, though I know Wreath will do a great job coordinating your wedding."

He chatted a few moments and moved on. Wreath watched him go then turned back to Grace, who was staring at her intently.

"Is he the guy? The former fiancé?"

"No. Micah is. . .an old friend. He's a good man. He'd never do something like leaving his bride at the altar." The truth of her words resonated someplace deep in her heart.

Grace glanced over her shoulder toward Micah, who was stepping into the main house. "Friends? Really?"

"Yes. Why?"

"Because the way he looked at you had nothing to do with friendship."

"No really. We're just friends."

Grace arched an eyebrow and grinned. "Brian and I were close friends in the beginning, too. And look where it led us." She turned and sauntered off, leaving Wreath with an uneasy sensation in her stomach.

A short while later, Wreath was in the garden room, a generous structure situated away from the main house, which hosted breakfast each morning and also served as a reception and dinner venue. The covered and heated patio allowed for events in any type of weather. Grace and Brian would be having their formal wedding dinner in this space. Micah came in, a smile on his face, and strolled toward her. "Still hard at work, I see."

She nodded to acknowledge his presence but didn't look at him. "The father of the bride added more guests. I have to find a way to squeeze in one more table."

"Anything I can do to make it work?"

Wreath laughed and held her arms straight out in front of her, toward the far wall. "If you could just push the kitchen back about ten or twelve feet. Thanks."

"I would if I could."

"It'll be fine." She smiled over her shoulder at him only to be caught in his blue gaze. There was a warmth, an affection there that made her heart skip a beat. Grace had suggested that there was something more than friendship in his eyes. Wreath had dismissed it, but now a rush of warmth forced her to look away.

He came closer, crossing his arm over his chest, drawing attention to his well-developed biceps under the knit shirt he now wore. He'd changed from the suit and tie to comfortable jeans and shirt. No matter how he was dressed, Micah always looked at ease, confident. It was a very appealing quality.

"I drove by your business yesterday. It's an incredible old church. No wonder you enjoy your work."

"Thank you."

"Speaking of church, I need to find one to attend. Any suggestions?"

"I go to Peace Community. I think you'll like it. The members are very active in the community. We have a singles group, and of course the choir. We're preparing for our Christmas cantata."

"So you still sing. Maybe I'll come and watch you perform." Micah cleared his throat. "Which brings up another topic. Christmas. I was wondering if I could impose on you for a favor."

"If I can."

"I realized it would be helpful if someone could give me a better understanding of the city, not just the restaurants and shops, but the things that make Natchez unique. Particularly the holiday celebrations."

"You mean like a tour guide?"

"In a manner of speaking. I've spent time studying the history of Monmouth and of Natchez, but what I need now is a boots-on-the-ground kind of exposure. If one of my guests asks about a special event, I prefer to know about it firsthand."

"What would you like to see?"

"Everything. Especially the romantic stuff."

Wreath frowned. "Why?"

"As you pointed out, Monmouth was voted one of the most romantic destinations in the South. How can I be an effective manager without knowing firsthand what makes it so romantic?"

He had a point, but she wasn't sure she wanted to be part of his romantic discoveries. "I don't know, Micah. I'm really busy right now. I'm sure Helen could give you a list of Christmas events and you could check them out in your free time."

The smile on his face faded. He let his hands fall to his sides and nodded. "Sure. I understand. Helen can tell me what I should see. Well, I'd better get back to work. You know where to find me if you need anything." He turned and walked out, and Wreath had the oddest feeling she'd hurt him somehow. She didn't like the idea of hurting him.

Chapter 5

The disappointment on Micah's face when she'd brushed off his request had nagged at Wreath's mind all evening. She wasn't sure why she'd turned him down. She was the perfect person to show him the ropes and acquaint him with the city. So why was she so reluctant to spend time with him? It had been several years since she'd taken in the holiday events. She was usually too busy, and with no one special in her life, taking a romantic carriage ride seemed pointless.

She picked up her soup bowl and carried it to the sink, rinsing it before placing it in the dishwater. A quick wipe of the counter and table tidied up the kitchen, and she moved to the living room to curl up with a book. An envelope on her desk caught her eye as she passed by.

The gala at Longwood.

She pulled two tickets from the formal invitation. It was one of the social events of the year. Many of the influential citizens of Natchez, the founding families, and garden club members would be there. The tickets had been given to her by the mother of one of her brides. She'd had no intention of attending, but now she wondered if it might not be a good way to apologize to Micah and at the same time introduce him to the social hierarchy of Natchez.

She remembered Micah's regret at introducing her to Jack, his lingering sense of responsibility for not warning her of what kind of man Jack was. It wasn't his fault. It never had been. She'd made the choice, and it was time to stop using Micah as an excuse for her own stupidity. Maybe showing him around Natchez would be a way to make amends.

She picked up the phone and called Monmouth.

Wreath tugged at the off-the-shoulder sleeves of her black dress again and smoothed down the body-skimming skirt. She shouldn't be this nervous. She'd been to numerous gala events in Natchez, both as a businesswoman and as the event planner. But this was different. This time she would be a guest with a handsome man at her side, the closest thing to a date she'd had in a while.

Being around Micah had dredged up deeper pain from her failed wedding—much more than Grace's theme had done. But his presence had also brought other memories to the surface, things about Micah she'd forgotten, like how sweet and thoughtful he was, what a strong Christian he was. Micah had been attentive, fun, and dependable. He'd possessed all the qualities she admired in a man. And then Jack had swept her off her feet.

The doorbell chimed, and she inhaled a deep breath to calm her nerves. This was so silly. It wasn't a real date. Simply an evening with an old friend. She opened the door and caught her breath. Micah stood tall and handsome in his dark suit. The expertly cut jacket draped his broad shoulders to perfection, and the appreciative gleam in his blue eyes sent her heart racing.

He looked her up and down, emitting a slow, soft whistle. "You look amazing. I'm not sure I should take you out in public looking like you do."

She smiled, cheeks flaming. She wasn't used to such blatant compliments. "It's just a simple black dress."

Micah shook his head and took her hand. "Oh no. There's nothing simple about that dress or you."

She pulled her hand away, struggling to find something to say. "I guess we'd better go or we'll be late. I have a lot of people I want you to meet."

An impish grin hooked one corner of his mouth. "I've met the only person I'm interested in."

Wreath's thoughts were so befuddled by Micah's admiration that she babbled like a schoolgirl the whole way to Longwood Plantation. Thankfully he didn't stop her; he merely smiled his make-your-knees-weak grin, as if he were enchanted with every word she said. Ensconced in his luxurious car, she allowed herself to enjoy the sensations. Dressed up, beside a handsome man, on the way to a gala event. It felt nice to be seen as an attractive woman, not just the person in charge with all the answers. Tonight she was the princess in the beautiful carriage, and her only objective was to have fun and introduce Micah to everyone.

The evening passed like a scene from a fairy tale. The

stately old home was resplendent in its holiday decorations, the perfect setting for the guests in all their glittering finery. Wreath knew many of those attending and introduced Micah. It didn't take long to realize that he was completely comfortable in this type of social setting. Warm, friendly, gracious, and charming, he never failed to include her in any conversations, keeping one hand on her back or arm, possessively. To her surprise, she liked the attention.

Jack had never mastered the niceties of dating. She'd never felt like she had his full attention. She couldn't remember one special event, one elegant dinner they'd shared. They'd spent most of the time at parties with his friends or at ball games. That should have given her a clue to their future.

As the evening wore down, Micah leaned toward her, resting his arm across the back of her chair. "Are you ready to slip out?"

She nodded, picking up her wrap and small beaded purse. After a quick good-bye to the hosts, they stepped outside. Wreath took Micah's hand. "Let's walk around to the front. I want to see the lights. This is one of the most beautifully decorated homes at Christmas."

Micah fell into step beside her as they followed the sidewalk around to the front entrance, stopping out away from the massive home for a better view. Unlike the Greek Revival style so associated with antebellum Southern homes, Longwood was an octagonal, Oriental Revival style. Five stories tall, the pinnacle boasted a large Byzantine-style dome. Christmas lights draped the Moorish arches along the front galleries, casting a warm glow over the grass and the nearby trees.

"Isn't it lovely?"

Micah slipped his arm around her waist. "Everything about tonight was lovely. Thank you for inviting me."

"You're welcome. I'm looking forward to showing you more Christmas events. Though I don't know how many we'll be able to fit in with our crazy schedules."

"We'll work it out."

Wreath looked up at him. He was gazing at the lights. His profile, outlined by the faint glow, reflected the man he was inside. The strong jaw, the straight nose and firm lips. He was a nice man, a special man. She'd been developing strong feelings for him when they were dating, until she'd gotten distracted by Jack, the dangerous bad boy she could save and tame. Jack had fit her romantic ideals. But Micah was a forever kind of man.

"Micah, why haven't you married? I can't believe some woman hasn't grabbed you up. You're a great catch."

An odd expression crossed his face when he turned to look at her. "There was a woman once. But she met someone else and walked away."

Her heart went out to him. He was too wonderful a man to be treated so cruelly. "She must have been blind."

"No. Just blinded by love."

Settled in the car once more, Wreath leaned back in the seat, content in the warm afterglow of the evening. She'd never enjoyed an evening more, and it was all because of Micah. She smiled as they drove along the winding driveway and under the lights draped between the trees overhead. The perfect end to a perfect evening.

The only sour note was learning that someone had broken Micah's heart. The woman obviously hadn't understood what a gem she had or she never would have cast him aside. A twinge of sadness settled in her heart as they pulled into her drive. She didn't want the evening to end. Ever the gentleman, Micah helped her out of the car and walked her to the door.

"I had a great time tonight, Wreath. I was the envy of every man there. You looked amazing."

She unlocked her door and pushed it open then turned to face him again. "I saw quite a few females giving you the eye, too. I don't think you'll have any trouble meeting new friends in Natchez."

"I already have a friend." He leaned down, his gaze locked with hers. She thought he was going to kiss her and she braced. But his lips touched her forehead, his hand resting briefly against the side of her face. "Sleep tight. I'll see you soon."

Watching him walk away left an empty spot in her chest. It couldn't be disappointment that he hadn't kissed her. It had to be her lingering sadness that the woman he'd loved had thrown him over for someone else. "Micah. I'm sorry you were hurt the way I was. I would never do that to you."

Micah stared at the ground a moment, slipping his hands into his pockets. "But you did, Wreath."

He turned and walked to his car as Wreath struggled to grasp what he'd said. The truth hit her with the force of a blow. She stumbled inside her townhouse and leaned back against the door as waves of shock washed through her. Nausea swirled in her stomach at her callousness. She'd dumped Micah without a second thought once she'd met

Jack. The same way Jack had left her for someone else the day of their wedding. No explanation. No apology. Just turned and walked away.

How could she have been so cruel? So thoughtless? It wasn't in her nature to willingly hurt people. Especially someone she'd liked as much as Micah. Wiping tears from her eyes, she took off her little black dress and prepared for bed, remorse settling like a stone in her stomach.

Wreath knew all too well the sting of rejection. The lingering questions, the deep need for some reason to justify the actions. She couldn't let Micah endure that kind of pain. She'd go to him tomorrow, ask his forgiveness, and explain everything.

She climbed into bed, tugged up the covers, and curled into a ball. Provided he'd even speak to her, let alone listen. For the first time, she allowed her long buried anger at Jack to surface. Not only had he shredded her heart, but he'd caused her to hurt someone she cared about. No it wasn't Jack's fault. It was hers. Jack may have walked out on her, but she had to take responsibility for hurting Micah. Her obsession with Jack had blinded her to everything and everyone else. How had she ever thought she loved him? A new thought rose to plague her as she teetered on the edge of sleep. If Micah had been hurt by her rejection, did that mean he'd been in love with her back then? And what about now? Why was he being kind to her? Was it possible he still cared?

❧

The small bag of round peppermint candies clutched in Wreath's hand felt like a lead weight. Her nerves were throbbing, her throat tightening, and her heartbeat erratic. She stood outside Micah's office door praying for courage to face him. After what she'd learned last night, she doubted he'd even speak to her, but she had to try, because she couldn't let him endure the same nagging questions she had for the last six years.

She stepped to the door and raised her hand to knock. All he could do was order her out of his life, which is what she deserved. The door suddenly opened and she found herself face-to-face with Micah. He had a warm smile on his face.

"Good morning. Helen told me you were on your way up. Come on in."

She walked past him, catching the scent of peppermint on his breath. She turned and held up her gift. "I brought you some candy."

"Thanks. I'm almost out." He gestured toward the jar on his desk, which held only a few pieces of the sweet. "What's the occasion?" He shut the door and motioned her to be seated.

"It's sort of an apology. For the past. I mean for what I did." She took a deep breath and started again. "I never meant to hurt you, Micah. Please believe me."

He laid the candy on his desk and sat down beside her. "I know that, Wreath. It's not in your nature."

"But I did, and I'm so sorry. You must hate me."

"I could never hate you."

"But you should. You should be furious. Why are you being so nice about this?"

"Because your happiness was more important to me than

my own. I was in—I cared about you. I still do."

Tears threatened to spill over, and she blinked them away. "Please forgive me."

"I already did." He took her hands in his. "Don't worry about that. It's over and done with and I survived. Just like you did. So are we still going to the Jeweled Christmas thing this evening? I'm trying to picture a tree decorated with jewelry instead of ornaments."

"You still want to go?"

"Of course." He held up the bag of candy. "We've made up. We'll check it out then have a bite to eat."

"It closes early, so we'd better go there first. I'll take you to the Cotton Alley Café afterward. You'll love it."

Micah smiled. "Sounds good. Do you want me to pick you up or meet me here?"

"Here. I have an appointment late this afternoon."

He stood and walked her to the door. "See you then. And thanks for the candy."

❧

Wreath stared out her office window, her chin resting on her hand. Micah had come to her cantata last night. She wasn't sure why that pleased her so much. Over the last ten days, they'd seen a great deal of each other between their hectic schedules. She'd shown him the Jeweled Christmas at the Towers, they'd taken in the arts and crafts fair downtown, and they'd attended the special production of *A Natchez Christmas Carol*. They'd even started searching out apartments for Micah. But nothing had given her as much joy as looking out into the congregation and seeing Micah sitting there while the choir presented their music. Having a friend to share the event had touched her deeply.

"Good afternoon. Hope I'm not too early."

Wreath glanced up as Grace Donovan walked into her office. "Not at all. I'll be right with you. I have a few entries to make for another bride. It'll only take a minute."

"No hurry." Grace sat. "How are things with you and the hunky manager?"

"What do you mean?"

"Are you still taking in all the Christmas events?"

"Yes." Wreath leaned back in her chair. "It's been fun. Micah is a great guy."

"How did you two meet?"

"We worked together and became friends. We had a lot in common, and it developed from there."

"That's how it happened with me and Brian. He started attending my church, and we became good friends. Then we both went to college at Belhaven in Jackson. Over time we realized that we had deeper feelings. But it started as a friendship. I think that's the key to a lasting relationship. Wouldn't you agree?"

"I suppose so." Grace's words had unleashed something inside her she didn't have time to examine right now. "Well, if you're going to learn to maneuver in this hoopskirt, we need to practice. Follow me. I have two styles for you to choose from."

In the large fitting room at the back of the shop, Wreath pulled out the two hoopskirts. "This one is the old-fashioned style. It's made from wire and it's rigid, meaning you'll have to learn to maneuver around in it the same way women did during the antebellum era. This one is a new version, made with flexible stays, and it will collapse and allow you to move and sit normally yet still maintain its shape when you're standing."

Grace examined the two hoops, bending and handling them. "Which would you suggest?"

"It's all up to you. It's your day. You can have whichever you want."

Grace stopped and turned to her, a thoughtful expression on her face. "I always thought that was wrong somehow. Should it really be all about the bride, like she's some princess who doesn't have to consider anyone else's thoughts or desires? I mean, shouldn't a wedding be about me and Brian? Not about the prettiest dress or the most extravagant decorations."

"I guess I never thought about it that way. Brides are my business, and they all want the day to be the most special and memorable day of their lives."

Grace nodded. "But what about the groom? He's shoved to the back and only comes out on the day of the wedding to play his part. That seems so sad to me. I want Brian to be part of things. I've seen my friends turn into. . ."

"Bridezillas?"

"Yes, and I hate that term. Brian and I agreed from the start that we'd decide as much of the wedding together as possible. He's my best friend. His opinion matters. I want to share everything with him." Grace reached out and held up the traditional hoopskirt. "Let's start with this one."

Wreath helped her into the wired contraption, which she

wore over her jeans. Grace laughed at the odd picture she made. Wreath led her out into the open area that had once been the fellowship hall. "First take time to walk around and get the feel of the volume of the hoop."

"Oh my." Grace walked the length of the room, setting the hooped cage swaying.

Wreath laughed. "It helps to walk slowly. But it'll be heavier once you have the dress over the hoop. Now come and sit on the chair. You'll have to lift the back of the skirt, but not too far, and then sit, letting the hoop collapse behind you."

It took Grace a few tries to get the hang of it. "I do like the idea of a real old-fashioned hoopskirt, but I think the newer hoop would be the best option."

"What is that thing you've got on?"

The women looked up to see Brian entering the hall, a bemused expression on his face.

Grace went to meet him, the hoop swaying back and forth as she moved. "Now that you're here, we can practice together." She took her groom's hand and pulled him toward Wreath, battling the hoop the entire way.

"I'm glad you're here Brian. You'll need a few lessons, too."

"What kind of lessons?"

"How to walk beside your bride, for one thing." Wreath positioned them side-by-side with Brian slightly in front of Grace. "If you walk a little ahead of her, you won't get tangled in the skirt." She watched as they mastered the walk. "Good. But it's a bit trickier when you dance."

"Am I interrupting?"

Wreath looked over at Micah as he entered the hall, unable to keep the smile from her face and the flutter from her heart. "Not at all. You're just in time to watch the bride and groom attempt their first dance in a hoopskirt." Micah came to her side, greeting Brian and Grace, then standing aside to watch.

"Okay, Brian, take Grace in your arms." The moment Brian pulled her close, the skirt swooshed up and out behind Grace, bringing chuckles from everyone.

"Oh man. What did I do?"

Wreath shook her head. "Exactly what you would normally do. But with your bride in one of these hoops, you have to keep your bride at arm's length so the skirt won't rise up in the back."

Brian frowned. "I don't think I like that. I want to hold you close. Not two feet away."

Grace slipped her arm around Brian. "I agree. Wreath, let's go with the new hoop. I don't want tradition getting in the way of my first dance with Brian. Come on, sweetie, help me out of this contraption."

Micah smiled and came to Wreath's side. "Nice couple. I can see why you've enjoyed working with them."

"I have. You're early."

"I can leave and come back."

"Don't be silly."

"You know, I never got to dance with you in your hoopskirt." He pulled her into his arms. "One of my greatest regrets."

Wreath melted against him, enjoying the strength of his

embrace and the sense of safety she felt in his arms. But she pulled away as Grace and Brian returned. Her feelings for Micah were so confused. She needed more time to sort them out.

After saying good-bye to the bride and groom, Wreath turned to Micah. He had moved to one of the large mullioned windows. "Beautiful, isn't it?"

"Yes it is."

"Would you like the grand tour?" Micah followed her through the old building asking questions, admiring the architecture, and complimenting her on her success. Wreath ended the tour in the back hall. "That's everything."

Micah pointed over her shoulder. "Do you sell wedding gowns here, too?"

She'd forgotten the rack of bride's gowns that needed to be stored. "Oh no. Those are gowns for my Bride's Closet. I have a small ministry that offers gowns to brides who can't afford to buy their own."

"So you give them away?"

"Sometimes, but mostly I offer them at a very low price, either to sell or to rent. Our church has a Career Closet, where we collect business attire to help women reentering the work force. Finding employment is hard enough, but the added expense of buying an appropriate wardrobe can be an obstacle. The Bride's Closet grew out of that."

"Where do you get all these gowns?"

"Donations mainly. Sometimes I find them at thrift shops or online." Micah looked at her intently, making her uneasy. "I just think every bride should have the opportunity to wear a lovely gown."

Micah smiled, taking a step closer. "You never cease to amaze me."

He cradled her face in his hands, tilting his head to one side and kissing her. It was a light, tentative kiss, but it sent a tremor of awareness deep into her core. Before she could fully grasp what had happened, he pulled back, his blue eyes dark and narrowed. He extended his hand.

"Come on. I have a surprise for you. Get your coat."

Quickly Wreath closed up the shop and took Micah's hand as they went down the steps and into the parking lot. She stopped in her tracks at the sight of a white horse-drawn carriage waiting patiently near the curb.

"What's this?"

"Your personal tour of the Christmas lights."

"Oh, Micah. Do you know I've never taken a carriage ride in all the time I've lived in Natchez?"

"Then I'm honored to be the first to grant you that pleasure." He helped her into the coach, settling her in under a soft blanket to ward off the evening chill. "I've brought you hot chocolate, too." He held up a thermos and two cups. "We can ride all night if you'd like."

Wreath snuggled in, letting the warmth of the blanket and the warmth of the man beside her fill her with a contentment she'd never known. "This is a wonderful idea. Thank you, Micah."

They rode slowly throughout the city, from Dunleith on the south side of town to Linden Avenue, with its row of Victorian homes. They passed by the Wedding Wreath shop on their way to the north side of town, and Wreath shared

Grace's opinion about brides.

Micah nodded. "I have to admit, the whole bride-as-queen thing always bothered me. As if she were the only one that mattered."

"I suppose it seems that way. It's just that the decisions being made are all things the bride is more comfortable with. Flowers, colors, decorations."

"What about afterward?"

"You mean the honeymoon?"

"I mean the day after the honeymoon when all the attention is over, the fantasy is gone, and they have to wake up each morning to the real world."

"Every couple has an adjustment period."

"But shouldn't a couple spend at least as much time on planning their marriage, something that will last for a lifetime, as they do on a ceremony that will last a few hours?"

"They do. It's called the courtship."

Micah shook his head. "No, that's the time when they're both on their best behavior. Not a true picture at all."

Wreath remembered when she was dating Jack. He'd been so fun, exciting. He'd kept her heart racing and her emotions in turmoil with his volatile personality. He hadn't given her a true picture of himself. She tried to wipe Jack's sudden image from her mind. The dark brown eyes, the cocky smile, the way he always stood with one hip listing to the side as if he owned the world. She didn't think of him often, but there were times when she wondered about him. Still wanted some kind of answer, some explanation for walking away.

Wreath hated for the evening to end, but work loomed for

both of them the next morning. After dismissing the carriage driver, Micah walked her to her car. "Thank you again. It was a wonderful evening. You're a good friend." She smiled up into his eyes, her heart catching between beats. The look in his eyes was the same one she'd seen before he'd kissed her earlier.

"Good night. Be careful driving home. I don't want anything to happen to you." He dipped his head, kissed her lips again in a soft, brief touch, then turned and walked to his car.

She watched him leave, wishing he'd kissed her for real. Silly idea.

Chapter 6

Grace Donovan's car was sitting in the parking lot when Wreath arrived at the shop the next morning. Mentally she ran down her schedule, searching for an appointment she might have missed, only to come up empty. That usually indicated one thing. A problem had cropped up that had to be dealt with immediately.

She jogged up the steps, hurried inside, and stopped at Bonnie's desk. "What happened? Where's Grace?" The bright smile on her friend's face wasn't what she'd expected to see.

"Grace has a surprise for you. She said it had to be done in person. She's waiting in your office."

Puzzled, Wreath hurried through the hall and into her office. "Grace. Bonnie said you wanted to see me?"

"Hello. Yes. I have something to show you." She took the lid off a florist's box. "I didn't tell you about this because I wanted it to be a surprise. I picked up the sample bridesmaid's bouquet this morning." Grace lifted out the twelve-inch floral arrangement and held it up.

"Oh Grace." The bouquet, a white wreath wrapped in delicate white tulle, with miniature white roses and sprigs of berries and greenery, made her gasp, and she touched her fingers to her lips. It was nearly identical to the bouquet her bridesmaids had carried, right down to the satin bow and the crystal beads. Her heart squeezed in an odd combination of sadness and appreciation. "It's beautiful."

"Won't these look stunning against their red dresses?"

"Gorgeous."

Grace stood and handed the bouquet to Wreath. "This one is for you. A thank-you for all your hard work and your friendship. Maybe you can hang it here at the shop or in your home." Grace gave her a big hug then picked up her purse and the thick notepad she always had with her.

"I'm touched, Grace. Thank you." Wreath smiled and gestured at the pad. "Still making changes? You don't have much time left, you know."

"This? Oh no. That's my love list."

"What?"

"My list of all the things I know and love about Brian and all the things we have in common. I add to it whenever I think of something new."

Wreath gently placed the floral wreath back in the box. "If you know them, why are you writing them down?"

"I intend to refer to this list frequently to help me remember what's really important in our marriage and why I fell in love with him."

Grace's open devotion and commitment to her groom

were inspiring. "Brian is a lucky guy."

"No. We're both blessed. That's why the Lord will be the most important guest at our wedding."

Chapter 7

Wreath, with Micah beside her, strolled the pebbled walking path on the grounds of Monmouth, now transformed into a sparkling garden of Christmas lights, and drank in the sight. The pergola, the arched bridge over the pond, every edifice gleamed with light, all symbolizing the night the Light of the World came to earth. Emmanuel. God with us.

Wreath had never thought about inviting God to her wedding. Grace's simple statement had lingered in her thoughts, like a pushpin holding an important reminder. If she had included the Lord in her wedding plans, would they have turned out differently? No. She and Jack were all wrong for each other. She knew now that she could never spend her life with a man who didn't love the Lord.

"You're awfully quiet tonight. Is everything all right?"

Wreath yanked her thoughts back to the man at her side. The weather had stayed warm for the last few days, and Micah had invited her to stroll through the grounds of Monmouth to view the light displays. "Yes. I was just thinking about something Grace shared with me today. She keeps a list of all the things she knows and loves about Brian. She's going to refer to it often to remind herself what's important in their relationship."

"She has a lot of wisdom for someone so young. She's right."

They stopped in the middle of the arched bridge. The lights sparkled, crystalline, on the water's surface in holiday hues. "What do you mean?"

"When you love someone, you want to know all about them. The smallest details become valuable—their favorite foods, favorite color, their dreams for the future. Love is about knowing and understanding. About caring what the other person wants. If a woman knew the important things about me, I'd know she really loved me."

Wreath thought back to those whirlwind months with Jack, trying to find one thing they had in common beyond physical attraction. Her heart clenched when she came up empty-handed. She didn't know Jack's favorite food, his favorite kind of music, or if he wanted children. She closed her eyes. Shame and regret raced along her nerves. She'd spent all her time creating the perfect fantasy wedding and not one second on her life with Jack.

Wreath looked at Micah. What about Micah? He stood now, hands grasping the railing, staring out at the fountain in the center of the pond. What did she remember about him? A kaleidoscope of memories emerged—in Memphis, a trip to the Peabody Hotel to watch the duck parade, an afternoon on Mud Island, and touring an old Victorian home. Weekend picnics, museum visits. She looked at him now, his brow creased in a frown, his jaw clenched, a muscle flexing rapidly. His normally warm blue eyes were a dark navy blue.

"What are you thinking about, Wreath?"

"Nothing." She inhaled a slow breath. "I'm just remembering."

Micah's lips pressed together into a thin line. "Yeah, that's what I thought."

"I was thinking about the day we watched the ducks march into the lobby of the Peabody."

Micah jerked his head up, a look of surprise clouding his eyes. "You remember that?"

She nodded. "I remember a lot of the things we did together. But you know what? I can't remember much of what Jack and I did. I can remember all the planning for the wedding, all the details, and I can remember the moment I realized he wasn't coming to the wedding. I remember wondering what was wrong with me that he'd leave me at the altar."

Micah took her hand in his. "There's nothing wrong with you, Wreath. Jack was the problem, not you."

"I'm beginning to see I never really dealt with that day. I've stuffed it into a box and never looked at it again. It hurt too much."

"But you're looking at it now. Maybe you can finally put it all behind you and look forward. What are your dreams for the future?"

She'd never thought about it. She lived her life from one event to the next. "I don't know."

"Are you content with your career? Is that all you want?"

"No." She tucked her hair behind her ear. "I think I'd like a family someday. Something more than a business to fill my life. What about you? Do you plan on staying in the hotel business?"

Micah smiled and shook his head. "No. I'd like to have my own small hotel someday, a place that would provide a good living but also be a home to raise a family." He leaned against the rail. "I've even toyed with getting into real estate."

Wreath smiled into his eyes, light blue now, reflecting the lights from the bridge. A subtle shift in mood made her aware of the growing attraction between them. He took a step closer, his hand gently brushing a strand of hair off her cheek then coming to rest on the side of her face. His eyes darkened and he tilted his head. He was going to kiss her, there was no doubt, but the thought sent a jolt of fear along her nerves. She backed away, heart pounding. "I'd better be going. I have a busy day tomorrow."

Silently, they strolled back up the sloping steps to the courtyard. Micah walked her to her car. She didn't dare look at him for fear of seeing his expression. He was probably angry, and she couldn't blame him. Wreath replayed their conversation all the way to her townhouse. She and Micah wanted the same things. Why did that scare her so much? And why had she backed away from his kiss when she'd wanted it so badly?

❧

The name on the file held Wreath's full attention. While searching her electronic documents for the folder on a former client, she'd stumbled upon the one that held all the precious details of her antebellum wedding. She'd considered deleting them several times over the years but had been unable to cut that last tie with her dream. Somewhere there was also a folder of pictures she'd never deleted. She'd put that at the top of her list to do right after the holidays. She clicked on her e-mails and responded to the first three. The next one stopped her heart. It was from Micah.

She didn't want to open it. The moment on the bridge last night when he'd almost kissed her had kept her up all night wondering why she'd pulled away when all she wanted was to step into his embrace and feel his arms around her. Until that moment, she'd not realized how deep her fear of romantic involvement actually was. Micah was a wonderful man, a sweet man, a man of character. Honorable and dependable. All the things she claimed to want. He'd made no secret that he wanted to spend time with her, that he was attracted to her, so why couldn't she let go of the fear?

With a deep breath, she placed her cursor on his e-mail, jumping when her cell tone shattered the silence in her office. Grace's name appeared on the screen. "Good morning. You're up early. I don't usually hear from you until after 10 a.m."

"Oh, Wreath, it's ruined. What am I going to do?"

Grace's deep sobs sent a surge of alarm down Wreath's spine. Her first thought was always the same when a bride called in a fit of hysterics. The groom had backed out at the last minute. She knew it was her own deep fears at work, and the truth was that not one of her brides had suffered that fate, but the thought rose up nonetheless. "Calm down, Grace, and tell me what happened. Whatever it is, we can fix it, I promise."

"No, you can't. There's not enough time. It's only a week until the wedding. I'll never find another one like this and get it altered. It was a one-of-a-kind designed for me."

Wreath clutched her phone closer, as if she could offer comfort through the connection. "Grace, is it your dress? What happened?"

"I got a call from the bridal shop this morning. She said there'd been a small fire in the back room where she stores the completed gowns, and four of the dresses were destroyed. Mine was one of them. Wreath, what am I going to do?"

Wreath's heart pinched tight in her chest. Nothing, short of being left at the altar, was as traumatic for a bride. "We'll think of something."

"But what? If it was just a regular wedding, I could find something else. I'm not that picky about the dress. But this has to be an antebellum gown, hooped skirt, historic design. I can't just walk in a store and buy another one."

"No, but we might be able to rent one." Another idea surfaced, one that left a fruitcake-sized knot in her chest. She'd consider it only as a last resort. "Grace, just sit tight and try not to worry. Let me make some calls and see what I can come up with. I'll call you back around noon, and we'll see where we are."

Bonnie stood at the desk waiting expectantly. "Was that a panicked bride I heard you talking to? What's wrong now? Wrong napkins? The candles aren't white enough?"

Wreath shook her head. "That was Grace. Her gown was destroyed last night in a fire at the bridal shop."

"Oh no. Bless her heart. How awful. This is a first for us.

Where do you want to start?"

"You start with local vendors, here and in Vicksburg, then try Jackson and Baton Rouge." She stood and glanced toward the storeroom, near the back of the building. "I'm going to check on something first."

The large cool and dry room, once a classroom in the old church, now stored oversized linens, delicate arrangements, and one very beautiful, very gently used antebellum wedding gown. Her heart pounding against her ribs, she pulled open the doors to the cabinet. Once a year she had it cleaned and then gently placed it back in the closet. She wasn't sure why, other than it had been her ultimate fantasy dress—designed in her imagination when she was twelve. Too precious a part of her dream to let go of yet too full of painful memories to look at.

Dress bag unzipped, she carefully slipped the bodice of the gown free then tugged out part of the full skirt. It was a beautiful dress. A quintessential antebellum gown. Grace would look perfect in it. But giving it to someone else wrenched her heart. She'd always believed, somewhere deep inside, she'd wear it someday. But now, looking at it, she realized it was all wrong for the woman she was today. If she were getting married today, she'd wear something sleek, simple, grown up, not a fairytale princess gown better suited for a Cinderella than a successful businesswoman.

"I thought I'd find you here." Bonnie came and stopped at her side. "Are you going to offer it to her?"

"I don't know."

"Wreath, don't you think it's time you stopped holding

on to the past and step into the future?"

"What are you talking about?"

Bonnie grabbed a small piece of the skirt and shook it. "This. Hanging on to that dress, the big vision of your perfect day. Let it go. You have so many more things to look forward to. And in the meantime, you're missing someone right under your nose who would sweep you off your feet if you'd give him half a chance."

Wreath shook her head. "You're not making any sense."

"Micah. In case you haven't noticed, he's got it bad for you. And he's a great guy. Handsome, successful, kind, thoughtful, and dependable. Yet you treat him as if he's just some ordinary Joe not worthy of your attention."

Wreath gently tucked the skirt back inside the bag. What would her friend say if she told her that falling in love with Micah was not only possible but probable? Trouble was she didn't know if it was love or just deep appreciation. "I know Micah is a great guy, Bonnie. It's just that he was buddies with Jack, he introduced us, and I'm not sure I feel the same way about him that I did when I was marrying Jack."

"Are you saying you're in love with Micah?"

"Maybe, I don't know."

"Well, when will you know?"

"Bonnie, you can't put a schedule on something like that."

"And you can't wait for some magical emotion to appear either. You need to sit down and start a list of the things you want in a husband then see how many of those things Micah satisfies. Write down all the things you know and love about him. Take a good hard look, because I think you're so blinded by your fantasy about Jack and that stupid wedding that you can't see what's right in front of your face." Bonnie took a deep breath. "Has he kissed you yet?"

Wreath turned away, rubbing her forehead. "Sort of."

"Sort of? Friend, when a man like that kisses a woman, there shouldn't be any questions left behind."

"Yes, he kissed me. But it was just a peck, the kiss of a friend."

"Did you kiss him back?"

Wreath shrugged. "Sort of."

"Oh good grief." Bonnie crossed her arms and glared. "Maybe the man is waiting for some signal, some sign from you on how you feel. A gentleman like Micah isn't going to push his attention on someone who isn't interested. Are you interested?"

"I don't know."

"Well you'd better find out, because you're going to lose that guy, and you'll regret it for the rest of your life."

Bonnie stormed off, leaving Wreath with a sinking feeling in her chest and a flood of unshed tears welling up behind her eyes.

Chapter 8

Wreath turned her attention back to the wedding gown. She and Bonnie never disagreed. They saw eye to eye on everything. Her idea had some merit, but she didn't have time to devote to listing Micah's good points right now.

But Bonnie was right about one thing. It was time to let go of the fantasy surrounding this dress. She'd grown and moved on. She picked up her cell and dialed Grace's number, surprised that her decision didn't hurt as much as she'd expected it to.

Within ten minutes, Grace was at the shop bubbling over with joy. "Oh, Wreath, it's more beautiful than anything I had ever imagined. But are you sure you want to loan it to me? I mean someday you'll want to wear it again."

Seeing Grace's delight in the dress dispelled any lingering doubts in Wreath's mind. "I'm sure. I think it should fit you, too. We're not that different in size. I've already talked to a seamstress I know who'll be able to alter it in plenty of time."

Grace touched the skirt gently then moved to give Wreath

a hug. "I'm so sorry for what you went through, but I think it might have been a blessing." She pulled back and looked her in the eyes. "Wreath, you could have made a huge mistake. He wasn't the one for you. Praise God, He saved you from that."

"I suppose. I hadn't thought about it like that."

"How else could you think of it, once the shock wore off, I mean? The man must have been a self-centered jerk or worse."

"He was, but he was exciting and handsome and—slightly dangerous." How could she explain what Jack had done for her, the way he'd made her feel like every moment was a thrill?

Grace went still, and Wreath looked at her. There was a puzzled and sad expression on her face. "Wreath, why have you saved this dress for so long?"

"I guess it was a reminder of my dream. My fantasy wedding. My Prince Charming. Silly, huh?"

"Extremely."

That's not what she'd expected Grace to say. "Excuse me?" How dare she trample on her dreams.

"Wreath, that sense of excitement and danger, that's not love. Those feelings only last a short while. They're the kind of feelings we have when we're young and foolish, when we think love is supposed to be a never-ending surge of emotions." Grace took her hand. "Love is deeper than that. It's two people who care about each other, who want what's best for the other and are willing to make sacrifices to ensure it happens. Marriage isn't a thrill ride, Wreath. It's a long up-and-down road. Even the vows remind a couple that there are troubles ahead. 'For richer, for poorer.' 'In sickness and in health.' "

"But how do you know he's the one?"

Grace squeezed her hands. "He should make you feel content, special. Someone who listens, who enjoys just watching you. Someone who, when you place your hand in his, you know you're safe, cherished, and protected."

With every word Grace spoke, one face came to mind. Micah's. Micah listening to her stories about brides, knowing he could care less. Micah drawing her out into the world again with his Christmas adventures. Micah always keeping his promises, always being there, always standing behind her.

The feelings she had for Micah were different from those she'd felt for Jack, so she'd dismissed them as mere friendship. But what if she'd been so busy looking for excitement that she'd mistaken her feelings for something else? Micah had carved out a place in her heart. But was it love? Micah had asked her about the day after the honeymoon, when the fantasy was over and real life began. Who would she want to spend her life with, wake up to every morning, find comfort and contentment in each night? Only one name came to mind. His.

❦

Wreath entered the old sanctuary and stopped at the west-facing windows. The late afternoon sunlight filtered through the stained glass, sending ribbons of color spilling across the worn wooden floor where the pulpit had once stood.

She'd never bothered to ask the Lord what His plans were for her life. Oh, she'd returned to her faith, but this was one stronghold she'd kept jealously guarded. Her shattered fantasy, her dream wedding. She'd held God responsible for that when she should have blamed Jack. Now she saw it for what it was. Her mistake but his decision.

It was time to give up the past. Time to let go of childish dreams and look forward with grown-up, realistic eyes. Closing her eyes, Wreath spread her hands wide, palms up, and invited the Lord to look into her heart and set her free. She allowed her heart to be silent, her mind open to whatever words the Lord had for her. She waited, letting go one at a time of the old chains that had bound her to the past. Her dreams, her expectations, her notions of love.

Slowly, she felt the burden of the past lift away, replaced with a sense of freedom. Peace swirled gently from deep within, bringing with it a new discovery. She loved Micah Broussard.

She smiled, pressing her fingers to her lips. She was starting a new phase in her life, the past having no place any longer. She'd start by getting rid of the things that kept her connected to the past.

In her office, she sat down at the computer and pulled up her document files, selecting the wedding folder she'd foolishly kept. One click sent it to the trash bin. Next, she opened her picture files and clicked on the folder with Jack's pictures. Her screen filled with his image. And for the first time, she didn't see a handsome rogue who'd made her heart beat faster, but the man he really was. A selfish charmer, a man with no regard for others, a man lacking in character. She looked into his eyes and saw no warmth, no compassion, no depth. Another pair of eyes filled her vision. A pair of blue eyes, warm with affection, sparkling with laughter, intense with compassion. Micah's eyes. What a fool she'd been. No better than one of her Bridezillas. So caught up in herself and a meaningless fantasy, she couldn't see the real thing when it came along.

It ended here. She moved her cursor to close out the file. A noise from behind drew her attention. Micah strolled into the room. Before she could speak, his expression hardened. His mouth pulled into a hard line and the muscles in his jaw flexed rapidly. His blue eyes darkened to navy. A shaft of fear shot through her. She followed his gaze and realized he was looking at her computer screen. Jack. She gasped and shook her head. "Micah I was just. . ."

His gaze scorched through her. "Longing for the past?" He shoved his hands into his pockets. "I don't get it. Explain it to me, Wreath."

She stood and took a step forward. "I was just. . ."

"Stop. What is it about the bad boys, the Jacks of the world that you women can't get enough of? They use you, they break your hearts, and you keep coming back for more. You whine and complain that all the good men are taken, but when a decent, God-fearing man stands in front of you with their heart in their hands, you brush them aside in favor of the abuse these jerks can dish out." He took a step forward. "Explain it to me, Wreath. I want to understand."

"Micah I was going to delete them. I didn't understand before, but now—"

Micah took her shoulders in his hands and jerked her close. "Understand this." He pulled her closer, capturing her mouth with his, kissing her with an intensity and passion that stole her breath and left her weak and shaking. He set her away, his blue eyes filled with anger and something else, sadness. She grabbed the desk to keep from falling. Micah took another step back, dragging his hand across his mouth.

"Decide, Wreath. Make up your mind what you want, because I might not be around if you take too long." He turned and stormed out, shutting the door with a loud bang.

Wreath sank into the chair as the tears spilled over. Her gaze landed on the computer screen and the picture of Jack. She deleted the folder with one firm press of a key, wiping his memory from her mind and shedding fresh tears for what her foolishness might have lost.

Chapter 9

Micah unlocked his car and reached for the door handle. His hand shook. Anger surged through him with a force he'd only experienced once before—the day Jack had left Wreath humiliated and heartbroken at the altar. He'd ached to plant a fist in the man's face. He'd done what he could that day, but there'd been nothing he could do to ease Wreath's broken heart. His own had been shredded as well. He'd longed to comfort her but lacked the right. His guilt over not protecting her from his friend had eaten away at him. He learned from his sister that when a woman's heart was involved, there was little anyone could do to change her mind. Love blinded her to the guy's faults. She became an expert at rationalizing his behavior. His sister had come to her senses before the relationship had progressed beyond the engagement. Wreath hadn't been so fortunate.

Micah shut the door and locked the car again. He was in no condition to drive. Maybe a brisk walk would calm him down. He started off down the street. He shouldn't have lost his temper with Wreath. His behavior hadn't earned him any points. Kissing her was the last thing he'd intended to do. He'd wanted to do that since he'd first seen her again, but kissing her in anger wasn't the way he'd wanted to tell her how he felt. Whatever slim chance he had with Wreath had gone up in smoke, but seeing Jack's picture on her computer screen had set off a wave of jealousy and anger that he'd been unable to control.

The Lord had given him a second chance to win her heart, and he'd failed. It was time to accept the inevitable and let her go. He rubbed his forehead, amused at the irony. He'd scolded Wreath for not letting go of her old feelings for Jack, and he was guilty of the same thing. He'd loved Wreath for years, holding out hope, but now it was time for him to let go, as well. There was only a week until Christmas. He'd make sure Helen worked with Wreath on the final details of the Donovan wedding. He'd keep busy elsewhere. After the wedding, they'd have less reason to see each other. And then there was the e-mail he'd received the other day. One he'd mentally dismissed but now might consider. His employer had offered him a new position. A chance to put a couple thousand miles between him and Wreath. But he doubted distance would change anything.

⸙

The day of Grace's wedding passed in a blur of activity. The weather cooperated by delivering a warm and sunny day. The detailed planning made for a hiccup-free event, from the ceremony under the pergola to the tossing of the bouquet from the front gallery of the mansion.

Wreath had been too busy to think about Micah, though

343

she'd caught sight of him a few times, her heart aching for what she might have lost forever.

She'd paused only once, when the ceremony had started. She'd listened to the vows, letting them sink into her spirit. She wanted to say those words to Micah, but how could she convince him of her love? Simply saying the words would ring hollow now. A new idea had formed in her mind. One she intended to follow through on soon. Maybe words were the answer after all. Just not spoken words.

∽∾

Micah walked into his office, the stress of the day weighing heavily on his shoulders. Grace and Brian's antebellum wedding had been a triumph, thanks to Wreath's skills and his staff's expertise.

He sat down at his desk and swiveled around to look out the window toward the pergola. The wedding guests had left and the staff was breaking down the canopies and clearing away the chairs and tables. He caught a glimpse of Wreath as she walked toward the courtyard.

Seeing Wreath but not being near her had been like a pebble in his shoe all day. She'd looked like an angel today in a long-sleeved navy-blue dress that skimmed her curves and gave her creamy skin a glow. Her brown eyes sparkled, attesting to her passion for coordinating weddings. And he had no idea how he'd be able to stay here and see her, work with her, and not go mad.

Dragging his hand over his face, he turned back to his computer. The e-mail from his old boss glared back at him. He had an out. A way to do what he loved—manage a small hotel—but do it away from Wreath. Far away. He had to make up his mind. Soon.

He picked up his suit jacket and slipped it on. He needed sleep. He closed up and headed out to his car. He stepped out of the building only to see Wreath walking across the parking lot. He started to call out to her but decided against it. It was time to let her go.

⌘

Wreath fingered the small box with the delicate china wreath inside. The symbol of forever. She didn't know how else to tell Micah so he would understand. If the wreath didn't say it, maybe the note inside would. He'd been cool and distant the day of the wedding. She'd been to Monmouth several times in the last few days but had been told he was busy elsewhere. He was avoiding her, and she couldn't blame him. Tomorrow was Christmas Eve. If her small gift didn't get through to him, then it was never meant to be.

⌘

Micah noticed the small box sitting on his desk the moment he entered his office late Christmas Eve morning. Wrapped in gold paper with a white bow, it looked out of place on his dark wood desk. Picking it up, he examined it for a note or card. He didn't know anyone here, with the exception of his staff, and of course Wreath.

He dropped his briefcase and coat in a chair, picked up the box, and pulled off the wrapping. Inside, he found a delicate porcelain wreath. The gold tassel at the top made it perfect for hanging on a tree. If he had one. He held it up to the light, smiling. It sparkled like the light in Wreath's golden-brown eyes. So why had she given it to him? A Christmas gift? He glanced back at the box, noticing a small note lying in the bottom. He pulled it out, a strange tightening feeling forming in his gut. He fingered it then set it aside.

He went to the coffeemaker and poured a cup. He stirred in a spoonful of creamer, trying to ignore the tension in the center of his chest. Back at his desk, he shrugged out of his suit coat, loosened his tie, and rolled up his shirtsleeves. He planned on spending the day working and forgetting it was Christmas. And he intended to ignore the note on his desk. He knew what he'd find inside. A good-bye letter. Wreath's let's-be-friends dismissal.

He sat down at his desk, shoving the box and its painful note aside. But it mocked him. With a grunt, he grabbed the paper and unfolded it, determined to get it over with.

It was a list. He read the first line, rubbed his forehead, and started again.

You love the Lord.
Peppermint candy helped you stop smoking.
You drink your coffee strong with a little cream.
Your favorite verse is "Be still and know that I am God"
      because it gives you a moment to find peace in a hectic day.
Your favorite dessert is pineapple upside-down cake.
Your brother Nathan is your best friend.
You want a family with three children.
You want to own your own small hotel someday.
You make me laugh.
You make me feel special.

The list went on. With each sentence, Micah's heart soared.

❧

The church had been packed for the Christmas Eve service. The voices raised in joyful praise still echoed in her memory as she entered her townhouse. The simple service had filled her with peace, chasing away much of the tension she'd been under the last week. It had even put her soured relationship with Micah into perspective. She had no one to blame but herself.

She trusted God with everything in her life, from her business problems to the choices she had to make daily. But when it came to her heart, she'd locked the Lord out because she hadn't trusted Him to keep it from being broken again. She'd decided she was more capable of protecting her heart than giving it over to Him to heal. As a result, she'd spent too long holding on to a dream that never existed and missed out on a chance at real love. Helen had told her about a job offer Micah had received. If he accepted it, he'd be moving to California, and she'd never see him again.

The weather had changed drastically. The balmy weather and sunny skies that had blessed Grace's wedding day had turned cold, gray, and blustery. What she needed was a cup of hot chocolate and a warm fire.

A knock on her door stopped her midstride. Who would be stopping by on Christmas Eve? Bonnie was with her family. She pulled open the door and froze. "Micah." Her heart pounded and warmth flooded up into her cheeks.

"Merry Christmas."

Despite her nervousness, she couldn't help but smile. She was so glad to see him. He looked gorgeous in a leather jacket and faded jeans. Her mouth went suddenly dry. "Merry Christmas."

"I missed you at church. You left before I could get to you." He shifted his weight slightly. "May I come in?"

"Oh, of course. She stepped aside to let him enter. His tall frame made her living room feel cozier than normal. Why was he here? She gestured for him to be seated in the living room. He shrugged out of his jacket and waited for her to be seated first. Always a gentleman. Her heart skipped a beat. It hit her then—he had come to deliver bad news. He was leaving, taking the job in California, or else he was coming to tell her that her note had arrived too late.

She sat down, drew her legs up under her, preparing for the worse. "It was a lovely service, wasn't it?"

He held her gaze. "Yes."

She clasped her hands together, her thumb rubbing the center of her palm nervously. "Can I get you something to drink? Coffee, hot chocolate?" He responded with a slow, lopsided grin that brought a light into his blue eyes and sent her heart tripping.

"Sure."

She stood and hurried to the kitchen, surprised when he followed behind her. Her hands shook as she slipped a cup of water into the microwave and took a package of hot cocoa mix out of the carton. She struggled to stay calm. She inhaled peppermint. Her heart lurched. She loved that smell. She turned to speak to him and found him only inches away, his gaze raking over her quickly before staring into her eyes. He pulled something from his pocket and held it up.

Her heart plummeted to the pit of her stomach. Her list. She started to move away, not wanting him to see her heartache, but he placed his hand on the counter, trapping her between it and him.

"Tell me about this, Wreath."

She refused to look at him, a wave of humiliation sucking the breath from her body. "Micah, please." She started to move again, but he blocked her way, pressing closer.

"I want to know what this is. Why you gave it to me."

She looked at him then. She had nothing to lose now. She crossed her arm over her chest, her only protection. "I wanted you to know that I've been paying attention."

"Why?"

"Because you're important to me."

"Why?"

"Because. I'm in love with you. I know it's too late. I've ruined everything. Grace helped me see I've been holding on to old dreams, afraid to find new ones for fear of getting hurt again."

Micah held up the note again. "You remembered what I said, about knowing me."

She nodded. "I remember more than what's on that list. I remember fireworks on the river, and the day at the park when we saw the baby birds, and the night we drove out to—"

Micah captured her mouth with his, drowning out all memories except the joy of being in his embrace. He ended the kiss, so full of promise and love. His hands cradled her face. "I've loved you from the first moment I saw you. I knew you were the only woman I could ever spend my life with."

Wreath slipped her arms around his waist, resting her head against his solid chest, listening to the beat of his heart. "I've been so blind and stupid. I've wasted so much time."

"Now we have all the time in the world. Marry me."

"Yes."

"I'll give you the wedding of your dreams."

"No. I want the marriage of my dreams. With you."

He kissed her again, with all the passion and promise of the future.

About the Authors

After retiring from BellSouth, owning a gift shop and tearoom, and working as a court clerk for the town of Pelahatchie, Mississippi, **Sylvia Barnes** penned a novel on a yellow pad, joined a writers group headed by Aaron McCarver, and started attending American Christian Fiction Writers conferences. Her first novella, *A Proper Christmas*, was included in the bestselling A Biltmore Christmas collection, published in 2011. Sylvia and her husband, J.W., live in the country outside of Pelahatchie, where they are active members of their church. They have two daughters and three wonderful grandchildren. Sylvia would love to hear from you. E-mail her at sylviajw@att.net.

Cynthia Leavelle teaches English and ESL at Belhaven University in Jackson, Mississippi. A native of New Mexico, she has two degrees from the University of North Texas. She has published one book with Crossbooks, *The Cord: The Love Story of Salmon and Rahab*, and has written numerous devotionals and short stories. She has been married for more than thirty-five years and has three grown sons. Cynthia would love to hear from you at cynthialeavelle@gmail.com or visit her webpage www.cynthialeavelle.com.

Virginia Vaughan worked as an investigator for the state of Mississippi before leaving to pursue her passion for writing. A divorced mom of two grown boys and one lovely daughter-in-law, she hopes to shine a light on the healing power of Jesus Christ through her stories. Virginia and her family make their home in Byram, Mississippi, and are members of Hillcrest Baptist Church.

Lorraine Beatty is a multi-published, bestselling author born and raised in Columbus, Ohio. She and husband Joe have two grown sons and five grandchildren. Lorraine started writing in Junior High and has written for trade books, newspapers, and company newsletters. She is a member of RWA, ACFW and is a charter member, and past President of Magnolia State Romance Writers. Away from writing she sings in her church choir, loves to garden, spend time with her grandchildren, and travel. I love to hear from my readers. Visit her at LorraineBeatty.com